RUFFLY
SPEAKING

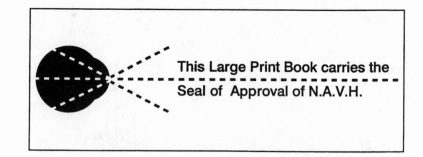

This Large Print Book carries the
Seal of Approval of N.A.V.H.

Ruffly Speaking

A Dog Lover's Mystery

Susan Conant

Thorndike Press • Thorndike, Maine

Published in 1994 by arrangement with Doubleday, a division of Bantam Doubleday Dell Publishing Group, Inc.

Thorndike Large Print ® Americana Series.

The tree indicium is a trademark of Thorndike Press.

The text of this Large Print edition is unabridged.
Other aspects of the book may vary from the original edition.

Set in 16 pt. News Plantin.

Printed in the United States on acid-free paper.

Library of Congress Cataloging in Publication Data

Conant, Susan J., 1946–
    Ruffly speaking : a dog lover's mystery / Susan Conant.
      p.   cm.
    ISBN 0-7862-0313-7 (alk. paper : lg. print)
    1. Large type books. 2. Winter, Holly (Fictitious
character) — Fiction. 3. Women journalists —
Massachusetts — Fiction. 4. Women dog owners —
Massachusetts — Fiction. 5. Dog shows — Massachusetts —
Fiction. 6. Dogs — Fiction. I. Title.
[PS3553.O4857R84 1994b]
813'.54—dc20
                                                    94-28127

To Wendy Willhauck
in memory of her beloved companion,
the miracle dog,
Ch. Frostfield Sweet Honcho (1976–1989).

ACKNOWLEDGMENTS

The wonderful people and spectacular dogs of NEADS, the New England Assistance Dog Service, Princeton, Massachusetts, helped me in researching the background of this book. Thanks, too, to Joel Woolfson, D.V.M., for clear answers to my veterinary questions and superb care of my dogs.

Many thanks to my fellow members of the New England and the Charles River dog training clubs, especially to those masters of praise and correction, Geoff Stern and Roseanne Mandel. I am also grateful to Bernard, mascot of Alaskan Malamute Rescue of South Texas, who bounded right into this book, and to Susan Cloer, who cheerfully leaped in with her dog. Thanks, too, to my perfect editor, Kate Miciak. Huzzah!

Frostfield Arctic Natasha, C.D., T.T., C.G.C., V.C.C., my first Alaskan malamute, *prima inter pares*, soul mate and godsend, died on March 31, 1993. Her grieving young nephew, Frostfield Firestar's Kobuk, who hitched himself to my sorrow, pulled as only a malamute can. I am grateful for his strength and graced by his life. He loved her, too.

The world of goodness is filled with fleas.

— *dictum of Chogyam Trungpa,*
called — Rinpoche, meaning "precious one"

1

If I come right out and ask whether you've been grabbed by evil-eyed aliens, whisked aboard their spacecraft, and subjected to grueling medical tests, you're going to say no, aren't you? Even if you remember every terrifying detail of the whole nasty business, you're probably too embarrassed to say so because you're afraid that people will think you're crazy. Besides, UFO experts agree that practically all abductees are left with only fragmentary memories of the horrid little gray-skinned medics who prodded and poked them and stabbed them with needles. No wonder people forget. Earthling doctors are bad enough; a gynecologist from outer space doesn't bear remembering.

It can't be easy to do research on UFO abductions, can it? The subjects who remember won't tell, and the ones who might spill all the fascinating details about the design of extraterrestrial hypodermics and speculums and stuff can't because they've forgotten. So instead of asking about the *experience* per se, the experts pose trick questions about epiphenomena — buzzing and whirring sounds that orchestrate the dance of weird lights, the sense that you've lost time and don't know where it's gone. Ah, but that happens to everyone, doesn't it? Certainly. But is it common to wake up paralyzed and sense a living presence lurking around in the room, looming over you, breathing close by your bed, watching you? Does everyone have the feeling of flying through the air without knowing how or why? Do we all feel as if we've left our bodies? And on returning, do we discover puzzling marks and scars on our torsos and limbs? Key indicator experiences, they're called, signs that maybe even unbeknownst to you, you've been the victim of an alien abduction.

Alternatively, of course, you spend your life with big dogs. The loudly respirating being in the bedroom? That sense of being *watched?* And just try walking two Alaskan malamutes in Cambridge, Massachusetts, on an icy winter day. Yes, flying through the air without knowing how or why, an out-of-body experience like none other, invariably culminating in abrupt reincorporation and the subsequent appearance of genuinely mystifying lumps and bumps, scoop-shaped, line-shaped, and otherwise, where none were before.

Amnesia, too. The last time it happened to me, I didn't remember a damned thing. One second, Rowdy and Kimi were leading the way down Appleton Street, and there was I, Sergeant Holly Winter of the Canadian Mounted Police, fearlessly daydreaming her way across the frozen Yukon wilderness; and the very next second, I found myself sprawled on a Cambridge sidewalk, watching a heavenly light show, but clinging nonetheless to the leather leashes of the Wonder Dogs, who were still after the same cat that had just precipitated my own precipitation, if you will. Thus, according to every key indicator, I am a bona fide abductee, and, in a way, the experts are right. What they miss, though, is a crucial difference: UFO abductees loathe and fear their alien captors, but, scars or no scars, I am wholeheartedly crazy about dogs.

So was Morris Lamb. For that matter, if experience continues beyond the great abduction, he's still wacky about dogs, and if Morris's heaven is truly his, he sits in perpetuity at the great eternal dog show in the sky. I see him there as clearly as I see the cream and terra-cotta of my own kitchen and the dark wolf gray of my own dogs, and I hear the raucous glee in Morris's laugh as Bedlington terrier after Bedlington terrier goes Best in Show, as is perpetually the case

11

in any paradise inhabited by Morris Lamb, who was an avid fancier of the breed and such a show fanatic that, regardless of even the most radical postmortem transformations of his soul, he undoubtedly continues to remember to bring his own thermos of coffee and his own folding chair.

In my own heaven, I won't be marooned outside the baby gates, and I won't be showing in conformation, either. Nerves or no nerves, I'll be striding briskly along over the mats of the Utility B obedience ring with a celestial Obedience Trial Champion at my side, an Alaskan malamute who eternally goes High in Trial or, on alternate days, the best obedience dog who ever cleared the high jump and never ticked it once. My last golden retriever, Vinnie, won't just meet me at the pearly gates, but will soar over them, Velcro herself to my left thigh, and precision-heel me through the portals and onto the streets of heaven, which are, of course, paved in . . . Well, let's just say that they are not paved in honor of the terrestrial obedience of the Alaskan malamute.

So there's Morris, content in the knowledge that his breed *always* wins. Also, if Morris's heaven is anything like Morris's earthly vision of paradise, you can bet that half the other men there are gay, too, or at least were when it still counted. Or, on second thought . . . I can't speak for Morris. Or God, either, for that matter. In fact, I know only two things about Morris Lamb's spiritual life. First, he was an Episcopalian. Second, as I've mentioned, he believed in Bedlington terriers. Otherwise? I have no idea. And my knowledge of God? Well, God and I have never actually discussed Morris Lamb — or sex either. Come to think of it, my conversations with God bear a striking resemblance to my conversations with everyone else, which is to say that we talk almost exclusively about dogs.

So if I'd gone to Morris's funeral, the Deity and I would probably have had an informative exchange about Rowdy and Kimi, but, as it was, I had the perfect excuse for missing Morris's funeral: I didn't know he was dead. I'd spent the weekend in Bethel, Maine, at the eightieth-birthday party of my grandmother, Lydia. She'd celebrated the occasion by getting an Irish wolfhound puppy and summoning the rest of us to come and admire him. We had. Early in the afternoon of Monday, May 11, I'd just arrived back in Cambridge and was puttering in the kitchen when Rita, my second-floor tenant, rapped sharply on the door.

Instead of applying the knuckles of her manicured right hand to the alligatored paint, Rita taps out a rhythmic beat with whatever collection of rings she happens to be wearing. Manicured? Yes, polish and all. Here in Cambridge, the typical educated woman gets her nails professionally painted only if she happens to be an anthropologist researching a book on female self-mutilation. But if you think about what Rita does for a living, it's easy to overlook almost any oddity she exhibits. Day after day, hour after fifty-minute hour, this poor woman has to sit in her office getting paid to hear stuff that's so awful that no sane person would listen to it free: trauma, misery, despair, terror, grotesque twists of fate — the whole catalogue of human suffering, and all of it inflicted on Rita. So in addition to having her fingernails filed and polished by a presumably unconfiding and uncomplaining manicurist, Rita wears clothes that not only match but coordinate with her shoes, which often have high heels. Even so, with the exception of Rowdy, Kimi, and their vet, Steve Delaney, Rita is the best friend I have. So if I'm defending her, what else are friends for?

When Rita's rings played her signature tune, her Scottie, Willie, must have recognized it from upstairs; one of his fits of owner-absent barking finally ended. Simultaneously, Rowdy and Kimi, who'd been sprawled on the fake-tile linoleum, quit gnawing their new Nylabones, leaped to their feet, and dashed to offer her the same joyous welcome they'd have extended to the Boston Strangler or a repo man come to claim all my possessions. The Alaskan malamute is the heavy-freighting dog of the Inuit people on the shores of the Kotzebue Sound, peaceful wanderers with no need for a watchdog or guard dog. My practiced eye, though, can spot the difference between Rowdy and Kimi's delight at the arrival of *any* visitor and the transported rapture they reserve for anyone who has ever treated them to so much as a miniature dog biscuit. After what happened the last time Rita did me the favor of feeding them when I had to be away — chaos but no bites — she's sworn never to do it again, but Rowdy and Kimi, oblivious to her vow, continue to offer Rita the ecstatic greeting owed to all incarnations of the supreme god in the Malamute pantheon, the many-named deity best known as Harbinger of Eukanuba.

So I shoved past the dogs, and before I even had the door all the way open, Rita was saying, "Holly, for God's sake, give me a drink, would you? I can't believe it. Christ, I've just been to the funeral of a total stranger."

2

"On purpose?"

In a futile effort to prevent the dogs from coating Rita's navy linen suit with dark guard hairs and pale underfluff, I grabbed their collars and hauled them back.

"What?"

"Were you in a funereal mood? Or did you —"

Rita's face broke into a wry grin. "Lease myself out as a hired mourner?"

As usual, Rita had just had her hair done. The back and sides were short, dark, and straight, but, on top, lightly blond-streaked waves and curls danced around and spilled onto her forehead. Rita is only about my age, not that much over thirty, so the streaking is what she calls a "preemptive defense."

"Do you really want a drink?" I asked. "Don't you have patients to see?"

"Not until four. I canceled everyone else. But I probably —"

"Coffee?"

Rita accepted, and, although I volunteered

to put the dogs in the yard, she said not to bother. Her suit didn't matter; she'd change before she went back to work. While I filled the kettle and fussed with French roast and mugs, Rita sat at the table and got treated to one of Rowdy and Kimi's see-how-adorable-I-am routines. Perfect wedge-shaped ears flattened against their heads, almond eyes open wide to display pupils the color of bitter chocolate, powerful hindquarters planted on the floor, they took up their positions on either side of her. When Rowdy had finished shaking hands, Kimi edged forward, sat up, and rested both of her ever-so-slightly smaller forepaws in Rita's hands, as if to say, "Well, if you think *he*'s cute, just take a look at me!" Then Rowdy unintentionally spoiled the performance by fetching his Nylabone, shoving ahead of Kimi, and presenting Rita with an already-tooth-roughened and still-wet end of his beautiful new toy. Although Rowdy has no difficulty in pinning pretend prey between his forepaws, he loves to have a person hold one end of a chew toy while he gnaws the other. Rita knew what he wanted. You'd think that a therapist would learn to keep her feelings off her face, but a flash of repugnance crossed Rita's. Real dog people, of course, recognize canine saliva for what it is: holy water — clear, clean, and blessed — but I took pity on Rita and put the dogs out.

When I got back to the kitchen, Rita had filled the mugs and put them on the table. Directly overhead, Willie's untrimmed nails tapped back and forth on the second floor.

I took a seat and drank some coffee. Then I pointed my thumb upward. "You want me to try trimming them for you? You hold, I cut?"

When I pointed upward, Rita probably expected another complaint about Willie's yapping and another offer to cure him of it. She looked baffled.

"It's the old rule. If you can hear them on the floor, they need cutting."

Rita's eyebrows rose. "I don't know what you're talking about."

"Willie's nails. On your kitchen floor. His nails need cutting."

"They can't be that bad. I don't hear them." Rita sipped her coffee, licked her lips, and then closed her mouth more firmly than usual.

Time for a change of subject. "So tell me how you ended up . . ."

Her smile reappeared. "My nine o'clock canceled. So I had a free hour, and it was a beautiful day and all that, so I went to the Square and bought the *Times*, and then I went over to Au Bon Pain and got some coffee and sat at one of the tables outside."

18

Which square? Porter, Central, Kendall? Here in Cambridge, if it goes without saying, it's like the letters that spell the name of God, best not pronounced aloud.

"And it was so nice out that you decided to go to a funeral," I said.

"At the table in back of me, there were these two men, and I couldn't help overhearing, and so one of them said something I didn't catch. And then the other one said something like, 'No, I can't. I have to go to Norris Lang's funeral.' Or, anyway, that's what I *heard*."

"He *died?*" Norris Lang, I should tell you, was — still is and ever shall be — Rita's analyst.

"No. Would you let me finish?"

"Of course."

"So I could hardly believe my ears!" Rita held out her hands, fingers splayed, palms up. "My analyst is dead, and no one's even bothered to let me know! And then, instead of looking in the *Times* to see if Lang's obituary was there, I turned around and said something like, 'Pardon me, but I couldn't help overhearing,' and then I said what a shock it was, and they said it was to them, too. So I asked when the funeral was, and it turned out to be today, and after all the work Lang and I have done on grieving, not to mention the unbelievable termination issues and simply

19

this overwhelming sense of loss and betrayal, I *had* to be there. So I got all the details, and it was at eleven thirty, and if I'd been thinking straight —"

"But, Rita, naturally, you weren't. I mean, if somebody mentioned Roz's funeral and I hadn't even heard she was dead —"

"Holly, Lang is my analyst. Roz is your *dog trainer*. It isn't —"

"It certainly is," I said. "So Norris Lang isn't d—"

"No! And I should've known, because, really, if nothing else, someone would've called to cancel our next hour, but I was so thrown that I . . . *Why* I was so ready to believe that Lang was dead is another matter. That one's going to take years. But what I did was go tearing back to my office, and I managed to reach my patients and cancel, and then I went flying over to this church on Brattle Street, which was jammed with people, and I should've . . ." Rita stopped to catch her breath. "But it never crossed my mind to ask if it was the right funeral. And there I was, sitting in this pew, and then, finally, I started looking around, and maybe a few faces looked a little familiar, but other than that, I didn't recognize a single person, which seemed kind of peculiar, because I should've known half the people there. So finally, *finally*, I looked at that little program they hand you, and there it was. I'd cancelled five patients to go to the funeral of this guy I've never even heard of. I felt like such a jerk. And what was I going to do? Get up and walk out?"

"Well, I hope it was at least a nice funeral," I said.

"Actually, it would've been right up your alley."

"I can't handle funerals," I reminded her. "You know that."

"Well, you could've handled this one. The priest brought her dog."

Gets me every time. "Oh. What kind of dog was it?"

"Cute." Rita is a person who refers to Shelties as "miniature collies." She recognizes dachshunds because she used to have one. She probably knew what a Scottie was even before she got Willie. She can tell a Dalmatian from a German shepherd, but probably not from a pointer or any other medium-size spotted dog. She's learned not to call my dogs "huskies," which malamutes aren't, and as I've informed her, even if they were, they'd be "Siberians" or Siberian huskies, but all she says when I tell her that is, "Then why aren't yours Alaskans?" Unbelievable. This woman has a Ph.D.

I refilled our mugs. "Rita, maybe I missed

something, but I still don't understand. How did you end up . . . ?

"Because of the *name*. The guy at Au Bon Pain was mumbling, plus, of course, my unconscious contribution. The guy who died was named *Morris Lamb*. Norris Lang? So it was —"

And that's how I heard about Morris.

3

At the risk of excommunication from the Dog Writers' Association of America, I spouted the inevitable my-God-I-wonder-what-happened-the-last-time-I-saw-him-he-looked clichés. As a matter of fact, Morris *had* looked fine. His young bitch, Jennie, had just gone Best of Breed out of Open, and Morris . . . Have I lost you? Well, if you don't speak dog, let's just say that Jennie had done well, and, if you're fluent, let me add that two no-show exhibitors had enraged all the other Bedlington people except Morris Lamb by breaking the major, but that Morris hadn't been more than slightly miffed. Morris was as competitive as any other terrier person, but he liked winning so much that, as long as he won something, he didn't particularly care what it was. If his bitch had taken first place in the Silly Dog Trick contest at a K-9 fun fest, he'd probably have been delighted.

Dog world relationships like mine with Morris are a little hard to explain to someone like Rita. For instance, any real dog person understands that since Janet Switzer is Rowdy's breeder, she is thereby my own blood relative, but Rita misses the critical point: If it weren't for Janet, Rowdy wouldn't exist, and if Rowdy didn't exist, I would be a person altogether different from who I am. Rita also fails to grasp why the act of entering even one dog in one show or obedience trial is tantamount to slicing open your palm and clasping the identically incised hands of every other person who has ever shown a dog. But it's a fact. We're blood brothers and sisters, like it or not; sometimes we do, and sometimes we don't.

"Morris wasn't a close friend of mine," I explained, "but *everyone* knew him." When I say *everyone*, I mean everyone-everyone, which is to say, those of us with the scarred palms. "Rita, *you* knew who Morris Lamb was. Winer and Lamb. In the Square?"

Cambridge must have one bookstore for every ten or twelve pairs of human eyes: The Harvard Coop, The MIT Coop, WordsWorth, Mandrake, Reading International, the Starr, the Book Case, McIntyre and Moore, specialty stores, Grolier, Kate's, Schoenhof's, Pandemonium, the Globe for travel books, and zillions of other bookstores, including Winer & Lamb — new and used cookbooks and a café, too.

Rita switched to her professional mode; her face and voice went dead neutral. "You're a, uh, valued customer? You bought cookbooks?" *(And how long is it that you've been Napoleon, Miss Winter?)*

My cooking consists mainly of picking up pizza from Emma's, which is on Huron Avenue, only about a ten-minute walk from where I live — Appleton and Concord — and has what must be the thinnest, crispiest crust and most compulsively delicious sauce this side of Sicily. Except in the North End, Boston's Little Italy, practically all the pizza around here is that thick-crust Greek stuff, not that I have anything against Greeks, but, look, do Italians go around selling moussaka?

I said, "I go to Winer and Lamb because of the dogs," thus in four simple words explaining — well, everything. "In good weather, when they have the little tables out on the sidewalk, you can sit there with your dogs, and they bring out your coffee, so you don't have to worry about what to do with the dogs while you go in to get it. Speaking of which, more?"

Rita threw me a glance of suspicion. "Is this decaf?"

"Of course not. I'm a writer."

"Do you have any Perrier?"

"Poland Springs?" I'm from Maine, not

France. Rita isn't from France, either. Maybe she assumes that Perrier is the name of a side street off Madison Avenue where water bubbles out of the concrete.

"Sure," she said.

When I'd poured and handed her the glass of water, I went on about Winer & Lamb. "So dogs are sort of allowed. Morris Lamb was a dog person." I made a connection. "Rita, *that's* why the dog was at his funeral. It didn't belong to the priest. It was one of Morris's Bedlingtons. Cute, right? Like a little lamb."

"What?"

"Like a little lamb," I repeated.

Rita still looked mystified.

"A *lamb*. A baby sheep," I persisted.

"No, it didn't look like a lamb. It looked like a dog."

"Well, then, it wasn't a Bedlington." True. Morris, in fact, used to refer to Jennie and Nelson as "my little flock." The deliberate similarity results from painstaking grooming. Morris's dogs always looked fabulous. He didn't groom them himself, either, so his grooming bills must have been astronomical, not to mention what he must've paid his handler, plus entry fees, and all the rest. Except for Doug Winer, who was Morris's partner in both senses of the word, Morris didn't have anyone but Nelson and Jennie, and he'd inherited the proceeds from some family cutlery business in New Jersey, so he had tons of money. "That's too bad," I added. "Morris would've wanted —"

Rita held up a traffic-cop hand. "Don't say it! Because, being the real dog person he was, he cared more about dogs than he did about —"

I felt offended. "No. Actually, he didn't. As a matter of — Maybe you even remember this. It was a couple of years ago. Some woman threw herself in the Charles, and once she started drowning, I guess, she changed her mind, and Morris jumped in and rescued her. This was in the early spring, so the water must've been freezing. And Morris was a big man, but he wasn't any great athlete or anything, and he must've been at least fifty. It sounds sort of corny, but it was a genuine act of heroism. Shit. I wonder what he died of."

Rita took a small sip of water. "If it had been something like that, the priest would've . . . But maybe she did. I was sitting way at the back, so I didn't hear very much." She rested an elbow on the table, leaned her head forward, and covered the lower half of her face with her hand. It was an odd, uncharacteristic gesture. She removed her hand. "Nobody could've heard from where I was."

27

"Rita, no one is accusing you of anything."
I could have been. The soundproofing between her apartment and the one on the third
floor is pretty good because I renovated the
two rental units when I bought the building.
Willie's owner-absent nuisance barking trav-
eled throughout the building, but the noise
produced by Rita herself was really bad only
in my kitchen. Whenever she talked on the
wall phone by her stove, her voice plummeted
straight down. Also, although I don't have
anything against public radio, I like to be able
to choose my own station instead of having
advanced adult higher education forced down
my ear canals every morning. After all, this
is Cambridge. If you want to start the day
by listening to an intelligent discussion of
world events, you open the window, and a
couple of passersby will be setting the events
in Bosnia in global perspective, and when
they've gone, others appear, and you overhear
a vicious argument about the economics of
sub-Sahara Africa. Cambridge is a city in
which you see graffiti in what I'm assured is
grammatically correct Latin. I like it here, but
I can wait until after breakfast.

When Rita and I had sat in silence for a
minute, I said, "Weren't you thinking about
having your hearing tested?"

She jerked herself upright. The little curls

on top of her head shook. She said nothing.

"Rita, can you hear Willie? He's walking across your kitchen floor. Can you hear him?"

She closed her eyes and concentrated. Her features aren't perfect, but she's very pretty and perfectly groomed, sort of like Morris's dogs, not that she resembles a lamb or even a Bedlington, and please don't tell her that I even suggested the comparison. What really shows on Rita's face, though, isn't the careful application of cosmetics. It's a promise that if you need to talk, she'll pay attention and take you seriously. She opened her eyes. "If I listen hard, I can." She rested her chin in her hands. "You know, Holly, a lot of people really do mumble." The truth of the statement seemed to cheer her. "And they talk too softly. Male psychiatrists are the worst. They don't bother speaking up because they expect everyone to hang on their every word."

I did not point out that Norris Lang, her analyst, was a male psychiatrist. I did not ask whether she ever had trouble hearing him. I eventually broke the silence. "Rita, I'm going to be blunt."

"*Mirabile dictu.*" Rita's mouth formed a sour line of worry. "And please do me a favor, would you? Do not, I repeat *do not* start telling me about how tactful and conflict-avoiding you used to be before you had malamutes,

29

because I am not in the mood for it right now."

"Damn it, Rita! Look, in the past six months, I don't know how many times you've been upset because you couldn't hear something that everybody else could, okay? You can't hear cats meowing or doorbells ringing, and you can't hear the turn signals on your car, so you keep leaving them on." By now, I was pleading. "And I know, I just *know,* that what you're going to do now is spend forever analyzing whatever psychological reason made you hear *Norris Lang* instead of *Morris Lamb,* and maybe you're going to say that you'll get your hearing checked, but you're going to end up not doing it. Rita, if Willie had trouble hearing, you wouldn't just complain about it. You'd find out what was going on." That's true. Rita knows nothing about dogs, but she's an outstandingly responsible owner nonetheless. Maybe she'd buy the argument that Willie's habitual yapping would impair his hearing. It would be worth a try sometime; so far, my other bids for silence had failed entirely.

"Have I been complaining?" she asked.

"Yes."

"I'm sorry."

"Forget it. Just get it checked, okay?"

She promised. Then I changed the subject. If the dog at Morris's funeral hadn't been one

30

of his Bedlingtons and really had accompanied the priest, a woman priest at that, I wanted the details. *Dog's Life* runs my column in every issue, and I was about to start substituting for a writer on whelping leave, but my editor, Bonnie DeSousa, is always crazy about free-lance articles on what she calls "interspecies bonding," and she pays pretty well for them, too. A female cleric with a canine acolyte? If you write for *Dog's Life*, that's the kind of story that brings home the kibble.

4

After Rita left, I checked the *Boston Globe* that had arrived that morning. Morris's long, newsy obituary must have appeared in the Sunday paper, which Rita or my third-floor tenants had removed from my doorstep to avoid advertising my absence. Monday's *Globe* had only a stark paragraph midway through the list of death notices.

LAMB — Of Cambridge, May 8, Morris Duncan, age 52. Devoted son of the late Harold and Mary (Duncan) Lamb. A memorial service will be conducted at St. Margaret's Episcopal Church of Cambridge at 11 A.M. Interment Mt. Auburn Cemetery, Cambridge. Late graduate of Harvard College. In lieu of flowers, donations may be made to The Bedlington Terrier Club of America Rescue Committee, 113 Fillmore Drive, Sarasota, FL 34236.

It seemed to me that Morris would have made

something of that "late graduate" business, but I couldn't think what. In groping for the right clever remark, I found nothing but Morris's absence.

Then I went to the guest room to start the work of filling in for Beryl Abrams, who edits the canine products section of *Dog's Life* and ordinarily writes most of the evaluations herself. Beryl has Papillons (average height at the withers about nine inches), and some of the products I randomly pulled from the two big cartons left by UPS would have to wait until Beryl's two bitches were safely delivered. A postpartum Papillon might enjoy recuperating on a tiny self-warming dog nest designed to retain body heat, but as soon as Rowdy and Kimi discovered what the little pillow did, they'd decide that, being warm-blooded and vulnerable, it was a fun form of dinner.

Another product I'd have to return to Beryl or farm out to one of my dog-training friends was a leash with a snap at one end for the dog's collar and, at the other end, a belt to strap around your own waist. The idea was Look-Ma-no-hands dog walking, but with *Alaskan malamutes?* My loyalty to *Dog's Life* does not extend to kamikaze missions. Equally unsuitable in somewhat less terrifying ways were a tremendous number of sure cures for problems that Rowdy and Kimi failed to ex-

33

hibit: chlorophyll drops to end bad breath, medicated pads to relieve itching, whiteners to eradicate tear stains around the eyes, enzyme tablets to reduce flatulence, a hot-oil kit to correct dry skin, foul-tasting furniture polish to discourage chewing, a package of Pee Wee housebreaking pads, and an ultrasound bark silencer and training device called the Yap Zapper. The Rowdy and Kimi Award for the canine product that a malamute needs least went to a flavor enhancer intended to tempt the appetites of finicky eaters. If I'd shined the Yap Zapper with the dog-repellent polish, seasoned it with chlorophyll drops and eye-stain eradicator, added a dressing of hot oil and enzyme tablets, and served the whole mess up to Rowdy on a bed of Pee Wee pads, he'd have wolfed it down, and Kimi would have fought him for her share, too.

The more I pawed through the remedies arrayed on the guest room bed, the more Rowdy and Kimi seemed like paragons of personal hygiene and canine good citizenship. Even so, I'd managed to identify a fairly large selection of products we could reasonably test out, including pet hair gatherers, pooper-scoopers, a newfangled version of the silent dog whistle, and — pity the poor manufacturers — a variety of toys, balls, and flying discs foolishly advertised as chew-proof and puncture-resistant. Hah! I wouldn't guarantee a steel girder safe in the jaws or claws of an Alaskan malamute.

When I'd ended my preliminary survey, I packed a small box with paraphernalia to return to Beryl, and a few products to forget entirely: old gadgets with new names, dangerous toys, and, believe it or not, a square of indoor-outdoor carpeting patterned with the head of a rabid-looking Doberman and the words *Go ahead. Make his day.* I stowed that box in the cellar, put everything else in the two big boxes, and dragged them to my study so they wouldn't get splattered with paint when I freshened up the guest room for my cousin Leah, who was arriving in a month or so to spend the summer with me.

Then I took the dogs for a short walk, answered a phone call from a pleasant-sounding woman interested in adopting a dog from Malamute Rescue, added a couple of paragraphs to an article about rabies, and dialed Winer & Lamb. I didn't expect Doug Winer to be back in the store on the day of Morris's funeral, but I didn't have any idea where Doug lived, and phoning Winer & Lamb seemed like the easiest way to get in touch.

The guy who answered had that lilting speech pattern that sounds so much like a regional accent that you'd swear that half the gay men in America came from the same hometown. Wherever it is, Morris originated elsewhere — New Jersey, in fact, as I've mentioned — but Doug obviously grew up there, as did several of the waiters at Winer & Lamb.

"I was a friend of Morris's," I explained. "I just heard, and I wanted to talk to Doug." To my amazement, the guy said that Doug was out back and that he'd get him for me.

When Doug got on the phone, I told him that I'd just heard about Morris and was very sorry. In case my mannerly mother happened to be wasting her celestial time by listening in, I refrained from mentioning that Doug was working and that Winer & Lamb was open on the day of Morris Lamb's funeral. I didn't make even the most oblique inquiry about the cause of Morris's death, either. When on earth, my mother, Marissa, directed her attention principally to golden retrievers, and when she wasn't training, grooming, showing, or tending to dogs, she was weeding her perennial garden, transplanting seedlings, laying tile in the house, or plastering walls. It's possible that the perfection of heaven has left Marissa with more free time than she used to have. If so, leisure could have turned her maternal and hovery, I guess.

Doug, though, eventually rewarded my virtue by answering my unasked questions. "You must think it's terrible for me to be here! We stayed closed until one." Doug's voice dropped to a whisper. "But none of them knows a *thing* about books, except Fyodor, and the silly boy has gone to Barbados! I was petrified someone important would have to pick today to drop in, and this is a dreadful thing to say, but we have been flooded with customers." I could almost see Doug cup his hand around the phone in case one of the employees read his lips. "Saturday afternoon, you just could not *walk* through here without stepping on someone's toes. To get to the register, I literally had to insinuate myself between bodies and slither through! And since we opened today, it's been almost as bad up here, and the café is *worse*. They *need* me here! They just can't cope. You never realize how many incompetent people there are in the world until you run a business. It's very disenchanting."

"Maybe it's better for you to keep busy," I said.

Doug evidently didn't need my support. "What choice do I have?" he exclaimed wildly. "They do terrible things! On Saturday, the afternoon of Morris's *death*, I found Victor *seating*, actually seating, two very desirable clients at a table with *soiled* linen! It was disgusting — big spots of grease and coffee all over the tablecloth — and I had to step in and say, 'Pardon me, ladies, but this table is very definitely *not* ready.' There's no excuse for that; you should just see our laundry bills. I sent Victor flying for fresh linens, and that's absolutely typical."

"Doug, every time I've ever been there, everything has been perfect." The tables in the café that occupied the front of the store and, in good weather, spilled onto the sidewalk, had pale pink tablecloths and napkins — cloth, not paper, and heavily starched. Even at the outdoor tables, the plates and cups were real china, white with a pink rim. Need I add that the silverware, although doubtless not sterling, was not plastic, either? Every table had fresh flowers.

Doug ignored my praise. "And you never can tell when SHE might appear, and Morris always dealt with HER himself. I couldn't manage it. Whenever SHE's here, I'm all nerves."

Cambridge is highbrow Hollywood. I was at Winer & Lamb once when it actually happened. This was last winter, so I was indoors. A friend and I were having lunch at the café when Julia Child walked through and up the little half-flight of stairs to the book section. She acted just like a normal person, and the rest of us tried to do the same, but everyone at the tables began discreetly whispering to everyone else so that no one would miss seeing her, and then one of the waiters, maybe the erring Victor, broke the spell by dropping a tray. Crockery smashed on the floor, and coffee splattered all over. I suppose that it was exactly the kind of incident that Doug didn't want repeated.

"She probably just wants to wander around and look at the books like everyone else," I told him. "She isn't going to need advice. If she finds a book she wants, she'll just need to pay for it. You can handle that, Doug."

"I can't! The last time she was here, I was so nervous that when she finally left, I was bathed in perspiration."

"Did she buy anything?"

Doug's sigh whooshed across the phone line. "Irony of ironies. A book on edible flowers."

The irony was lost on me. "Uh . . . ?"

"You didn't *know?* Morris *poisoned* himself with them."

"But if they were —"

Before I had a chance to say *edible,* Doug went on. "But they *weren't.* We think he was creating a *mesclun.*" Doug must have remembered that I was one of Morris's dog people, not one of his food people. "Mixed baby greens —"

"A salad," I said. "I know."

"You know how random Morris was," Doug said affectionately. "And he hadn't even read the book, of course — he never did; he created — and he must've traipsed around the yard snipping here and there, and then tossed it all with a *chèvre* vinaigrette." Doug paused. I had the sense of time passing. "I found him in the bathroom." As an afterthought, he added, "Naked."

"Doug, how awful for you. Was he . . . ?"

Perhaps because Doug had spent so much time surrounded by recipes, he gave a nauseatingly graphic account of Morris's death, almost as if I'd requested directions on how to recreate it myself right in my own kitchen — and bathroom, too, I guess — as I assume that you don't. The gist of Doug's story was that although Morris lived on Highland, only a few blocks from a fancy greengrocery on Huron, he'd spared himself the walk and the expense, too, I suppose, although Doug didn't say so. In Cambridge, and probably elsewhere, tiny greens cost more per pound than lobster. Maybe they're worth it. They taste good, and the ones you buy won't make you sick. Anyway, when Morris finished harvesting a variety of infant salad greens from the raised bed garden that Doug had built for him, he'd foolishly added the leaves of what turned out to be a lot of poisonous plants.

Because of dog writing, I know a little about poisonous plants. Grass is harmless, but to be safe, don't let your dog eat the leaves, stems, or flowers of any houseplants, shrubs, perennials, or annuals. A few — nasturtiums, for instance — are fine, but watch out for an alarming number of harmless-sounding things like azalea, rhododendron, lupine, delphinium, hydrangea, and foxglove. Foxglove? Digitalis. So make Rover stick to his Purina, and if you get in a creative mood and decide to make a really exotic salad, toss a few Pro Plan croutons on your lettuce, and leave the hydrangea — especially the hydrangea — out in the yard where it belongs.

According to Doug, however, Morris didn't die of poisoning, at least not directly. As Doug explained in detail I didn't want to hear, the plants made Morris so sick that he became dehydrated. Sometime on Friday night, he passed out. Then he aspirated his own vomit. Sorry. Compared with Doug's description, mine is appetizing.

The part about spicing up the salad sounded like Morris. Also, in spite of the Bedlingtons, Morris wasn't the kind of owner who reads up on all the latest news about canine diseases and household hazards. Morris almost certainly knew not to substitute a choke collar for a regular buckle collar, and I'm sure he knew better than to feed chocolate to a dog, but that was probably about it. So Morris was responsible but not supereducated, Harvard or no Harvard. When he studied the dog magazines, I'm sure that he concentrated almost exclusively on show results. And the aspiration? It happens to dogs all the time. It's one of the approximately two hundred solid reasons not to debark a dog and one of the main reasons a lot of veterinarians won't perform the surgery, which leaves a dog vulnerable to — well, to aspiration. So, all in all, Doug's story was improbable but credible. Even so, I didn't believe it. As I soon learned, almost no one else did, either. We were dopes, of course. We assumed that since Morris was gay, he must have died of AIDS.

5

Sometime around Memorial Day each year, the prestigious Essex County Kennel Club sponsors Boston's answer to the Westminster Kennel Club Dog Show. But I prefer Essex County, and so does every dog there who's ever endured the heat, crowding, and chaos of Madison Square Garden. Essex is Westminster with the calendar turned back a thousand years, a medieval tournament instead of a twentieth-century teleplay, and all the better for it. It's a gorgeous pageant that really earns the name *show*. Although the site in the past few years has been a college campus in suburban Boston, when you approach from a distance, you'd swear it's Camelot. The beauty of the multicolored striped tents and the intense green of the acres of lawn will fool you into expecting a pair of armored knights on horseback to charge up and start jousting, and if the women in pastel dresses turned out to be princesses with cone-shaped hats instead of breed handlers dolled up for the ring, you wouldn't be surprised at all.

A thousand years ago, knighthood was strictly limited to males, who rescued — and certainly never vied with — females. Times change. On the morning of Saturday, May 30, a month after Morris Lamb's death, the champion who bore my colors entered the ring and got trounced by a damsel in no distress, which is to say that Rowdy gallantly joined the round table of Alaskan malamute dogs who'd gone Best of Opposite while the invincible Daphne once again took Best of Breed. Alien? Best of Opposite Sex to Best of Breed. If a bitch — right, a girl — wins BOB, then BOS goes to a dog. Lost? Stick around, anyway. Before long, you'll be talking about Bred-by dogs and Open bitches as if you were one yourself. In the meantime? Relax. Everyone's welcome at a dog show.

Even Daphne. More or less.

After Rowdy's defeat, while he rested in his crate in the shadow of Faith Barlow's Winnebago, I made the rounds of the concession booths (yield: eight sample packets of dog food, two Nylabones, an attention-getting squeaker, a bottle of Mela Miracle pet luster-izer spray, and two welcome-back-to-dog-heaven presents for my cousin Leah, a twenty-one-inch heeling lead and the video version of Bernie Brown's *No-Force Method of Dog Training*). Faith Barlow, by the way,

44

handles Rowdy in breed. Why? Faith is a first-rate professional handler. I like my dogs to win. Any more questions?

When I'd finished stocking up, I headed for the breed rings, which formed two temporary buildings, each consisting of a long, wide, awning-covered central aisle with a row of four or five rings — roped-off rectangles — out in the hot sun on each side. You don't have to go inside to watch, of course — you can work on your tan while you follow the judging — but I grew up on the coast of Maine, and I'm still not used to the hellish climate this far south of God's country. Besides, it's fun inside. The aisle I entered was crammed with cool spectators watching the activity out in the hot rings; exhibitors spraying and brushing last-minute winning glints into the coats of sparkling dogs; and keyed-up, next-in-the-ring amateur handlers nervously shifting their feet and snapping rude accusations at innocent strangers.

I was meandering down this aisle of paradise — dogs, dogs, and more beautiful dogs, sweet sight, O beautiful vision, do not cease — when I was bashed from the rear by a hugely overweight woman cuddling a Maltese terrier about a tenth the size of one of her breasts. Thus I didn't exactly run into Doug Winer; I got rammed into the back of his folding chair.

"I'm sorry!" I said, untangling myself.

Now, if you're new to dog shows, I should warn you that when you get shoved into someone and there's a dog nearby, as there's inevitably going to be, what you're apt to hear even before your words of apology leave your mouth is, "Oh, yeah, I'll bet you're sorry! Didn't mean to step on his foot and make him go lame, did you? Number one dog in the Western world until *you* had to go and . . ." Stage fright. Ignore it. It's not dog fanciers at our best. And if you're already one of us? Well, then, I just have to ask you: Who brings these people up?

But Doug Winer wasn't a real show type and didn't have a dog at his side, anyway. Doug not only accepted my apology, but introduced me to the person seated next to him, namely, his father, an extremely short, stocky, and completely bald man of seventy-five or eighty who bore an uncanny resemblance to the dogs parading around in the ring only a few yards away. Guess? Certainly. Bull terriers. True gentlemen. Mr. Winer, Sr., rose from his folding chair, shook my hand, and — a dog-show first — offered me his seat.

Doug had dark, curly hair all over his hands, arms, and head, and so ineradicable a growth of beard that hourly razoring would still have left him looking in perpetual need of a shave.

His thick build was his father's, but when Doug stood to greet me, he moved with the agility of an athlete. I seemed to remember that he played tennis. At any rate, he wore white, a polo shirt and pressed pants as spotless as the linen at Winer & Lamb. Doug gestured to his empty chair and threw me an imploring glance. "Holly can have mine." Addressing his father and me, he was starting to explain that Bedlingtons were next in this ring.

Mr. Winer's face suddenly took on a look of alarm and confusion. "Where's your mother?" he demanded.

Children are always getting lost at shows, but our octogenarians don't have time for mental failure. They're too busy training and grooming dogs, whelping puppies, and traveling to shows. The only thing elderly dog people ever seem to forget is how old they are. But Doug's mother? The two big awning-covered breed ring areas looked identical. To Mrs. Winer, maybe the dogs did, too.

But Doug seemed unperturbed. "Mother had some errands to run," he told his father matter-of-factly. "She was going to do some shopping. She's home by now." He turned to me, leaned close, and quietly confided, "Stealing some time alone."

I can take a hint, and I don't mind doing

favors. I gave Mr. Winer a big smile. "I'd love to sit down, if you don't mind."

When Doug had excused himself and promised to be right back, his father practiced the courtly art of helping a lady to her seat. The folding chair and I must both have challenged him, and, of the two, I was probably the greater challenge. I'd ironed my shirt but not my jeans, which were, however, clean. My old Reeboks weren't. I usually smell like training treats and dog shampoo. Mr. Winer's courtesy deserved Joy — the perfume, naturally, not the dog chow, which, as far as I know, at least, is made by a totally different company, but, in its own way, is very good nonetheless.

"Is this your first dog show, Mr. Winer?" It was as close as I could come to asking the gentleman about himself.

He nodded.

"And Doug is showing one of Morris Lamb's dogs?" I was genuinely curious. Doug used to accompany Morris to shows, but I'd always had the impression that he was there for Morris, not the dogs.

"They've moved in with us." Mr. Winer sounded surprised, as if the two Bedlingtons had shown up at his door only seconds earlier. "Nelson and . . ." He groped.

I pretended to search my own memory.

"Jennie, isn't it?"

"Jennie," Mr. Winer confirmed.

"They're living with you? With you and, uh, Mrs. Winer?"

I almost expected Mr. Winer to ask *who* was, but he didn't. All he did was nod again.

"Doug can't have dogs?" I waited a second and rephrased the question. "His landlord doesn't allow dogs?"

Mr. Winer looked really bewildered now.

"Oh." I'd finally caught on. "Doug lives at home? With you?"

"Brookline," Mr. Winer answered. "Francis Street." Unasked, he went on to give me first the address, and then precise directions for driving there and advice about where to park. The recitation of the familiar details seemed to comfort and reassure him. His voice lingered fondly at every turn and stoplight.

When he'd finished, I said that the area, Longwood, was lovely — it is — but Mr. Winer wasn't paying attention. He twisted restlessly around and looked here and there until he caught sight of Doug, who was five or six yards behind us listening to an impeccably groomed young woman with the brisk, confident air of a professional handler. Her blue-flowered dress matched the thin blue show lead in her hand. At the dog's end of the lead pranced Ch. Marigleam's Canadian

49

Lovesong (Nelson to his friends), who paused midfrolic to lick the pretty woman's hand, then Doug's.

Want some free advice? If so, ask a real dog person. You can't shut us up. Here it is: With some breeds, amateurs do fine in conformation, but if you want to show your terrier, hire the best professional handler you can afford, because if you go out there and stumble around yourself, no judge will so much as look at your dog. Too bad, but that's the truth. Morris Lamb knew it. So, evidently, did Doug Winer.

I glanced at Doug's father, who was beaming so jovially that his entire hairless head practically glowed. He turned toward me, winked, took another look at his son and the pretty handler, and in proud paternal tones murmured, "Doug has his eye on that one! Just you watch!"

Any object of Doug's amorous regard would so absolutely, totally, definitely, and unconditionally have been male that I found it almost impossible to imagine how anyone could suppose otherwise. But Mr. Winer wasn't just anyone.

Kennel blindness takes all kinds of forms. In dog fancy, of course, it means the inability to see the faults of your own dogs. Daphne's owners, for example, probably don't realize that her ears are a little big and slightly high set, at least by contrast with Rowdy's, which are small in proportion to the size of his head and set exactly where they belong, on the sides, just as the standard says. Also, Daphne's tail is rather short, and she doesn't have the best neck I've ever seen, either. But then some judges either don't read the standard or don't recognize it even when it materializes in the ring. You've seen Rowdy, right? You've seen him *move?* Incredible dog. The standard incarnate.

But the point about Doug and his father isn't that Doug had a major fault in terms of the standard for human beings, because there isn't any one standard for all of us. There couldn't be, any more than there could be a single standard for Saint Bernards, Bernese mountain dogs, Chihuahuas, and all the others. We don't vary in size and shape as radically as dogs do, but in our own way, we're equally diverse, aren't we?

Am I making myself clear? Suppose the standard you're using is for the Great Dane, when, in reality, your dog is a Chesapeake Bay retriever. Enter kennel blindness. Love that dog enough and before long, you're going to convince yourself that, according to the standard, your Chessie is a flawless specimen of an entirely different breed. Maybe he *is* faultless, but that's not the point. The point is that you're using the wrong standard.

And if your Chessie has the option of barking out the truth? That you've made a fool of yourself? That you don't know the first thing about your own dog? Caught in that situation, any Chessie with any sense is going to worry that if you find out, you'll be heartbroken. Maybe you'll even decide that you don't want a Chessie at all. Maybe you never liked Chessies, or never thought you did, anyway. Maybe the shock will be more than you can take. So if your Chessie really loves you? And knows how much you need him? Well, then, maybe he's going to act just like Doug. He's going to let you go right on admiring your perfect Great Dane.

6

Late on a Friday afternoon a couple of weeks after the Essex County show, the dogs and I were heading back from the river. According to Rowdy and Kimi, we were supposed to be retracing our steps and taking the direct route by following Appleton Street from where it begins, at Brattle Street, to where it ends, at Concord Avenue, home being 256 Concord Avenue, the barn red house at the corner of Appleton. I, however, had led us to Fayerweather and then onto Reservoir Street. Just when Rowdy and Kimi had more or less reconciled themselves to Reservoir, though, we came to the intersection with Highland Street, where they balked and I coaxed. Highland Street was not one of the direct routes home, I conceded. Highland did, however, intersect with Appleton, I added, and it happened to be where Morris Lamb had lived. Furthermore, I felt like walking down it, and we were damned well going to do so. Malamutes might worship monotony, I said; I did not. If I decided that this was the way we were going, then this *was* the way we were going, and that was that. The dogs continued to balk. Then I reached into my pocket, pulled out a fistful of freeze-dried liver, smacked my lips, and, having firmly re-established myself as the alpha leader of the pack, made the turn onto Highland with Rowdy and Kimi bouncing and leaping along beside me. You think I'm kidding? Alpha *means* the one who gets her own way.

After Rowdy and Kimi had swallowed the liver, they threw me a few more of those bi-peds-are-so-stupid looks, but soon got dis-tracted by the olfactory traces of a dog who'd left his mark so high up on the trees and fences that Rowdy and Kimi, who aren't exactly minis, nearly toppled over trying to cover his scent with theirs. Irish wolfhound? Great Dane? My dogs lingered at shrubs and pressed their noses together at tree trunks as if to share information about the big fellow and decide what to do about him. Meanwhile, I looked around. Dog-walking makes the perfect ex-cuse to linger in neighborhoods that are tonier than you are.

Highland runs parallel to Brattle for two long blocks — Sparks to Appleton, Appleton to Reservoir. Like Brattle, it has houses that the inhabitants might justifiably refer to as mansions, but never do. Off Brattle is just what it sounds like, the neighborhood off Brattle Street, but it's also a way of life and a way of language. Off Brattle, you don't inhabit a mansion; one has a big house. You didn't go to Harvard, either; one was an undergraduate. It must be a required course, for God's sake. Cambridge 101, Advanced False Modesty: The Linguistic Pragmatics of Less Is More.

So Highland Street is Brattle without the traffic: big houses painted in earth tones, soft mauve, or a warm, pale yellow like homemade mayonnaise, old brick and natural stucco, and none of the aqua vinyl siding and gray asbestos shingle that still survive in my neighborhood, Fresh Pond, which is only a few blocks down Appleton from Highland, but on the opposite side of Huron, where a big house is just that and isn't apt to be all that big, anyway. But don't get me wrong. Despite the muted mauve voices — earth tones, old brick — and the educated hues of the paint, Off Brattle is an intense study in color, and that color is green. In early June, Highland Street is like the masterpiece of an artist who worked green to its verdant limits, Henri Rousseau without even the ladies or the lions. Vegetable opulence.

But here and there amid the wisteria-trimmed piles of stucco, the Victorian arcs, and the vast, restrained colonials resides the evidence that sometime not all that long ago, someone ran desperately short of cash and had to sell land. Morris Lamb's house was one of the tattletales. To judge from its architecture, the era of need must have been the mid or late nineteen fifties, when Morris's flat-roofed cube with its heavily framed plate glass windows must have looked daringly modern. Morris or one of the previous owners had tried to force-fit this angular peg into the curves of the neighborhood by painting its harsh uprights and cross beams an ultra-toned-down pale tan with just a hint of lavender, and by planting a miniature forest of low-maintenance, fast-growing shrubs around the foundation and all over the front yard. The camouflage was about as successful as ripping the tail fins off an old Caddie, soldering an upside-down peace symbol on the hood, and expecting the result to pass unnoticed in the new car lot of a Mercedes dealer.

Rowdy and Kimi applied their noses to the leathery leaves of a rhododendron at the edge of the sidewalk in front of Morris's house. Pleated blinds covered the windows. The two-car parking area next to the house was vacant. The shrubs were trimmed, and fir bark the color of redwood had been spread under them so recently that the air smelled strong and woodsy. The house looked neither inhabited nor uninhabited. There was no For Sale sign in the yard. Having learned nothing, I called to the dogs and moved along.

Just beyond Morris's, separated from his modern misfit only by a weed-free path and a narrow shrub border, was a three-story house with peeling cream-yellow paint and stark, handsome lines. The color was softer than the bright yellow of the Longfellow House on Brattle Street, and the Longfellow House wasn't in desperate need of a gutter and roof job, but, properly renovated, this place would have had the same festive look of a three-tiered wedding cake. And, although there were stretches of lawn, the yard was mainly devoted to border after border of perennials. I stopped. My mother grew perennials. In fact, Marissa was a terrible snob about flowers. Not about people, I should add, or dogs, either, really, but flowers. She would have loved this place. Delphiniums were everywhere, along the front of the house and in profusion in the long, wide borders, where the heavily budded spires were beginning to stretch upward, but weren't yet in bloom. Bleeding hearts and candytuft were on their way out, and the main sources of color were the blue forget-me-nots, columbine, and alpine asters, the pink coral bells, and the spreading clumps of magenta-flowered geranium sanguineum. Delicate white azaleas were in bloom, and the peony buds were about to open. Espaliered against a tumbledown carriage house visible at the rear of the deep lot was what I guessed might be a quince tree. Clematis vines climbed the twin trellises that flanked the front door of the house. Along the sidewalk ran a shabby but graceful white fence that came to an abrupt end at Morris's property line.

While I was admiring the garden, Rowdy and Kimi followed an invisible track across the damp concrete to one of the carved posts of the peeling white fence. Like most dominant malamute bitches, Kimi can lift her leg with the best of the boys — and did so on the shabby white fence. When she'd finished, the Best of Opposite sniffed the post, brushed past it, veered around, sniffed it again, turned around yet one more time, and at last began to cock his leg.

At the exact moment that Rowdy's hind foot rose from the concrete, a true Cambridge type suddenly emerged from the depths of a thick clump of peonies in the side yard and marched toward us like a tiny Caesar toward the Gauls, and, in case you think I'm being fanciful, let me add that her nose was distinctly Roman and that her short, straight steel-gray hair zoomed directly down from the crown of her head to her brow, just like you-know-who's. She wore a pair of khaki canvas work pants and a short-sleeved white shirt that looked like the top of a coffee shop waitress's uniform. On her feet were a pair of L. L. Bean Original Maine Hunting Shoes, which aren't shoes at all, but the longest-lasting and most incredibly ugly boots on earth, guaranteed to keep your feet dry, comfortable, and one hundred percent hideous from the first wearing to the last resoling of your Bean boots or the final resouling of you, whichever comes first. If you're looking for sin, I guess you can find it anywhere, even Off Brattle, and I was perfectly willing to believe that lust, avarice, and pride might thrive in private behind the delphinium spires and the colonial facades, but damned if I could imagine a real Cambridge type guilty of personal vanity.

"What beautiful delphiniums you have!" I called out brightly. "I've never seen so many in one garden."

About ten feet behind the white fence, the woman came to an abrupt halt. She was small and rather bony, and the weathered skin on her face seemed stretched over oddly flexible iron. Brandishing a six-pack flat of delphinium seedlings in her trembling right hand, she delivered a lecture on the history and architectural significance of the fence that now separated us. She was an animated speaker who projected her voice with skill and vigor. Maybe she'd had training. In fact, as she went on, I began to suspect that this woman had been taught that the secret to conquering the fear of public speaking was to imagine something silly about the audience, that everyone was naked or that the listeners weren't people at all, but heads of cabbage. At any rate, she certainly didn't acknowledge that only three people had shown up and that two of the three were Alaskan malamutes. She looked neither at the dogs nor, I might add, at the fence post they'd just finished marking. I didn't look at it either. Why look? I see dog urine every day. I don't need a refresher course. And damned if I was going to apologize. True Cambridge types aside, reality *is* reality: Fences are fences, and dogs are dogs.

The woman's head turned back and forth on its axis. Her eyes swept upward. Perhaps she addressed God. Perhaps God listened. If so, the Deity had to hear it all. You don't. Here's a sample: "Central to the dispute as to the precise year of its erection is, as one might suppose, the War of 1812, i.e., did Theodosius Smith merely place an order for it before taking up arms, or was it, in point of fact, not merely commissioned but actually crafted, delivered, and erected in its entirety prior to his departure?"

With every word she said, I seemed to shrink. I should have walked away.

"Alternatively," she continued, "could it possibly be, as Milligan posits, that Agatha Smith, the eldest of the surviving daughters, supervised the construction during her father's absence?" She paused. Maybe I was supposed to be taking notes. "We shall probably never know with any great degree of certainty, although . . ."

Her blue-gray eyes cold with outrage, she went on and on. At the end of what seemed like an hour, when I felt about two inches high, she threw Rowdy a single glance of scorn. Then an expression of sudden sweetness transformed her face. It smoothed the wrinkles, even diminished the jut of her jaw and chin. She softly cleared her throat and reached what she evidently felt was a climactic conclusion. Her voice was very soft and infinitely censorious. "Longfellow is reputed to have admired it."

Cambridge! I mean, what's the most Longfellow could've said? *Nice fence,* right? And when you consider the eminent people, including highly qualified AKC judges, who've admired Rowdy and Kimi? Well, you're bound to conclude that, all in all, my dogs were a lot more praiseworthy than her stupid fence. And, of course, the dogs didn't mean the fence any harm. In fact, all they did was admire it, just like Longfellow. But in a different way, of course. Or so one assumes.

7

An hour later, Rita was smashing her fist on my kitchen table. "So you've got the perfect comeback! And what do you do? Stand there and let this old snob make you feel *small*." Bang! The spectacular Emma's pizza that Rita and I were sharing for dinner practically leaped up, as if a misguided chef were tossing the finished product instead of the dough.

I replied with dignity. "I didn't have to say it aloud. Thinking it was enough."

"Would you not *shout* at me?" Rita's slice of pizza dropped to her plate, and her hands flew to her ears. Her hearing aids whistled. "Christ, I hate that sound! You know what it is?"

"Feedback. It happens when —"

"Wrong," Rita snapped. "It's the sound of old age."

"Rita, there are *children* who wear hearing aids, and, as a matter of fact, there are dogs —"

"So instead of being an old lady, I get to be a *dog!* Hallelujah!"

63

If you know Rita, the first thing that'll hit you is that she didn't sound like herself, and, as it turned out, the foreign sound of her own voice was one of her approximately seven thousand complaints about the hearing aids, which she'd picked up from the audiologist that morning and had been dutifully wearing all day.

"But in dogs," I said, "they're implanted in the ear. *Dogs* don't have the option of taking them out when they've had enough."

Rita shook her head. Her sleek hair danced. "I'm not supposed to. I'm supposed to . . . Christ, how am I going to see patients like this? I'm going to turn into one of those silent types. Twice an hour I'll utter a single word: *Um.* I can't believe people pay for that." She took a bite of pizza and chewed. When she rested the slice on her plate, her eyes filled with tears. Emma's pizza is good enough to make you weep, but the effect isn't usually literal. "Holly, I can't chew right! And when I smile . . . When I move my jaw, these things feel like stones being jabbed in my ears."

Rita and I have been through some tough times together, but I'd never before seen her look defeated. I felt terrible.

"You just got them this morning," I reminded her gently. "You'll get used to them." My tone was the one I use for dogs forced to wear those horrible Elizabethan collars that prevent postoperative animals from ripping out their stitches. When the incision heals, though, the Elizabethan collar comes off. Rita was supposed to wear the hearing aids for life.

"Talk to me," Rita ordered. "Distract me."

Rita is a born psychologist. What distracts her is mental life. Those jokes about therapists asking about mothers? All true. Fathers, too, sometimes. Early childhood. Links to the present. Therapists are loopy about connections. So to cheer Rita up, I talked about Marissa and her delphiniums and also about her ever-so-slightly authoritative approach to the obedience training of small human beings, and then, since Rita was still looking glum, I used her favorite phrase. "I had this fantasy . . ." I began. As usual, Rita perked up right away. I continued. "When I saw the woman marching up with her flat of delphiniums, I had this fantasy that she was going to offer me some. I was going to tell her about how my mother grew them, and she was going to be really impressed that someone even knew what they were."

"Someone?"

"Me. She was going to be impressed with me. And she was going to insist on giving me a tour of her garden. And then she was going to sort of press this flat of delphinium seedlings on me, with complete instructions." My sense of minor humiliation returned. "It didn't quite work out like that."

"The resurrection fantasy is your own," Rita said, "but the reality is that it was *her* loss." She sounded like herself again, at least to me, but as soon as she'd finished speaking, her eyes refilled with tears.

"Her name is Alice Savery," I went on, still trying to distract Rita. "S-a-v-e-r-y, Savery, only she isn't. Very."

"Introductions followed the indirect tongue-lashing?"

"Definitely not. I ran into Doug Winer on my way home. He was just turning onto Highland, and he pulled over. Doug was Morris Lamb's partner — Winer and Lamb — and also . . . Anyway, Morris lived on Highland, and Doug has inherited Morris's house, and he was on his way over there to check on something. Doug isn't living there. He lives with his parents. Someone's renting Morris's house. Anyway, Doug told me who this woman was. Alice Savery. He says she's sort of obsessed with the fence. Also, apparently I got off easy. She hates dogs, or she's afraid of them or something. She thinks they come in and ruin her garden, and she's paranoid about rabies."

Rita was nibbling pizza as if searching for

some way to masticate without moving her jaw. The return of appetite is a sign of health, or it is in dogs, anyway. She stopped chewing. "Phobic," she said. "Paranoid is —"

"Okay. Phobic. Anyway, her brother was some kind of famous professor."

"Savery," Rita said, as if the name should mean something to me. "She's Savery's sister?"

"Whoever he was."

"Alfred Savery was a Harvard professor who was an expert on Pope. Alexander Pope translated Homer. The *Iliad* and —"

"I know who wrote the *Iliad*. So her brother was sort of, uh, third-hand?"

"No, he wasn't . . . Okay. Look, Holly, I'm sorry. These damn things. I'm just — Shit! This is like some kind of sensory bombardment experiment! And why the hell did I have my hair cut so short? Take one look at me, and what do you see? *Handicapped.* Poor handicapped person."

"You aren't —"

"*Aurally challenged.* Shit! You know what? The CIA probably makes listening devices that'll fit inside the head of a pin —"

"Look, I am very sorry that you have small ear canals." She was supposed to get those tiny Ronald Reagan gadgets that go right in the canal, but she'd had to settle for aids that were infinitesimally more visible than those. "But, Rita, the fact is, they practically don't show."

"The fact is, they are this disgusting *prosthetic* pink!" She brushed back her hair and turned her head to display her left ear.

"Well, what do you want? Purple?" Not tactful. Rita's lips quivered, and she burst into tears, but crying evidently didn't help. "Holly, nothing sounds normal! It isn't just that it's noisy; it's noisy and horrible. The whole world sounds like a cheap radio."

"Rita, people *do* get used to them."

"I don't want to get used to them."

"Maybe you have them turned up too loud," I suggested. "Or . . . Rita, do you have to wear *both* of them?"

She sighed and grimaced. "There's this whole thing about binaural hearing. You're supposed to —"

"Let me try them." I stretched out my hand. "I want to hear what it sounds like."

Rita looked as if I'd asked to borrow her toothbrush. "They won't fit you right. They're made —"

"Just take them out! It's no different from trying on earrings, okay?"

She conceded. Rita found the aids disgusting. They weren't, really, except for the color, which I'll admit was a little repulsive, like the rubber fake-flesh on a Halloween mask. With Rita's help, I fitted them into my ears. Boom! The refrigerator roared like a diesel engine. My head filled with cracking, snapping, buzzing, shrieking, and screaming.

When Rita spoke, her voice sliced through my eardrums. "Well?"

"This is . . . These things are really weird." Imagine trying to talk while your voice is being bounced off the moon and piped back into your own ears. I sounded loud and hollow, like an eerie stranger.

Without actually saying that she'd told me so, Rita nodded in satisfaction. "You thought it was just vanity, didn't you?"

"Yes. How do you get these things out?" The impulse to rip them from my ears was almost irresistible, but Rita had paid a fortune for them, and I was afraid of breaking them.

Rita let me keep suffering. "Now we both know why so many people who get hearing aids end up leaving them in a drawer somewhere."

The whirring and humming or maybe just the unnatural quality of sound made it hard to pay attention to her words.

The stranger's voice that was mine spoke again. "Rita, this can't be right." I stuck my thumbs in my ears and pried the aids out. The world returned to normal. "Leave them out for a while, okay? I didn't get it before. I do now. Give yourself a break."

While Rita carefully stowed the aids in a little gray pouch that she tucked in her purse, I began to clear the table. Every dog in the house must have been listening for the telltale scrape of chairs on the linoleum, the clatter of plates, and the flow of water at the sink. From the yard, Rowdy and Kimi yelped and *woo-woo*ed. Overhead, Willie's sharp Scottie yaps echoed the smooth malamute pleas. When I let my dogs in, they barreled ahead, slammed into each other, and leaped and pranced in what I took to be a ritual dance aimed at appeasing the great god of pizza crust, who occupies a high place in their pantheon, right up there with Harbinger. And who is this doughy deity? I am, of course. Play it right, and you're everything to your own dogs.

Deity or not, I never neglect a training opportunity. "Stand!" I told them. They froze on all fours. I was tempted to ask Rita to play judge and run her hands over them, but she wasn't exactly in a playful mood, so I praised the dogs, doled out the crust, and released them.

Then I rejoined Rita at the table. "Rita, I was just thinking. When the dogs bark like that?" Tact. Rowdy and Kimi's extraordinar-

70

ily varied and fascinating vocalizations range from woos to yelps to whines to growls to howls. Universal truth: Your own dogs *communicate*. It's other people's dogs that just plain *bark*. Willie, for example, *barks*. "Isn't that going to . . . I was wondering. If the hearing aids amplify all that, isn't it going to damage your hearing? You know, noise-induced hearing loss?"

Rita shook her head. "They cut off. Otherwise it could happen, but there's a built-in device."

It seemed to me that built-in cutoff was exactly what Willie's vocal cords needed. I didn't say so. As I've mentioned, I don't believe in surgical debarking.

"And if they're not turned on," Rita continued, "they're just like earplugs." She stood up. "Holly?"

"Yeah?"

"I've had it for today. I'm going to leave these things out and go and take a hot bath. You know, what you did helped a lot. Thank you."

"I didn't do anything."

"Trying them. It helped a lot."

I shrugged.

Rita rested both hands on the back of the chair, straightened her elbows, and leaned forward. "I've been thinking. You know what

71

it's like? This, uh, sensory bombardment? It's exactly like what William James wrote." She paused. "About what the world is like to a newborn. He wrote that it was 'one great blooming, buzzing confusion.' Maybe that's how I need to construe it." *Construe.* Now she was really herself again. "As a rebirth," she added. "Learning to wear these things is like being reborn. So if it feels traumatic, maybe it's because it *is* traumatic, because, in terms of sensory input, it *is* a kind of birth trauma."

"I like the phrase," I said.

"Birth trauma?"

"Uh-uh. 'A great booming, buzzing confusion.' That's beautiful."

Rita waited.

I smiled at her. "I love it. It's perfect. 'A great booming, buzzing confusion.' "

"Well, I'm glad you're pleased," Rita said.

I was, too. "One great blooming, buzzing confusion." The perfect description of a dog show. Birth and rebirth. Life itself. I like it all.

8

Leah and I are first cousins on the human maternal side; our mothers were sisters. But superficial human kinship means little to either of us. What really makes us blood relatives is that Leah handles Kimi in obedience. Until the previous summer, Leah's parents, Arthur and Cassie, had kept Leah in strict quarantine from the highly contagious world of purebred dog fancy, but it took Rowdy and Kimi about five minutes to infect her, and after three months with us, she was a hopeless case. When her parents first sent Leah to us, she called all sled dogs *huskies,* thought of *heel* as something on the rear of her foot, and imagined that a *camelback* had something to do with mountains. By the end of August, all she talked about were paddling gaits, snap tails, standoff coats, Dudley noses, clean lips, deep briskets, CHD, PRA, HITs, BISs and bitches that didn't take; and when she liked something a whole lot, she produced the ultimate doggy compliment: *typey.* By then, Leah's supposedly educated parents could no longer understand a single word she said, and I'm convinced that they began to feel inferior, but the last straw, so to speak, came when Leah mentioned the possibility that she and Kimi might one day become OTCH fodder, and Arthur and Cassie decided that since the phrase sounded dangerously reminiscent of *cannon fodder*, it must be communist and that she'd better get out of their house and begin to outgrow her socialist youth as soon as possible.

(What *is* OTCH fodder, you ask?) Well, okay, here we go. A dog that continues to compete after he earns his U.D. — Utility Dog title — accumulates championship points for each first or second place in Open or Utility, Open B, of course, and Utility B, if it's divided. When the dog has 100 points, he becomes an OTCH dog, Obedience Trial Champion, and, having done so, keeps on competing for OTCH points against dogs that aren't earning any because, of course, he is. Those dogs, the ones that make it possible for him to get the points, are — you guessed it — OTCH fodder. And while we're on the topic, let me add that far from being socialist, communist, or even vaguely communal, OTCH competition is the ultimate in capitalism. It's survival of the fittest, sociocanine Darwinism, and the only thing even remotely pinko about it is nature's tooth and claw red, in other words, the sharp teeth and well-filed claws of the top handlers.

Where were we? . . . Oh, so Arthur and Cassie would probably have been glad to have Leah leave Maine for Cambridge in mid-June so they wouldn't have to listen to her talk above their heads all summer, but with intelligent malamute opportunism more characteristic of Kimi and Rowdy than of me, Leah had taken triple advantage of Harvard's ungodly tuition, her parents' tightwad tendencies, and their academic snobbery to get a paying job at what I innocently called a day camp, but what Leah patiently explained was not a mere camp but the Avon Hill Summer Program. Once Leah spelled out the difference, it made sense. Privileged Cambridge children do not squander their summers rallying round the flagpole; they take courses. They don't go to camp; they attend programs. Camps, of course, have counselors. Schools have teachers. Summer programs? Leah's official job title was, I swear to God, *mentor*.

Leah was due to arrive here on Friday, June 12, and to begin work on Monday, the first of two days of intensive staff training that would prepare the mentors for the arrival of the children — mentees? on Wednesday. Although Leah wanted Arthur to drop her at the bus station in Portland, he insisted on driving her here, why, I can't imagine — on the rare occasions we've met, Arthur has acted even more afraid of me than of my dogs — but he won out, and at five o'clock on Friday, into my driveway pulled his dented old blue Volvo wagon with one window half-full of the brightly colored campus parking permits that Arthur collects the way I collect show trophies, or did back when I had golden retrievers, anyway; and not a single bumper sticker anywhere expressing anything that might be misread as enthusiasm about anyone or any cause. Good old Arthur. Fortunately, Leah takes after our side of the family — my mother's red-gold hair — and as for her personality, well, for a start, in sharp contrast to Arthur, she has one.

Anyway, when Leah and Arthur arrived, Rowdy and Kimi were indoors, the driveway-side door of the fenced yard was open, and I was making the rounds with the pooper-scooper. Yes, it was another thrilling episode in the romantic saga of My Life and Adventures with the Legendary Wild Dogs of the North. But back to Arthur. He used to remind me of a wooden spoon, but when he half-opened the Volvo door, I realized that what Arthur actually resembled was a rudimentary sketch of a chromosome, the long, slim outline devoid of genes, nothing but slimy, blank protoplasm, a true recessive type. He peered nervously around, and rightly so, of course. Alaskan malamutes are friendly to people, but they'll happily devour garbage, sticks, plastic, anything at all. Song birds caught on the wing. Wooden spoons. Chromosomes.

Before her father had finished easing open the car door, Leah had sprung from the Volvo, dashed around it, hurtled toward me, knocked the pooper-scooper from my hand, and practically bowled me over on top of it. In the two seconds before I returned her embrace, I caught a glimpse of flamboyant red curls and had a vague impression of something different about Leah. Make that some *things,* and I was right. The first difference to hit me was the perfume, Calvin Klein's Obsession, as I later learned, and if you'll pardon an aside, let me remark that the next time your dog gets sprayed by a skunk, go ahead and try the tomato juice, the vinegar, the New Dawn detergent, the Skunk-Off, and all the rest, but, after exposure to Leah, I'd pit only one fragrance on earth against a skunk's, and that's that damned Obsession.

"You look *wonderful!*" I told Leah. "You're so, uh, sophisticated!"

Last summer's multiple layers of sport-specific clothing — running shoes, tennis shorts, hiking anoraks, biking shirts with pockets in the back, footless dance tights, and all the rest, each specific to a sport in which Leah did not participate — had given way to solid black, as if Leah had gone into unwitting mourning for the child she had so recently been. Her hand clutched a tattered paperback copy of a novel by Jean-Paul Sartre, one I'd tried to read at her age, but only in English: *Nausea*. Leah's, though, was in French: *La nausée*.

Leah smelled and looked new, but sounded like her old self: "I am *so* glad to be here!"

I grinned at her, but when my eyes caught her ears, I almost gasped. She'd pierced the right lobe in five places, the left in three. One more hole, and she'd have had half a golf course. And eight different earrings, one gold stud, one small gold hoop, one huge silver hoop . . . Well, you get the idea — ritual scarification, the symbols of a rite of passage.

The rear of the Volvo held an even larger collection of Leah's possessions than it had last year — suitcases, a backpack, a duffel bag, an assortment of cardboard boxes, a boom box, and a CD player. Real dog person, are you? Compact disc. As far as I know, there's no such thing as a Companion Dog player, but if there is, do let me know; *Dog's Life* is always interested in new and unusual canine products. Regardless of what Leah's stuff was,

Arthur offered to carry it in. I declined. I offered him a cup of coffee. He declined.

Leah seconded his refusal. "It's a long drive back. He doesn't have time." I frowned at her, but her father looked more relieved than hurt.

Fifteen minutes later, when Arthur must have been fighting the Friday traffic north, Leah was unpacking, and Rowdy and Kimi were still in a state of paralyzed bliss. At their first sight of Leah, they'd wagged all over, fallen to the floor at her feet, bounded up, and again hurled themselves to the linoleum. After they recovered, they merely collapsed on their backs, tucked in their paws, and let their tongues loll out while she scratched their tummies. Then she smacked her lips and said, "Gimme kiss!" Rowdy and Kimi will do anything she asks. They scoured her face. She was home.

When Leah saw the guest room, her room, she looked genuinely surprised and made a big effort to sound happy. "You redid it!" I had: fresh white paint, white miniblinds picked up for virtually nothing at Grossman's Bargain Outlet, paisley Laura Ashley comforter discovered at Marshall's at one-third the original price, all chosen for the person Leah had been last year. If only I'd known, I'd have replaced the bed with a bohemian pallet on the floor. French novels would have barricaded the windows. Candles tucked in Chianti bottles would have provided the only light.

Fortunately, though, Leah has a sunny disposition. Also, she hadn't yet realized that black is the color created by God to display the undercoat and guard hairs of Her chosen breed, the Alaskan malamute. Beryl's packages had contained a couple of defurring gadgets. While I prayed that they worked, Leah merrily unpacked a tremendous number of black garments and tried to reassure me that the redone room was very pretty.

"It's a little, uh, unsophisticated for you," I said, looking around. "But it's also my guest room, when you're not here." I tried to imagine my father curling up on a pallet, blowing out a Chianti-bottle candle, and resting his head on a stack of existentialist novels. After five insomniac minutes, he'd end up in a red-blooded American L.L. Bean sleeping bag outside in the yard, and in the morning, he'd have a serious talk with me about moving back to Owls Head, Maine.

"Really, I like it a lot," Leah said for the tenth time.

Within a few days, however, Leah's room was so shrouded in black clothing, so thick with dog hair, and so stacked with unreadable books that my misguided redecoration didn't show. Let me point out that I did not nag her to clean up her room. I train dogs; I knew better. As any sane dog person realizes — *Sane* dog person. Oxymoron. As any *wise* dog person realizes, nagging gets you nowhere. If you don't like it when your neutered male mounts your bitch? Don't watch. So that's what I did with Leah: I kept the guest room door shut.

Besides, Leah and I had better things to do than clean and nag. We talked. We trained the dogs. Last summer, I'd been the expert. Over the winter, I'd merely been living with dogs, working my dogs, attending obedience classes, going to shows and trials, and writing for *Dog's Life*. Leah, however, had undergone a religious conversion experience, seen the light, and opened her heart to Bernie Brown, proponent of the "no-force method" of dog training, the only trainer ever to earn more than 5,000 OTCH points — 1,472 points last year alone — revered instructor, lively dog writer, and altogether a guy worth taking into your dog-loving heart.

On Saturday night, when Steve and I went out to dinner, I got a break from the unrelenting "Bernie Brown says . . ." but when we got back, Leah and her last summer's boyfriend, Jeff Cohen, were on the sidewalk on Appleton Street, and the first words I heard when I opened the car door were,

"Jeff, Bernie Brown says . . ."

Jeff is absolutely everything you could ask for in your cousin's boyfriend — lovely kid, great sense of humor, blond curls like a Renaissance angel's, Celtics fan — and, as if all that weren't enough, he'd just put a C.D.X. — obedience title, Companion Dog Excellent — on his Border collie, Lance, brilliant breed, splendid dog. (Border collie. Not Lassie. Smaller. Black and white, tough and wiry, world's best herding breed, top agility breed, Frisbee genius, obedience natural.)

"The underlying philosophy," Leah was saying, "is that you don't give the dog a chance to screw up. You structure everything so that the only thing the dog can do is what you want."

As Leah droned on, Kimi was pulling on her leash and using her front paws to excavate a giant hole at the base of a Norway maple. Meanwhile, Lance, the object of Leah's pontification, sat in flawless heel position at Jeff's left side, black and white body perfectly straight, head turned to take in Jeff's face. If a flock of sheep had turned onto Appleton Street, Kimi would have torn the leash from Leah's hands and murdered them all. Lance, C.D.X., born with sheep on the brain, wouldn't have let his eerie Border collie stare wander from his master's eyes until Jeff had released him. And *Leah* was the one playing instructor.

Jeff was going away for the summer, but what if Leah bored him senseless and drove him permanently off? Well, I just hated the thought. We'd lucked out once: a perfect Border collie. But twice? Two *perfect* Border collies? Forget it. If fortune favored us, though? An Airedale. Possibly a Norwegian elkhound. A Keeshond, wonderful breed, long life span, more energetic at age ten than most breeds are at three.

And if heaven frowned? A skulker, a carpet soiler, a submissive urinator, or, worse, a fear-biter or even a fight-starter! I mean, you try to educate kids, teach them the difference between right and wrong, but when they're caught in the throes of adolescence? When the hormones are raging and their judgment's shot? Well, it's not easy. In fact, it's nerve-wracking. You can absolutely never tell what they might bring home next.

9

Rita's old dachshund, Groucho, was a sweet, cooperative little guy who provided her with a myriad of seasonal excuses to avoid dog walking. Summer was too hot for Groucho. Winter was too cold. Spring was wet. Autumn was unpredictable. Toward the end of Groucho's life, he actually became too feeble to enjoy an outing and thus offered Rita her first legitimate reason never to take him for more than a one-block bathroom trip.

Her present dog, Willie, however, is an energetic young Scottie who needs vigorous daily exercise. More to the point, Willie is simply not the kind of individual who would passively and cooperatively submit to being used as an excuse. After all, he's a Scottie. He's also himself. Double whammy. If Rita showed any sign of enjoying their walks, he'd probably fall flat on the sidewalk and refuse to budge as soon as his paws hit concrete. As it is, the more ardently Rita tries to avoid dog walking, the more intensely Willie revels in it. In fact, what Willie loves isn't so much walking as winning.

Willie: short for Willful.

What's going to save Rita from ruining Willie's walks by learning to love them is her irrational insistence on dressing up whenever she leaves the house. When you walk a beautiful dog, what you wear doesn't matter because anyone worth meeting is going to look at your dog, not at you. Rita disagrees and refuses to compromise even in the small matter of shoes. This is Cambridge, postfeminist *now,* not China a hundred years ago, but at six-thirty or so on Monday evening when Rita and Willie rounded the corner from Concord and trotted down Appleton, she wore a white linen suit and a pair of what she tells me are called *spectator* pumps. To walk a dog. But Rita looked great, and so did the recently trimmed Willie.

Grooming, though, is an entirely superficial process that has no impact on character, especially what's called "real terrier character." Willie's bushy eyebrows, correctly combed forward, failed to hide the fire in his black-hearted eyes. Am I getting the message across? Let me warn you: Willie doesn't just bark. Well, I'll hedge. Willie ponders biting. He mulls it over. He imagines it. He savors the prospect. He plans. To the best of my knowledge, however, he has not translated his impulses into action since he's lived with Rita.

85

What he does is eye people's ankles and, given the opportunity, fly at them, too. For some reason or another, perhaps the scent of Rowdy or maybe even the scent of my own non-spectating soul, Willie really goes for mine.

When Rita and Willie reached our drive-way, I'd finished tidying up the tiny bed of impatiens next to the fence and was thinking how much prettier delphiniums would look there instead and wondering when Leah would get home. At the sight of me, Willie began his inevitable growling and barking, and Rita made her usual futile attempts to restrain him and to get him to keep quiet while she also fished around trying to turn off her hearing aids.

"I'll take him," I bellowed over the din. I reached for his leash, but Rita didn't trust me.

"I can cure him of that, you know," I shouted to her. "He has the right to learn how to be a good dog."

Rita had finally located the dials on her aids and hence missed most of what I said. "Yes, he really is a good dog," she replied happily.

That horrible stereotype of the comical old deaf lady who keeps making a laughingstock of herself? And all because of Willie. Well, not because of Willie himself — key distinction — but because of his rotten but eminently eradicable behavior. Yes, eradicable. How? Lots of ways, of course, but I'll confess that what danced through my head was a sharp vision of the Yap Zapper in my own skilled hands. Why? Because no one makes a fool of Rita, not if I can help it.

As usual, it didn't take Willie long to settle into a silent but eager contemplation of my high-top Reeboks. Then Leah appeared — and not alone, either — and, black eyes blazing, Willie started up again. So, in her own way, did Leah. Without a single glance at Rita, Leah swooped down on Willie, wrapped her hands around his muzzle, clamped his jaws shut, and thus reduced his ear-shattering racket to a bewildered whine and, within seconds, to stunned silence.

"What a good dog!" Leah told him. "Good dog, Willie! Willie is a good, good boy." The Bernie Brown method? *Make* the dog do exactly what you want, and then make him glad he did. But pouncing on other people's Scotties? It's like reaching out to knock someone else's elbow off the table. Besides, if you try this kind of thing with the wrong dog, you're likely to get bitten, by the irate owner if not by the dog.

Leah's unpardonable violation of the rules of polite society worked maddeningly well. She kept crooning softly, and before long,

Willie was watching her face instead of her ankles, and his little tail was zipping back and forth. Leah has a wonderful voice for dogs, much better than mine, a voice identical to my mother's: sweet, confident, and utterly genuine. The flame in Willie's eyes softened to a glow.

I suddenly remembered my own manners. "Hi," I said to Leah's companion. "I'm Holly Winter. I'm Leah's cousin."

He squared his shoulders, held out his hand, and stiffly shook mine. In a bland way, he was a good-looking kid, medium height, medium build, medium-length medium-brown hair, medium-blue eyes . . . Well, you get the idea. He was a clean-cut guy about Leah's age dressed in a blue oxford shirt and chino pants.

Still crouched next to Willie, Leah apologized for failing to make introductions and went on to make amends. Her companion's name was Matthew Benson, and he was what any normal summer camp would have called Leah's cocounselor. Unlike Jeff, Matthew lacked the rare gift of treating adults as full-fledged human beings. He was so rigidly polite that I immediately began to wonder what he was like when grown-ups weren't around. Oh, one other thing about Matthew. As I've mentioned, practically everything about him was medium. The exception was his expression, which, far from being medium, was supercilious in the extreme, at least when he managed to take his eyes off Leah. When he looked at her, though, I saw the same soft glow that now warmed Willie's black eyes. Possibly, just possibly, Leah had already muzzled this guy, crooned to him, and told him what an infinitely good boy Matthew was. Or maybe he'd just plain fallen for her.

If Rowdy and Kimi had picked up a bland, supercilious companion on one of our walks, I'd have immediately ordered the hanger-on out of my sight: "You go home right now!" With Matthew Benson? The temptation definitely presented itself.

Before long, however, Matthew was installed at my kitchen table drinking in the sight of Leah pouring fruit-flavored water down her deep seventeen-year-old throat while I fished around in the refrigerator and meditated on a favorite subject of Rita's, namely, the odd and unpredictable relationship between reality and fantasy. In particular? The reality of this stolid youth and my fantasy of the free-roving character who would trail Leah home if Jeff departed. Jeff and Lance, you see, were hiking the Appalachian Trail, and, in the meantime, here was Matthew, the object of a moist, refrigerated mediation that led me to conclude that reality is what never crossed your mind.

So what's your guess about Matthew's breed? Another Border collie? Wrong. A Chinese crested dog? The Scottish deerhound that went Best of Breed at Westminster? An Irish water spaniel with weirdly human eyes, a Staffordshire bull terrier, a Tibetan spaniel, a puli, a briard, an Ibizan hound, two basenjis, an OTCH flat coat? Wrong, wrong, wrong! Reality, as I've said, is what never crossed your mind.

Consider Matthew, installed here in my cream-and-terra-cotta kitchen at seven o'clock on the evening of Monday, June 15. Has there ever been a blue-eyed calf? If so, its eyes are Matthew's, and they are trained on Leah, whose red-gold curls spill down the back of the only nonblack garment she owns, a brand-new Avon Hill Summer Program T-shirt, white with red letters. Her glorious laugh ripples as she chatters to this godless bovine clod. A reality. Matthew is clean and wholesome, and, almost exactly three months hence, like Leah herself, will pass through the Gate into the Yard, which is to say that the kid is going to Harvard. . . . But draw your own conclusions.

Enter my cream-and-terra-cotta kitchen two magnificent specimens of a flawless breed, bright-eyed, plumy-tailed living proof of universal love, ambassadors of divinity, heavenly perfection made flesh and blood and fur, radiantly celestial and all-forgiving incarnations of the Great God Malamute. Suck in your breath, sigh in awe, sing their praises, reach out your hands. What do they offer? Redemption, salvation, momentary union with the infinite, life's one absolute assurance that God does not, after all, expect us to make it on our own. We have not been deserted; we are not bereft. Reach out your hands! Touch them! But Matthew does not. Rebuffed, they prostrate themselves at his feet. He does nothing at all. Yes, friends, the literally god-awful truth: Matthew is an atheist! He does not believe in dogs.

10

"There doesn't seem to be much here," I said from the depths of the refrigerator. Its principal contents were a gigantic red box of dog biscuits — stored safely out of reach of dogs and food moths alike — a twenty-one-ounce plastic bucket of Redi-Liver — the same — two plastic bags of Vermont cheddar cut into bite-size cubes, and a half pound of thick-sliced low-sodium roast beef that would have done for sandwiches if it hadn't been a little squished from being shoved in my pockets. As you'll have gathered, I train with food. The cheese might have done okay for Matthew and Leah — it looked all right — but I somehow suspected that the last time I'd used it, I'd been teaching Rowdy to watch my face by filling my cheeks with cheddar. If you're a real dog person, you know the rest, and if not, by all means don't miss my forthcoming article in *Off-Lead*, "Secrets of the Pros: Top Handlers Spit It Out."

I closed the refrigerator door. When I stood up, so did Matthew. "I could run down to

Emma's," I offered.

"My mother's expecting me," Matthew said, "but thank you."

Nonetheless, when I took a seat at the kitchen table, he sat down again. I was hungry. I wished that he'd eat with us or go home, one or the other. On the theory that there's nothing most adolescents hate more than a determined interrogation by a parental adult, I asked him whether he lived nearby. His reply was more interesting than I'd expected.

"Highland Street." He glanced briefly at me and returned his eyes to Leah.

"Oh," I said enthusiastically, "I used to know someone who lived there. He died this spring. Morris Lamb. Did you know him?" Highland is only two blocks long. Besides, Morris was hard to overlook.

"My mother's renting his house." Matthew's voice registered nothing.

To Leah, I said, "Morris had Bedlingtons." For Matthew's benefit, I added, "Bedlington terriers." Matthew still looked so blank that I stupidly said, "Dogs." Leah squirmed in her seat and examined her fingernails.

I changed the subject. "Highland Street is beautiful." Scintillating. "So you're going to college right near home?"

Matthew's eyes shifted; he looked unaccountably uncomfortable. Before he could reply, Leah, ever voluble, said, "Not really. His mother just moved here. They used to live in New York, and Matthew thought his mother was staying there, but he isn't living with her after the summer. He's in Weld, too."

All Harvard freshmen live in halls in the Yard. When they're sophomores, they move to houses. *Halls* and *houses,* mind you, not mere *dormitories,* because the word would obviously condone the possibility of permitting one's intellectual powers now and then to lie *dormant,* whereas at Harvard, even in sleep, the mind never rests.

"Oh," I said, "with Leah."

Kimi, who had evidently decided to return snub for snub, had retired to my bedroom, but Rowdy never gives up. His latest offering to Matthew was a polyester lambskin ball that he happily retrieves or simply transports from place to place. When Matthew showed no interest in the toy, Rowdy dropped it at his feet and left the room. I'm not sure that Matthew noticed him at all.

Meanwhile, Leah was talking. "And, Holly, you won't believe what his mother does! You know what she is? She's a *rector!* Just like in Jane Austen. Isn't that incredible? A *rector!*"

Matthew finally cracked a smile. "My mother's an Episcopal priest. Leah thinks —"

She interrupted him. "And she has a hearing

dog, and I'm going to get her to bring her dog to the program and do a demonstration. You want to come?"

Matthew had tightened up again. "Leah, she hasn't —"

"But she will!"

As I've explained, the Avon Hill Summer Program offered courses, and if you're thinking gimp, think Cambridge. Poetry workshops. Black-and-White Photography. Beekeeping. The Art of the Blacksmith. The Suzuki Method, which, thank God, Leah was not teaching. You know what the Suzuki method does? Takes innocent little children and teaches them to torment adults by squealing out "Twinkle, Twinkle Little Star" on quarter-size violins. Spare me. Urban Flora and Fauna — weeds and cockroaches? — taught by Matthew, who was also doing something about computers (not, I assumed, a module on user-friendliness), and, like Leah and all the other mentors, assisting in the program's showpiece, a play that the children were writing and producing themselves. Leah had been hired to teach, of all the damn things, Conversational Latin, and at her own initiative was also giving a course on guess-what that included a demonstration by an arson-detecting Labrador retriever, a field trip to Steve Delaney's veterinary clinic, a guest speaker with a dog from the Seeing Eye, and a hands-on grooming session from which Rowdy's coat would, I hoped, eventually recover. Matthew was not, of course, coteaching the unit with her.

"I've heard of your mother," I said to Matthew. From Rita, of course. Morris Lamb's funeral. Now I finally understood the presence of the dog with the priest.

Matthew nodded politely. Rowdy reappeared with a red rubber Kong toy. He opened his jaws and watched the toy bounce across the floor. Matthew stayed as focused on Leah as if he'd just done an eight-week attention course with Terri Arnold and graduated at the top of the class.

"Well," I went on, "it really would be great if your mother would visit Leah's course. Those dogs are amazing, and they usually have such wonderful personalities." As soon as the words left my mouth, I could feel color rush to my face. I remembered a book I'd noticed on one of Rita's shelves. I hadn't read it, but the title had hit me: *The Betrayal of the Body.* I wondered whether this kind of blush was what the book was about. I heartily wished that Matthew would leave. Before long, he did.

"Nice kid," I told Leah.

She lounged in her chair and stroked Kimi's

head. "You didn't like him."

"Of course I did," I lied.

"You did not! You thought he was boring."

"How can you say that? His mother is a priest with a hearing dog. That's the last kind of person I'm going to find boring. Maybe he, uh, talks more when adults aren't around."

"You shouldn't have said anything about being near home."

"What was wrong with that?"

"Matthew wanted to go to Stanford, and he got in, but when he got into Harvard, too, his mother made him turn down Stanford, and *then* she moved here, so . . ."

"Leah, *I* didn't know that."

"And Matthew is shy," said Leah, softening. "But isn't he *gorgeous?* Didn't you think he was gorgeous?"

A more ordinary-looking human being has never crossed my gaze, I wanted to say. Fortunately, I was leaning over gathering up the collection of toys that Rowdy had vainly offered Matthew, so Leah couldn't see my face. "Yes," I said. "And I'd love to meet his mother."

"So you can write about her," said Leah, obviously accusing me of something.

"Yes," I admitted. "Among other things."

"For *Dog's Life.*"

"Probably."

"With a pun in the title."

"Hey, let me tell you something," I said, staring Leah in the eye. "I have a mortgage to pay, two big dogs to feed, and an old car to replace one of these years, and if my editors want cute, then cute is what they get, okay? This may come as a big surprise to you, but the fact is that we can't all teach conversational Latin."

Leah looked genuinely abashed. "Holly, I'm sorry. I'm very sorry. I didn't mean —"

"Oh, yes, you did." I waited a second. Sometimes I forget how young she is. "But it's okay. Leah? I'm sorry, too."

She brightened up, smirked a little, and said, "Um . . ."

"Yes?"

She mumbled.

"What?"

"I was thinking . . . But maybe you'll, uh, be offended."

"No I won't. What?"

"It's kind of corny."

"Say it!"

The title she came up with was pretty sappy, I'll admit, not to mention obvious, but she was, after all, an amateur. For an article about a priest with a canine acolyte? Not bad.

"Say Your Prayers."

We were friends again.

11

My determination to meet the rector, whose name was Stephanie Benson, had as much to do with Rita as it did with mortgages, kibble, and cars.

Rita's initial agitation about the hearing aids lasted only a few days. What followed was a shift that I found alarming. I saw less of Rita than ever before. She quit dropping in and never felt like hanging out. After a couple of rebuffs, I asked directly whether I'd done anything to offend her, and what happened made me regret raising the issue. Tears spilled out of her eyes. She threw her arms around me and sobbed. But she refused to talk about her hearing loss or the aids, except to insist that she was adapting. She wouldn't even talk about her analysis, and if you know Rita, you'll realize that that was the worst sign of all. Her face and body took on the tight, steely look of grim determination. She kept her teeth locked together and her lips immobile, like someone waiting for novocaine to wear off. Her eyes were huge with raw feeling.

What Rita lacked, it seemed to me, was a positive vision of the possible, in other words, if you'll pardon the expression, a positive role model. Yuck. But I'm serious. Try to name a single attractive or appealing character in anything — book, movie, TV show — who's anywhere near Rita's age who wears hearing aids. Name a celebrity who does. The few who've come out are a million times better than no one at all, but can you imagine going to Rita and telling her that the aids were no big deal because, gee whiz, look at Ronald Reagan? So I hoped that Matthew's mother was brilliant, charming, and gorgeous. I hoped her dog was, too.

I didn't have a chance to learn anything about Stephanie Benson until Rowdy and I returned from Thursday night services at the religious institution of our choice, the Cambridge Dog Training Club, to which, like Hasidic Jews on *Shabbat*, we'd made our way on foot. We arrived home to find a note from Leah that read, "Kimi with me. Back soon. *Lava* you. L." Leah actually can spell *love*. "I lava you" was the punch line of a joke she'd learned from one of her students at Avon Hill, a nine-year-old boy named Ivan — pronounced EE-*vahn*, Cambridge being Cambridge — who was the terror of the group led by Leah and Matthew. Cambridge being

Cambridge, this group, a sort of summer-camp version of homeroom, was called a "core cluster," but, just to prove that they were human, Leah and Matthew both referred to EE-*vahn* as Ivan the Terrible.

The students had started the program the previous day, and Leah had arrived home with the joke and had repeated it nonstop all the previous evening and throughout breakfast. I was hoping that the terrible Ivan had supplied her with a replacement today, but soon after Rowdy and I got home from dog training, when Leah and Kimi burst into the kitchen, the first thing Leah did was sink her fingers into Rowdy's thick ruff, stare into his eyes, and ask for the millionth time, "Hey, Rowdy, what did the mommy volcano say to the baby volcano?" He dropped to the floor, and while Leah administered a vigorous tummy scratching, she gleefully delivered the inevitable "I lava you."

"He *lavas* you, too," I said sourly. "So does Kimi, who also *lavas* to go to dog training, where you were supposed to take her tonight. Where were you?"

"Roz is away," my cousin said dismissively.

"Funny," I said, "that if Roz happens to be away and there's no advanced class, then Rowdy and I go right ahead and —"

"Bernie Brown says —"

101

"Bernie Brown says that if you're training a malamute, you need all the help you can get." Principally in the form of a golden retriever.

By then, Kimi had joined Rowdy on the floor, and despite the masses of undercoat that were rapidly turning Leah's black spandex tights and miscellaneous layers of funereal tops a woolly white, the three of them made a beautiful if somewhat sentimental girl-and-her-dogs portrait. Leah's contribution to the charming scene was, it seemed to me, entirely contrived. I'd been successfully set up. Instead of taking Leah to task for failing to do what she'd promised, and instead of getting her to answer my initial question about where she'd been, here I was enjoying the picture of my lovely cousin cozily at home with my beautiful dogs.

As if to confirm my sense of being shamelessly manipulated, Leah changed the subject. It's even possible that Bernie Brown recommends the tactic. "Matthew's mother says she'll be glad to talk to you," Leah announced, "and her dog is *so* cute. His name is Ruffly. He's a little mixed-breed, and he has great big ears, and he's really adorable, and you should see him work. He's amazing."

Another thing about the Bernie Brown method: It's very effective. Leah had my attention. "So what's she like?"

"The rector?" Leah gave a wry grin.

"Stephanie Benson."

"This is totally unlike you."

"What is?"

"I start telling you about Ruffly, and you're asking about the rector? Are you all right?"

"Yes," I said. "But Rita isn't."

While I outlined what Rita herself would probably have called my "treatment plan," Leah rummaged around in the cupboards, which were no longer a sort of dog lover's twist on Old Mother Hubbard's. On Tuesday night, Leah and I had gone to the Mount Auburn Star Market, where she'd filled our cart with hardtack rye crackers, edible seaweed, canned beans, balsamic vinegar, red cabbage, fruit-flavored water, and enough packages of ramen noodle soup to provide the first course at a banquet for the entire population of Greater Tokyo. The package she selected that night was pink. Pink is shrimp.

By the time two cups of water had come to a boil, I was saying, "So what Rita needs is an encounter with a possibility that's become a reality, because this whole thing is totally alien to her. There's no reason why it shouldn't be, because if you grow up the way most of us grew up, the whole thing is strictly theoretical. Like creatures from outer space,

103

okay? Maybe in theory you might agree that there could exist intelligent life on other planets, and maybe all along you would've agreed that there could exist a successful, attractive professional woman your age who wears hearing aids, but you're about as likely to meet someone like that as you are to run into a space woman. Only what's really happened, I think, is that Rita feels as if, all of a sudden, she's *become* one of these aliens, and, before, she wasn't even sure they existed."

"With the rector, it's no big deal." Leah peered at the pan and poked a fork into what looked like a rectangle of freeze-dried curly white worms. "She wears her hair pulled back; you can see her hearing aids. Besides, Ruffly's leash has 'hearing dog' printed in big letters, and his tag says he's a hearing dog, which is how she gets to take him to restaurants and stuff, where dogs aren't allowed."

I caught the glint in her eye. "Don't even think about it," I ordered her.

Leah indignantly plopped a bowl of noodles on the table in front of me.

"So what is Stephanie like?" I asked. "Or, really, would Rita . . . ?"

"Oh, yes. Definitely."

"Great," I said. "And is she going to come to your course?"

Leah nodded. "But not next week. Maybe the week after. Ruffly's having problems. He isn't used to the new house yet. But the rector said to tell you to call her."

Ramen noodles taste better than you might imagine, kind of like spaghetti in oversalted bouillon. "This isn't bad," I said. "She said to *call* her?"

"So you can —"

"I know why." I drank some broth. "I just . . ."

"Holly, is something bothering you?"

"Can she hear enough to . . . It's okay to call?"

"They have an amplifying phone. Matthew hates it because his mother always forgets to turn down the volume, so when he answers the phone, it blasts in his ear. But it rings really softly, because they don't need to hear it, because no matter how soft it is, Ruffly does. You should see, when the phone rings? That's one of Ruffly's sounds, and he goes berserk."

"And, uh . . . Stephanie. You can, uh, have a conversation with her?"

Leah looked disgusted with me. "How could she be a rector if you couldn't talk to her? And she sounds just like everyone else. Actually, she sounds like Rita. She's from New York."

Having finally put it all together, I addressed Leah sternly. "You were there tonight, weren't you! At the Bensons'? You *knew* there was a hearing dog there, and you took Kimi with you? Leah, I'm not positive, but I don't think —"

"They got along great," Leah assured me. "Ruffly even let Kimi eat out of his dish."

"And if Kimi had gone for his food, and he'd tried to defend it?"

The Alaskan malamute has jaws that can crush the muzzles and backbones of canine adversaries, but if Ruffly had decided to defend his food and Kimi had accepted his challenge, she probably wouldn't have left a mark on him. With one quick shake, she'd have broken his neck.

"They liked each other," Leah said defiantly.

"Even so, Leah. A hearing dog isn't a pet. Or isn't just a pet. Those dogs have work to do."

"Kimi didn't stop him. I told you. When the phone rang, Ruffly went crazy."

"And what did Kimi do?"

"She helped," Leah bragged. "She ran right after him."

"Leah, at a minimum, you should've asked first, or better yet, why didn't you leave Kimi here?"

"I didn't even know Ruffly would *be* there.

How was I supposed to know the rector was home?" Leah leaves few pauses in a conversation, but a heavy silence fell. "I didn't know if anyone would be there," she added. Her expression was serious and practical. "You want me going all alone to empty rectories with guys I just met?"

"Leah, really. It isn't a rectory. It was Morris Lamb's house, and take it from me, Morris was no rector."

Undeterred, Leah picked up an imaginary book and held it dramatically at arm's length. "Her delicate, sensitive heart pitter-pattering in her moist and ivory-skinned yet richly ample and curvaceous bosom, our heroine raps timidly yet boldly upon the massive oaken portal of the somber *rectory*." She cleared her throat and continued. "The hollow ring of manly footsteps thuds from within the manse and reaches the tender and quivering drums of her shell-like pale pink ears. The ancient door creaks inward upon hinges unoiled for countless generations."

"Morris's house was probably built about 1955," I said, "and —"

"And in the dim light of the single votive candle that casts mysterious yet oddly thrilling rays of flickering illumination in the vast cavern of the great hall, our heroine descries —"

"What?"

"You're interrupting!" Leah resumed her narrative. "Descries that it is HE — Matthew! the noble rector's noble son — who languidly intones, 'Enter, my pretty! So you have not forgotten our assignation.' "

"Enough! I get —"

"Stop interrupting! You're breaking the flow. We're just getting to the good part." Leah continued: "Languidly stretching forth all twelve highly-inbred yet unmistakably aristocratic digits, he seizes . . .

"*Twelve?*"

"Twelve," she repeated. "Inbred."

"Twelve."

"With all twelve inbred digits, the better to bodice-rip, my dear, he seizes the lacy and demure yet —"

"*Yet* again?"

"Yet again tantalizing bodice of her pale-green watered silk, puff-sleeved, shimmering gown and petrifyingly but thrillingly rips it to passionate shreds." With a gasp, Leah put a protective hand across the intact black jersey that stretched across her own ample and curvaceous bosom. "But wait! Hark!"

"*Hark* isn't romance, is it? It's —"

"Hark! Out of the deep and looming blackness that hovers o'er the rectory, and up its steep and winding steps, thunder the massive paws of a gigantic hound of hell. Slavering at the mouth, the great beast springs and leaps. Within mere nanoseconds, the would-be rapacious Matthew lies pinned to the time-worn timbers he so recently trod, all thoughts of present and future bodice-ripping forever banished by the righteous fangs of canine justice. So the moral of the story is —"

"Romances don't have morals," I said. "The romance *is* the moral."

"This one does." Leah closed the imaginary book and set it firmly on the table. "When keeping assignations with sons of rectors, always remember your own bitch."

12

Late on Monday afternoon, I rang what still felt like Morris Lamb's bell. To make sure that *Dog's Life* hadn't scheduled a competing story about some other dog-assisted member of the clergy, I'd phoned Bonnie, my editor, who called the idea "fresh and novel." For obvious reasons, fastidious dog journalists avoid the word *scoop*.

Where Morris Lamb had found the door chimes, I can't imagine. There can't be much call for the theme from *Canadian Love Song* anymore. You always knew when Morris was approaching the door. He sang along. So did his older Bedlington, Nelson. That last time I was there, his young bitch, Jennie, hadn't yet learned to join in, but Morris felt optimistic about her progress. Terriers have little aptitude for singing tricks, but even if Jennie had spent years without producing so much as a little yowl, Morris would have maintained his faith in her. I once overheard someone — it must have been Doug Winer — accuse Morris of always thinking that the glass was half full. I remember Morris's rejoinder. Yes, indeed, he replied, half full of Sapphire Bombay gin.

The high-pitched barking that now accompanied the chimes was loud and intent, if not melodic. The little dog who produced it proved to be what the vernacular styles a Heinz. At a guess, Ruffly had some Papillon, Chihuahua, foxhound, toy Manchester terrier, and beagle, possibly mixed with some basenji. But if you want a clear picture of him, imagine a Sheltie-size smooth fox terrier body; a black-and-tan coat; and the bright, intelligent dark brown eyes of a Pomeranian. Ruffly's most striking features, though, were his rounded, stand-up Cardigan Welsh corgi ears, one perfectly upright, the other folded slightly at the tip, both utterly immense in proportion to his head and body, like two gigantic flexible satellite dish antennas on a tiny cottage, one mounted solidly on the roof, the other listing as if fixed in the act of clutching some invisible signal. Oddly enough, Ruffly's serious expression and those mammoth, improbable puppy ears gave him the distinctive beauty of a dog perfectly suited to fulfill his purpose. Fifty-seven varieties and all, Ruffly was an unmistakable purebred, A.K.C. — All Kinds Combined — the perfect prototype of the all-American hearing dog.

When I'd rung the bell, Ruffly's prancing and yapping had been audible, but by the time Stephanie Benson opened the door and welcomed me, the dog was frozen in a sit-stay with nothing moving except his bright eyes and those sound-grabbing ears. Leah had said that he was having problems. I saw no sign of them at all.

Like almost everyone else who lacks a major physical or sensory disability, I practically don't notice those of other people and am immediately relaxed and comfortable with anyone who has one. Furthermore, all my friends will testify that if, instead of being someone with hearing aids, the woman who greeted me had had no head or if she'd been a ringer for my deceased mother or even an obvious clone of me, I'd still have looked at the dog first. Having studied the dog, Ruffly, I did not then stare rudely at Stephanie Benson's hearing aids, which were larger than Rita's but had the same kinds of little switches and dials. Their color was the same, too, what Rita vilified as "prosthetic pink." But, as I've said, nothing about disability makes me in the least bit ill at ease, apprehensive, or self-conscious. I'm never afraid that I'll do or say the wrong thing. What happened as I followed Stephanie Benson across the foyer of Morris's house was a meaningless accident. That I have executed thousands of about-turns in obedience rings covered with torn, taped, curly-edged rubber mats without once falling on my face is irrelevant. I just plain tripped.

I've liberated myself from stereotypes about priests, too. It's thus unnecessary to point out that when Stephanie Benson kindly knelt down to make sure that I hadn't broken anything, I did not imagine that she would chant prayers over my bruised and recumbent body. I was, however, a little surprised to hear her say, "These bare floors are just hell on rubber soles." Rita would have made something of it, of course. *Hell* and *soles* in a single sentence? But, then, Rita makes something of anything. "I've got to put a rug down here," Stephanie Benson added. "Are you sure you're all right?"

I scrambled to my feet. "Fine," I said.

Stephanie Benson smiled. She was a tall woman with a large frame and substantial muscles, bosomy, too, but not heavy. She had strong features and unusually square, widely spaced teeth that looked as if she'd just brushed them. Her face looked freshly washed, too. Her skin was thick and leathery, something like the insides of Ruffly's ears. She wore no makeup, but, in its stead, a heavy coat of shiny moisturizer. Each of her hands was about the size of the dog's head, and on

113

the fingers of both, she wore silver and turquoise rings that were nothing, absolutely nothing, compared to the heavy Navajo squash blossom necklace that almost covered the top half of her white jersey dress. Her eyes were almost as turquoise as the stones. Her hair was black, with only a few strands of white, pulled straight back into a knot at the nape of her neck.

As I gaped at Stephanie Benson's jewelry, struggled to regain my composure, and checked out my camera and tape recorder, she covered my awkwardness by telling me how happy she was to help with the article. "They tell us we're pioneers," she said. "Everyone knows about guide dogs, but hearing dogs are equally remarkable, and part of our job is to get the word out about them."

Before long, Stephanie Benson had supplied coffee and settled me in Morris Lamb's big living room, which still, of course, had its same old floor-to-ceiling windows and sliding glass doors, open today to let in leaf-filtered sunshine. The room now held a collection of formal furniture that honestly seemed better suited to a rectory than to Morris's cube: maple tables, pale yellow wing chairs, an ottoman, two upholstered couches with no fireplace to flank, a museum-quality highboy with shiny hardware. Stephanie Benson's Oriental rug was too small for the living room floor; and in the adjoining dining room, the ladder-back chairs jutted up discordantly, and the long, wide oval table created the impression of a dance floor so elevated that would-be waltzers would need a step stool to reach it. Morris had furnished the place in stark wood and vivid colors, but he was such a hopelessly indulgent dog owner that, in his day, every piece of furniture not actually occupied by a Bedlington at least bore the marks of one, puppy-chewed legs or telltale splotches where a stain remover had reneged on its manufacturer's promise.

Stephanie had seated me directly opposite her on one of the couches. The coffee table between us held, in addition to two delicate violet-patterned white cups and saucers, my little tape recorder, which Stephanie gave me permission to use before I even had the chance to ask. When I interview people who are self-conscious about their voices, I end up trying to scribble down what they're saying instead of being free to listen. Stephanie said, "You want to tape this? Go ahead. Then you won't have to bother writing, so we can *talk*." Ruffly stationed himself on the floor next to Stephanie. As she and I talked, his eyes darted back and forth between us as if following the ball in a conversational tennis match.

115

Before I could begin the interview by making warm-up small talk about Matthew, Leah, and the Avon Hill Summer Program, Stephanie took the initiative. "First," she said, "I'm going to tell you why I have a hearing dog. Everyone always wonders. Here I am, the rector of St. Margaret's. We spoke on the telephone. When you talk to me, I hear you. And I may sound slightly ministerial, but I don't sound *deaf*. Did I cheat?" Her turquoise eyes watched me. I wondered whether she could hear me catch my breath. Ruffly could: Those waving ears held momentarily still. His owner's smile widened.

"I assume not," I answered.

"Well, the answer is simple, Holly. Virtually no one can manage hearing aids twenty-four hours a day. It's unendurable, and you end up with ear infections. So you take them out at night, and the dog is your smoke alarm. Your burglar alarm. Your alarm clock. That's literally true. I set the clock for Ruffly; it's no good to me. When it goes off, he wakes me up. That's part one of the answer, the simple part. The other part is that if I'm walking down the street, I don't necessarily hear a car even when it's right next to me, but Ruffly does, and if someone calls my name from a block away, there's not a chance I'll hear it, but Ruffly knows my name, and he knows every name anyone's likely to call me, so if someone hollers 'Mrs. Benson' or 'Stephanie' or whatever, he lets me know. Or if my back's turned. It's . . . I don't know how to explain it — it's nothing he was specifically trained for — but he can tell if someone's talking to me. Before Ruffly, people must've thought I was a terrible snob! Because I'd muddle along listening and lipreading, which is mostly guesswork, you know, and then someone would start a conversation, and I suppose I just wouldn't answer, or they must've seen me on the street and tried to say hello, and I'd just go sailing off ignoring them."

"Is that how you happened to get a hearing dog?"

Stephanie laughed. "The precipitant actually was teakettles. I'd burned out something like twelve in a row, and then I really did it. One of them must've whistled itself dry, and then, well, it didn't actually go up in flames, but the fumes set off the smoke detector, and, meanwhile, I was in my office merrily working away, and by the time Matthew got home, the teakettle had melted — well, melded, really — into the element on the stove. And also, before Ruffly, I was managing *talking* on the phone, but the problem was knowing when it was ringing. If I didn't have my aids in, forget it, but the rest of the time, we had this bell rigged up that was so loud that it drove Matthew crazy. And the other thing was sirens."

I must have looked puzzled.

"Fire engines," Stephanie explained. "Ambulances. That's one of Ruffly's sounds. Sirens. When I'm driving, he sits next to me, and when there's a siren, he puts his paw on my shoulder, and I know to look around and pull over."

I asked for Ruffly's life story. Stephanie had mentioned lipreading, and that's probably the main reason she watched my face, but my knowledge of the practical purpose didn't spoil the flattering effect. She'd had Ruffly, her first hearing dog, for a little more than a year. He'd been rescued from a pound and intensively trained in basic obedience and in his specialty by the agency that had placed him with Stephanie. His exact age was unknown, but he was somewhere around three. "But we celebrate his birthday nonetheless," she said. For the first time, Stephanie looked a little unsure of herself.

"Yes?"

"It's ridiculous. Really, it started as a joke. Well, I might as well say it. If it's too corny, just don't use it."

I told the truth. "The chances of anything

being too corny for *Dog's Life* are pretty slim."

"July Fourth," Stephanie said abruptly. "That's Ruffly's birthday." She paused. I was too slow for her. Before I caught up, she said, "Independence Day. Is that too much?"

I smiled. "My editor will love it."

"Actually, though, last year was his first year with me, and I didn't think it out, and the choice proved a disaster. The problem was the fireworks. I was stupid enough to take him out, and, believe me, it was no hearing dog's idea of a holiday. I assume this year will be better, at least right here."

I said, "He might hear something in the distance. There are fireworks on the Esplanade, and he'll probably catch a little of *The 1812 Overture*. It's at the Hatch Shell, in Boston, on the other side of the river, and it must be a couple of miles from here. It should be all right."

Stephanie shrugged. "Let's hope so. Ruffly gets thrown easily these days. The move has been hard on him, I suppose, or that's what they keep telling me. First we moved from the city, in April, and then here, just a couple of weeks ago, and the agency where I got Ruf- fly has been wonderful, but all they say is that it's the transition. Let him get used to the new house, and he'll settle down."

Ruffly, who'd settled peacefully on the floor

at Stephanie's feet, looked perfectly at home, at least to me, but Stephanie's face was worried.

"That makes sense," I told her. "I suppose it takes him a while to figure out what's just background noise he can ignore, and what's new, something he has to tell you about."

"Exactly. That's what they keep saying. And Ruffly is still working his sounds, the phone, the door. I burned some toast the other day and set off the smoke detector in the kitchen, and Ruffly certainly didn't miss *that!* If he weren't doing his work, everyone would be really worried, but he is. The problem is . . . Well, *one* problem is that he's *apprehensive*. It's hard to describe, but working with a hearing dog, you really do become part of each other."

For the first time ever, it occurred to me there were people who felt even closer to their dogs than I did to mine.

Stephanie continued. "And a lot of people don't understand. They think, oh, the dog's trained to do this list of specific things. Listen for the phone, whatever. But it's a lot more complicated than that, because, yes, Ruffly knows his sounds — the phone, the teakettle — but it's impossible to train a dog to listen for every single sound that you might need to know about, and it's unnecessary, because *listening* is exactly what a hearing dog does. But what makes the whole thing work is that *you* respond. He listens, I watch him, I check things out, and, believe me, if Ruffly wants something checked out, he won't take no for an answer. That's one of the things they *drill* into us: Watch your dog! Trust your dog! Really, it's more like: Obey your dog!"

"Tracking is like that," I said. "When a dog is following a trail, you have to remember that he has this incredible nose that's telling him absolutely everything, so most of your job, really, is to trust your dog. Trust his nose. And it's easy to think, oh, well, no, the track layer couldn't possibly have gone that way, so the dog must be wrong. But if you trust your little brain instead of the dog's big nose, will you ever be sorry."

Stephanie smiled in recognition. "But with a hearing dog, you need both. I need his ears. He needs my brain. And my hands. He needs me. The word is *bonding,* of course, but that's so *au courant* that it trivializes it, I think. But . . . Maybe you can understand it. Ruffly and I have spent all day every day together from the second he entered my life, and I am convinced, I am absolutely *convinced,* that something is bothering him now."

Ruffly continued to look — dare I say it? — completely unruffled. Sorry about that.

"Is there anything, uh, specific?" I asked. "Any specific behavior?"

Stephanie sighed. "Well, since you're *here*, of course, he isn't doing it now. For some reason, it's usually in the evening. It's almost a fit of some kind. An attack. A bizarre attack. He jerks his head. He winces."

"In pain?"

"No! Not that I can tell. That's what's so frustrating about it. It's very frightening, terrifying, but I have no idea what it is."

"Does he fall down?"

Stephanie leaned forward. Ruffly's eyes followed her. "No. It's . . . It is *not* epilepsy," she said emphatically.

"If it were," I said gently, "not that it is, but if it were, it wouldn't necessarily be a big deal, you know. Seizures can be scary to watch, but —"

"It's not epilepsy. I've seen people having seizures, and that's not what this is. I am positive."

Well, I'm not, I thought. "You've asked your vet?"

"I don't have one here yet. Actually, I meant to ask you about that. We saw our regular vet just before we moved, only a couple of months ago, and she did his heartworm test and a physical and all the rest, so he isn't due for anything, but —"

"Did she check for parasites?" *Worms.* Sometimes I think you can't take me anywhere.

But Stephanie Benson was unfazed. "She always does. Did, I should say. It was negative. No parasites."

"You might want to have it repeated." I avoided *stool sample.* Fecal terms are like artichokes and oyster forks, best left to the hostess to touch on first. "In situations like this," I added, "no matter how sure you are that it's a behavioral thing, it's usually a good idea to rule out the physical stuff, just in case."

Stephanie Benson nodded. "I was going to ask you," she said again. "The truth is, I'm worried sick about Ruffly. I thought I understood everything about him, and these strange episodes have really thrown me. You don't happen to know a good vet around here, do you?"

"Do I ever," I said. "I know the best there is."

13

When I'd written down Steve Delaney's name and the phone number of his veterinary clinic, I asked Stephanie Benson about photographs to accompany the article. Although my camera seemed to have survived my crash onto the hall floor, Stephanie spared me the need to use it. As a photographer, I'm barely adequate, and I'd have photographed Stephanie at home in mufti. The pictures Stephanie offered me had been taken in church, and she wore clerical garb. I selected two. One was a lovely close-up of Stephanie and Ruffly in which the two dissimilar faces had an identical expression of alert intelligence. In the other, Stephanie and Ruffly stood in front of an altar. Stephanie was raising her draped arms upward in what looked like an instruction to her congregation to rise in joy. The wonderful thing about the photo was the way Ruffly's big, dark ears echoed the sleeves of Stephanie's black gown. I was surprised and abashed to learn that the gifted photographer who'd caught the identical expressions and that repeated pattern of owner and dog reaching toward heaven was Matthew Benson.

"Matthew has quite a good eye," his mother commented, when I complimented her on the pictures. "It came as a surprise when I first noticed it. In most ways, Matthew is so scientific that it's almost impossible to tell what he's feeling, but I really do think that his photographs reveal a rather unexpected aesthetic sense." Stephanie's face was proud and puzzled.

"These show a lot of feeling," I said. "And, technically, they're amazing."

"With Matthew, that more or less goes without saying. If it's technical, he masters it. The question for Matthew is never about the machine itself. It's whether there's a spirit in there, too, a ghost, or whether everything is wheels and gears and microchips." She gazed steadily at Ruffly as she spoke. I wanted to ask whether that was how Matthew saw Ruffly — as wheels and gears and microchips — but the unspoken question felt rude. In any case, Stephanie went on to answer it. "Matthew still hasn't entirely reconciled himself to Ruffly. Before — before Ruffly — Matthew was a tremendous help with all the assistive devices, ghastly bells for the phone and lights here and there for this and that, and then I'd forget to *look* at the lights, and

125

Matthew would be disgusted with me. And now, ever since Ruffly, I don't need all that paraphernalia. Poor Matthew! I'm afraid he sees Ruffly as a sort of John Henry who's beaten his machines."

If Rita had been there, she'd have said — or at least thought — a lot of far-fetched things about sibling rivalry and the Oedipus complex and the symbolism of men and machines. I felt happy to be a dog writer instead of a psychologist. Stephanie Benson must have wondered what I was smiling about. "Dogs are stiff competition," I said.

"That's what's so funny about Matthew's attraction to Leah." Stephanie shook her head. "Although, of course, he doesn't see it that way, and if you point it out to him, he is not amused. But she is such a darling! And with that big, beautiful dog? They're adorable. How could he resist?"

It was obviously my turn to say something flattering about Matthew. *What?* "They seem to be having a good time," I said. "And it really is okay for her to bring Kimi here? I was a little worried that Kimi would, uh, bother Ruffly."

"Not at all. They play little games together. Kimi is just as cute as she can be," Stephanie added.

Darling. Adorable. More than any other domestic breed, the Alaskan malamute retains the anatomical characteristics associated with the wolf's powerful bite, including the broad muzzle and the sagittal crest along the skull. A malamute that bites your arm breaks your arm. I always expect the worst of my dogs; I never forget what the darlings could do if they felt like it.

In lieu of a full explanation, however, I just said thanks. I also thanked Stephanie for talking with me. As she showed me to the door, I mentioned that I'd known Morris Lamb, the previous occupant of the house. To my surprise, Stephanie had met Morris. Off Brattle isn't exactly a rental district; as I should probably have realized, a personal connection explained why she was in Morris's house. Doug Winer's cousin, Sheila something, who lived in Brookline, had been Stephanie's roommate at Smith, and they'd stayed friends. In April, when Stephanie arrived in Cambridge, Sheila and Doug had taken her to have tea with Morris, who was one of her new parishioners. In referring to Morris, Stephanie used words like *warm, interesting,* and *generous,* and she said that Morris was one parishioner she could count on not to object to women clergy or to the presence of a dog in the sanctuary. She didn't say that Morris never actually showed up in church; she didn't have to. Morris showed his dogs all the time, all over the place. The only services he attended on Sunday mornings were conducted by the American Kennel Club.

"I felt terrible about his accident," Stephanie said.

"Terrible," I echoed, but *accident* hit me as a peculiar word for a fatal AIDS-related illness. I wondered whether Stephanie actually believed that trumped-up death-by-salad story, or whether Doug or his cousin had somehow persuaded her to promulgate it. If so, I couldn't understand why. Doug obviously hadn't come out to his elderly father, but if his cousin had known Morris, Doug had obviously come out to her. Morris was so outgoing that it was impossible to imagine that he'd ever gone in anywhere to begin with.

"It must be odd for you," Stephanie said. "To see us here? In his house?"

"It's a lot better than seeing it empty. That would be really strange." We were in the front hall now. I imagined Stephanie buying a rug for the bare floor, closing the big windows in winter, arranging to have them washed, making the house her own. "And Morris would have been glad to have a dog here," I went on. "I mean, I am, too. . . ." I let it go at that. Without a dog, the house might not have felt like Morris's, but it seemed unnecessary to say so.

"It's an unlikely house for me," Stephanie acknowledged. "It's not really my style, and I'm used to an apartment, but the location is perfect — a ten-minute walk from St. Margaret's — and the neighborhood was irresistible. After the city? I still can't get over it." Stephanie opened the front door, looked up, and smiled. "Trees. A real garden. We actually have a backyard. It seems like a miracle. It's the most bucolic place I've ever lived."

I looked up and down Highland Street. Even by my rural standards, it was remarkably verdant. Furthermore, unlike the country, it was all ivy, flowers, and well-pruned shrubs and trees, and it lacked the dented mailboxes, discarded beer cans, and torn-open plastic bags of rubbish that are the garden sculpture of the average back road in God's country, the beautiful State of Maine.

"Highland is one of the prettiest streets in Cambridge," I agreed. "And it's so quiet." As soon as I said it, I felt stupid. What did Stephanie care whether it was quiet or not? But maybe she did. I remembered the horrible roaring and buzzing that had assaulted me when I'd tried Rita's hearing aids. I couldn't reconcile that bombardment, which seemed to be defeating Rita, with Stephanie Benson's poise and self-confidence, and especially with her obviously cheerful outlook. Although Stephanie was chatting and lingering, she was also ushering me out — we were at least half way down her front walk. On impulse, I suddenly said, "Please tell me if this is an imposition or an intrusion, but I have a big favor to ask. One of my best friends has just started wearing hearing aids?" Why is it that women turn everything into questions? Rita had just started to wear the aids; there was nothing questionable about it. I rushed on. "And she's having a rough time getting used to them. And I don't know how to help her." Confession. What are priests for?

I guess Stephanie was a good priest. Her big, wide face warmed immediately. "Would you like me to talk to her? I'd be glad to."

I was thanking Stephanie and starting to explain a little about Rita when I caught sight of three boys huddled together on Highland Street. They seemed to have appeared out of nowhere, but now formed a tight little group on the far side of Alice Savery's property. They weren't making any noise — they seemed to be whispering together — and they were almost motionless. What grabbed my attention, I suppose, was their unnatural silence and stillness. *Ambush posture:* Your dog is trotting along minding his own business, sniffing

130

a utility pole, bouncing around, and then suddenly another dog appears, and instead of leaping ahead to greet it or behaving himself and ignoring it, your dog drops flat to ground. His legs go right out from under him. He doesn't make a sound. His hackles don't rise. He freezes. Then WHAM! He springs. It isn't called ambush for nothing.

But only one of the three boys actually sprang — a scrawny kid of seven or eight, I guessed, with straight brown hair that stood out in tufts all over his head. His two companions sank almost to their knees and sheltered themselves from view in the branches of a flowering shrub, but peered out to follow the dash of their tufted friend, who bolted down the sidewalk in front of Alice Savery's house with his arms outstretched like the wings of an airplane, and deliberately and repeatedly whacked the top of Alice Savery's fence along its entire length.

At the end of his first pass through what I suspected was enemy territory, the boy was heading straight for Stephanie, Ruffly, and me. His eyes were in most respects entirely different from Rowdy's, which are, of course, almond shaped and very dark brown — the boy's were violet-blue circles — but I'd seen that glint before. It's the sparkle that appears in the eyes of a creature who's right in the delicious midst of getting away with something good. Rowdy, though, is always decently groomed. This boy had the vaguely neglected appearance you see in a lot of the children of Cambridge intellectuals — the uncut hair, the battered athletic shoes, the jeans with holes in the knees. The only fresh piece of clothing he wore was a white T-shirt with bright crimson letters that spelled out "Avon Hill Summer Program."

I half expected the boy to smash into Stephanie or me, or to trip over Ruffly, but at the last moment, he veered, zoomed away, and once again administered a series of passing blows to the fence. Then, after what looked like a brief conference with his buddies, he zipped back toward us, but suddenly turned, dashed up Alice Savery's walk, and made for her front door, to which he delivered a single hard blow of the fist. Until then, the whole performance had been absolutely quiet, but the second his hand slammed against the door, the two boys lurking safely in the shrubbery burst into wild catcalls, and a shrill but not terribly loud alarm began to sound from Alice Savery's house.

By now, the boy who'd triggered it had sped out of the yard, and he and his eggers-on had switched from whoops and howls to raucous imitations of the alarm. To my mind, though, the star performer was Ruffly. At the first wail, the little dog danced across Morris's yard, yapped at the shrub border demarcating the edge of Alice Savery's property, then fled back to Stephanie, wheeled around, and reran the route, just in case Stephanie had missed the point, I guess. When Ruffly returned to Stephanie, he positioned himself to face the noise and, on the off-chance that Stephanie still hadn't gotten the message, gave her a hard nudge. She did her part. "I'll take over now," Stephanie told Ruffly. Accompanied by the excited dog, whom she kept praising for his good work, she walked calmly down the sidewalk to the beginning of the eminent fence. She made a show of carefully observing Alice Savery's big, shabby yellow house, the lovely garden, and the shouting boys. Ruffly's work had been flawless; I wondered what could possibly be wrong with him.

At last, the alarm quit. Stephanie briefly raised her hands to her hearing aids. "There. I'm back in business again. Sometimes it's perfectly lovely to turn the world off."

"Does this happen often?" I asked, joining her.

She smiled and shook her head. "The alarm's new, I think, but those boys pull something or other on a fairly regular basis. This is their most spectacular effort to date. The poor woman who lives there has a real gift for keeping them going. If she'd ignore them, they'd leave her alone. She doesn't seem to understand that the worst thing she can do is to make it interesting for them. The fence is their favorite target, not that they actually do it any harm, but poor Miss Savery is inordinately proud of it, for some reason."

"Longfellow admired it," I said pompously.

Stephanie smiled in recognition. "You know her?"

"No. We had one little encounter. My dogs were with me. I got the fence lecture."

"Oh, dear. Miss Savery is very definitely not a dog lover. Doug warned me about that, but so far she hasn't uttered a word of complaint. Doug marched me over and explained all about Ruffly, but all she did was treat us to a disquisition on the fence. It's apparently standard fare. I gather that the children have it down almost word for word. They dare each other to brush their hands along the fence, and then they take off, or they hang around and wait for her to deliver the lecture about the fence. The thing that provokes her most is . . . She's an avid gardener, as you can see, and it drives her wild to have them run through the yard. Matthew tells me that the ultimate dare is to pick her flowers."

"How does Matthew . . . ?"

"Because of Ivan," said Stephanie, pronouncing the name as Leah did, EE-vahn. "Haven't you heard about Ivan?"

"Ivan the Terrible. Yes, of course. Leah talks about him all the time."

"Matthew and Leah," Stephanie said rather pointedly, "are so cute talking about him. Leah keeps pretending to propound some dog training theory about how to settle Ivan down, and she's joking, but Matthew is such a serious soul. Leah can't resist teasing him, and the more she kids him, the more *logical* and *sensible* he becomes. Poor Matthew. Emotion always comes as such a surprise to him. He must be a little overwhelmed right now. He's absolutely smitten with her."

14

"Stephanie Benson says that Matthew is absolutely smitten with you," I told Leah. "Those were her exact words."

"Matthew is being sort of a jerk," Leah said.

It was Saturday morning, and we were heading south on Route 128 on our way to a show-and-go at the Canine Emporium in North Attleboro. I was driving. Leah, still half asleep, was drinking coffee. I'd been awake for hours. By eight o'clock, Steve and I had had breakfast and taken a shower. (Always, always shower with your vet. Clean profession.) When Steve left for work, I walked the dogs, tidied up the house, and made two unsuccessful attempts to rouse Leah, who was displaying that notorious sign of incipient moral dissipation, sleeping late when you ought to be out showing your dog. The salvation of youth requires radical measures. Rapping on the door and calling her name had done no good at all, and the dogs were pestering to get into her room, anyway. All I did was open the door. The credit for wresting Leah's slothful soul from Satan belongs exclusively to Rowdy and Kimi.

"How is Matthew being a jerk?" I asked.

"He thinks that Stephanie should go back to New York."

"You can't really blame him. How would you like it if your parents had just suddenly decided to move to Cambridge?"

"He doesn't mind that much that Stephanie's here."

If so, it seemed to me that Matthew Benson was the first freshman in history to be perfectly happy that his mother had followed him to college. I didn't say so.

Leah continued. "What he doesn't understand is why his parents don't work it out. And also, Stephanie and Phillip — that's his father — gave him this whole line about *the family* and not going too far away. So what he thinks is that since they weren't going to stay together anyway, they might as well have let him go to Stanford."

"Maybe they didn't know they were going to split up," I pointed out.

"That's what I said."

"So that's what he's being a jerk about?"

"It's more about the rector, because Stephanie only got to be a rector by moving here, and Matthew thinks that she should've just stayed in New York instead of advancing her career."

"So his parents just separated? Recently?"

"When the rector left. Stephanie got offered this job, and she packed up and left. Really what Matthew thinks is that since Phillip is a physicist, and she's a rector, Phillip's work is important and hers isn't. Matthew doesn't say that, but you can tell that's what he thinks."

"I wonder whether St. Margaret's knew."

"Knew what?"

"That if Stephanie took the job, she'd leave her husband."

"What does that . . . ?"

"Nothing. I just wondered. Anyway, it sounds as if Matthew really confides in you."

"Of course he does," Leah said smugly. "He's utterly smitten with me." She drank some coffee and made a soft noise of discontent. "This car smells funny. It smells like . . . like orange rinds or something. Lemonade."

"Lime. It isn't the car. It's Kimi."

I'd spent the week writing the article about Stephanie Benson and working on the product evaluations. The previous day, Rowdy had been my guinea pig for yet one more new line of Australian miracle coat revitalizers, shampoos, conditioners, and grooming sprays

— dog fancy is high on Down Under these days — and Kimi had been allotted the equally trendy citrus goos and glops. An obedience show-and-go is the lowliest link in the Great Chain of Being Shown, just above a run-through and below a fun match, so I didn't have to groom the dogs at all, but they're inevitably the only malamutes entered in any obedience event, and I like them to serve as good ambassadors of the breed. The Aussie shampoo I'd used on Rowdy had disconcerted me by failing to foam or bubble, but it had done a good job. Kimi's citrus products had left her looking terrific, too, but she smelled like a gin gimlet.

"Didn't you notice it when Kimi and Rowdy woke you up?" I asked.

"The dogs didn't wake me up. Rita's radio did."

"I'm sorry. I'd speak to her about it, except that I keep complaining about Willie's barking and I hate to do anything to make things worse. Rita's not doing very well these days. It's the hearing aids — she hates them. That's why the radio's so loud in the morning. She doesn't like to put her aids in until she's been awake for a while."

"I don't know why she's making such a big thing of it. Stephanie wears hearing aids and it doesn't bother her. Rita's being a big baby."

No one asked your opinion, I longed to say. The task of explaining Rita's distress to a seventeen-year-old was beyond me, especially because I didn't fully understand it myself. Instead of trying, I changed the subject by asking what Ivan had been up to in the past few days. After observing his assault on Alice Savery's door, I'd taken increased interest in what Leah called "The Amazing Adventures of Ivan the Terrible," and Leah was always happy to relate new episodes. As I'd heard earlier in the week, although Alice Savery hadn't appeared during the raid, she'd evidently been at home and had certainly seen enough to read the lettering on Ivan's shirt. On Tuesday, she'd presented herself at the Avon Hill Summer Program and insisted on seeing the director. She hadn't complained directly about the boys, but had stated that she wanted to make a gift to the program, a gift that turned out to be a stack of photocopies of a page from a walking guide to Cambridge architecture, the page that contained a capsule description of her fence with notes on its historical significance. The director was, of course, mystified by the visit until Matthew Benson made the connection.

Ivan's latest prank at the program, the one Leah told me about in the car, involved Matthew himself. As I've mentioned, Matthew was teaching a course — or maybe a seminar, workshop, or module — about urban flora and fauna, and one of the fauna had, indeed, turned out to be the cockroach, which, as Matthew had explained to me, was a zoologically fascinating insect of ancient and noble lineage. The topic put Matthew in an unusually talkative mood, and he became outright animated as he went on about it. I wasn't very responsive, but Steve, who was there, too, caught Matthew's contagious enthusiasm, and the two had a long, technical discussion about evolution and adaptation that almost sent me rushing to call the exterminator.

Steve commented afterward on what a bright kid Matthew was. I had to agree, but couldn't resist adding that as companion animals, Border collies were a few million evolutionary steps ahead of roaches, and how would Steve like it if his clients started showing up with little portable kennels crawling with vermin for him to spay and neuter? Steve said that he, like every other veterinarian, would be happy to find a new area into which he could expand his practice, and he claimed to welcome the challenge of mastering microsurgical techniques. Furthermore, Steve said, neutering roaches couldn't be any worse than de-scenting skunks.

But back to Matthew. The Avon Hill Summer Program followed a hands-on, learn-by-doing approach. Consequently, instead of just reading about roaches and listening to Matthew lecture about them, his students watched them in the flesh, if *flesh* is the right word for what insects have. In the shell. In the shell surrounding some revolting mess of squishy, roachy slime. Whatever. The point is that Matthew's roaches lived in some sort of dry aquarium in the AHSP science lab, or they did until Ivan liberated them.

"And then Matthew and the director asked Ivan why he did it," Leah said, "which turned out to be a mistake, because Ivan can explain anything, anyway, and his mother — she's a single parent — is a professor of socioecology at B.U., and —" B.U. Boston University.

"Of *what?*" I asked.

"People and the environment. Rain forests. Trash recycling. Lots of things. Ivan can tell you all about it. She's a really good parent that way, and she reads Shakespeare with him, things like that. Otherwise, she's pretty oblivious, but she tries. Where was I? Oh, so they asked Ivan why he did it, and he had this great explanation about how they'd been studying the cockroach's beautiful adaptation to varied natural environments — they don't have to keep evolving, basically, because they're perfectly adapted now — but how were you supposed to observe it when the roaches were trapped in a glass box?"

"The director bought that?"

"Not really. Matthew made Ivan sit down and work out how fast roaches reproduce so Ivan would understand the quote significance of his act unquote, and the director kept wringing her hands and wondering about whether to spray now or wait and see what happened. It was Matthew's fault, really."

"What was Matthew supposed to do? Put a training collar on Ivan and bind him to his left side until —"

"Bernie Brown is not meant to be taken literally," pronounced Leah. "The roaches should've been locked up."

"Listen," I said, "could we get something straight? First of all, Bernie Brown would take one look at Ivan and find that kid a good home and get himself a better prospect. Second, the no-force method isn't about how to correct behavior problems. It's about how to score two hundred instead of a measly one ninety-nine, okay?"

Two hundred? Perfection. Let's start from the Beginning, 1933, when Mrs. Whitehouse Walker returned from England and, instead of issuing the usual complaints about the lousy British food and the warm beer, said, "Let there be light."

And there was light.

There were, however, neither apples nor serpents, no original sin at all, and, really, it's a religion of endless forgiveness, too. Every time you enter the ring, you start out with all two hundred points. Your only task is to stay perfect. I should warn you, though, that strait is the gate that leads in and out of the obedience ring. And narrow the way. What did you think canine cosmology was? Some quack religion?

15

Here's proof that I am less dog-obsessed than is commonly supposed. Kevin Dennehy had been my friend and next-door neighbor for quite a few years before I noticed his almost unbelievably precise conformation to the American Kennel Club standard for the Mastiff. Amazingly enough, I never made the connection at all until I was researching an article on the breed. Then, all of a sudden, the words hit me. "Forechest should be deep and well defined." Kevin's forechest. "*Shoulder and Arm* — Slightly sloping, heavy and muscular." To say the least. "Legs straight, strong and set wide apart, heavy-boned." Kevin's own. But here's the clincher: "*General Character and Symmetry* — Large, massive, symmetrical, and well-knit frame. A combination of grandeur and good nature, courage and docility." Kevin's hair is even an acceptable color, for God's sake! Well, the standard says "apricot," not the word Kevin would choose, but his hair is a light enough red so that no sensible judge would disqualify him, and, all in all, Kevin Dennehy really is the ultimate Mastiff.

What impeded my recognition of Kevin's essential Mastiffness, so to speak, is that in the flesh, my next-door neighbor looks nothing whatsoever like a dog, and if he did, the probable breed would be an Irish terrier, Irish wolfhound, or Irish anything else. As it is, Kevin looks like exactly what he is: a Cambridge cop, a lieutenant, in fact. The original purpose of the Mastiff? Watchdog. I can't imagine how I missed it for so many years.

"Accidental death," I told Kevin. It was early on Sunday afternoon, one day after the show-and-go (Kimi, 185; Rowdy, don't ask) and Kevin and I had both found excuses to hang around outside and enjoy the combination of warm sun and a cool breeze that occurs in Cambridge about once every thirty years. Kevin was massacring the barberry hedge that separates his mother's property from my driveway. I was washing my Bronco. "Everyone has been assuming that Morris died of AIDS," I continued, "or some AIDS-related illness, but then I heard someone call it a terrible accident. Morris died on the night of May eighth or maybe early on May ninth. I remember, because it was my grandmother's birthday. Late Friday night or early Saturday morning. He was found on Saturday. You

know anything about it?"

"What was the guy's name?"

"Lamb. Morris Lamb. Winer and Lamb, in the Square?"

"Guy pulled a lady out of the Charles a couple of years back?"

"Yes! So —"

"He's dead?"

"Yes. I was wondering . . . This woman, Stephanie Benson, the woman who's renting his house . . . I just wrote an article about her. She's an Episcopal priest. She has a hearing dog. Anyway, she just casually mentioned something about Morris's *accident.* So I wondered. But maybe it was AIDS after all."

"Deaf lady." Kevin jabbed the shears at the hedge. "Over on Highland."

"Yeah." My sponge made big swirls of soap on the side of the car. "She's renting Morris Lamb's house. It's that sort of glass cube, right next door to the run-down one that looks a little like the Longfellow House."

"Crackpot House." Kevin's voice capitalized the words.

"What?"

"Crackpot House," he repeated. " 'Cause there's a nut that lives there. Crazy lady who —"

"Stephanie Benson isn't a nut," I said. "Far

from it. She has a hearing loss, and she's a priest, but —"

"Lady next door. Miss Alice Savery."

"Oh, her," I said. "I ran into her. How do you . . . ?"

"How? Because she calls us. Been doing it for years. Royal pain in the butt." Kevin's voice was oddly tolerant, almost affectionate. "Help! Police! House across the street's being broken into, and then you get there, and there's a furniture van and a guy delivering a sofa. First time I get called there, I'm on the force all of maybe three days, and I'm all dressed up in my new uniform, I march up with my chest all puffed up, Officer Dennehy to the rescue, at your service, ma'am, and I'm, Jesus, I'm Sir Galahad charging out of the cruiser, and my partner sees fit not to warn me, 'cause that'd spoil the fun. 'You handle this one, kid,' he says, and puff, puff, my chest swells up more, and my head does, too. So I go charging up to the big front door, and first thing that happens is — Jesus, that son of a bitch, pardon my French, should've warned me — this tiny little lady comes to the door, can't be more than five feet tall, but that doesn't stop her! She *still* looks down her nose at me, and she says, I never forgot it, she says, 'Constable,' just like that, 'Constable,' she says, 'I am going

148

to make an exception in your case, but, at this house, service personnel are expected to call at the rear.' "

"My God," I said.

"And Cardello, my partner, Cardello's standing there just waiting, because he knows what's coming, and when I turn around, he's got this big smirk on his face, and he's just standing there splitting a gut."

"What a nasty woman," I said. "So what did she want? Why did she call you?"

"Something *dead*." Kevin's voice was flat but ominous. I quit scrubbing the Bronco and looked toward him. He was looming over the hedge with a wicked grin on his big freckled face.

"An animal?" I asked.

"Something *dead*." Kevin's voice dropped to basso profundo and lingered on the word. "*Dead*," he repeated.

"Well, what was it? A squirrel or . . . ?"

Kevin let me suffer and then, obviously pleased to have suckered me, said, "Not a damn thing. That's all it ever is, nothing, but that's not how Alice sees it."

"You're on a first-name basis?"

"Alice in Wonderland. Not to her face, but that's a, uh, kind of a nickname."

"So what was her problem?"

"Well, according to her, something — she

doesn't say what, but *something* — is . . ."
Kevin paused to clear his throat. "It seems
like, according to her, all of a sudden, there's
some kind of a bad smell in the house, and
the way she's worked it out, what it's coming
from is that something's died." Kevin tilted
his head to the side and rapped two big fingers
against it. "Nut case," he explained. "She calls
all the time. Calls about everything. Helicop-
ters. Charcoal. Clothes dryers. Got to watch
out for them. In winter, where they're vented
outside, they give off this steam, and the way
she sees it, the house is on fire. Her house,
neighbor's house, anyone's house. *Men.*
Strange men. They break into her house all
the time. Dig up her garden. Bury things in
it. Pollution. Guy walks down the street smoking a cigarette, and she calls us. Dogs. Kids.
She hates kids. The sun comes up, she calls
us. Like I said, nut case."

Thinking of my own tax dollars, the ones
Alice Savery was wasting, I said, "And you
still have to . . . ?"

"The one time we don't —"

"It'll be real."

"And the thing of it is," Kevin said somewhat apologetically, "according to her, the
way *she* sees it, it *is* real, because how's she
supposed to know it's all in her head? So you
gotta feel sorry for her. You can't help it."

150

"I guess so," I said.

"And she goes through, uh, phases. She has these fits of calling us. And then she lays off for a while. And a lot of the time, she just wants someone to complain to, so she calls and complains, and they listen, and that's the end of it. For now."

"Kevin, when I was there the other day, these kids ran in her yard. . . . Well, one kid did, but he had a couple of friends with him, not that they did any harm, but it was pretty obvious that they just did it to get her goat. So some of her complaints probably are justified, in a way. I think the kids probably do torment her."

"Course they do," Kevin said. "Same as this dog of yours probably *does* run over and pee on her flowers, but, like they keep telling her at the station, there's no law against it. It's just human nature. But one thing about Alice is, she's always right. Won't listen to a word you say."

"Which dog of mine? Did Alice Savery actually call? And it is not *human* nature to —"

"This deaf lady's dog. That's her latest." Kevin sounded like a happy owner describing a naughty puppy's newest trick. I'd finished soaping the Bronco and was hosing it off. While I let the water run over the rear, I glanced at Kevin. The pride in his voice and

151

on his face was both personal and civic. Alice Savery, I realized, was a condescending, arrogant nuisance, but she was Kevin's nuisance and probably the pet eccentric of the rest of the Cambridge police force as well.

"She complains about . . . Kevin, I don't know what she says, but that is possibly the best-behaved dog in Cambridge, and if Alice Savery starts trying to make trouble — Well, you know, really she can't. That dog does not run loose, and, also, the laws about guide dogs for the blind apply to hearing dogs, so —"

"It defecates on her lawn," Kevin said, "or so I'm told. Alice isn't my personal responsibility anymore. It's one of the prices you pay for promotion around here. They take away your uniform, and you don't get Alice anymore, either, so all's I know these days is what I'm told, but what I'm told is that it defecates on her lawn, and it does a lot else, too." Kevin gave a sly smile and narrowed his eyes. "But I can't swear to the *else*, because that's not what she showed up at the station with." He studied me.

"You're joking," I said.

He solemnly raised his right hand. "Scout's honor. In a Ziploc bag."

16

"A pot of Earl Grey, please," I told the waiter, whose name, I remembered, was Fyodor. Harvard Square abounds in my-name-is-and-I'll-be-your establishments, but Winer & Lamb wasn't one of them. Fyodor's name stuck in my memory because Morris Lamb, who always added Homeric epithets to the names of his waiters, invariably referred to this one as *Fyodor with the mad Russian eyes.* Morris liked to dramatize. The waiter's bright-blue eyes looked perfectly sane to me, and the only thing Russian I'd ever noticed about Fyodor was his name. "Leah?"

It was four o'clock on that same Sunday afternoon, and Leah and I were seated indoors at a pink-draped table for two. Taking tea in the Square had been Leah's idea. Sometime during the preceding week, Doug Winer had shown up at Stephanie's while Leah was visiting. He'd come to repair a light switch, unstop the garbage disposal, and perform a few other landlordly tasks, I gathered. He'd also used the occasion to announce that henceforth

Winer & Lamb would be doing Sunday teas. Leah had arrived home with a large and rather formal invitation to the gala tea that would launch this entrepreneurial ship, and I'd agreed to accompany her.

When we tried to make a little party of the event, everyone we invited made excuses. Kevin didn't actually say no; all he did was make a show of crooking the gigantic little finger of his right hand and raising an imaginary china cup to his lips. Steve said bluntly that tea wasn't his cup of. Rita begged off, too. Her aids amplified the clatter of dishes and the background noise, so restaurants drove her crazy. I said we'd sit outdoors. She still said no. Another time? Stephanie had an obligation at St. Margaret's, and Matthew was attending a conference at MIT with his father, Phillip, who was in town for the weekend. I'd counted on the dogs, who would've been allowed under one of the sidewalk tables, but in the midafternoon, a heavy cover of gray-black clouds blew in, and by the time Leah and I were ready to leave, big drops of rain were pelting down, so Leah and I got dressed up and went alone. I wore a white jersey dress and carried a black umbrella. Leah bound her hair back from her face with a wide black band that matched the rest of her existentialist funereal chic. We felt grand.

"An espresso, please," Leah told Fyodor, who scribbled down the order, removed the invitation card that entitled us to a free platter of goodies, muttered deferentially, and took off.

The café was already quite crowded with what looked to me like a principally Harvardian clientele — alumni, alumnae, and faculty, women with intelligent faces, no makeup, and simple clothes, men who spoke in educated tenor voices and would have been outraged at the accusation that they adored women who were good listeners. I heard scraps of French, Spanish, and a couple of languages I didn't recognize. A man with African blue-black skin and ritual scars on his cheeks spoke British English to an elderly Caucasian woman dressed in a pale blue sari. At the table next to ours, a couple nibbled cucumber sandwiches and discussed feminism in relation to the next presidential election. She had a blotchy-looking scarf messily draped around her neck. He wore a neatly folded ascot. He argued that it was meaningless to speak of the women's vote. She agreed with him.

"This is what Rita calls a 'civilized occasion,'" I told Leah.

Doug Winer, who'd been drifting from table to table, overheard and happily repeated the phrase. "Civilized occasion! I may borrow that

155

sometime," he said playfully. "Sunday tea at Winer and Lamb. The ultimate civilized occasion." As usual Doug's face showed his apparently ineradicable black whiskers. He wore a boxy white suit that somehow narrowed and elongated his low, muscular build. Murmuring a perfunctory apology to the three people at a nearby table for four, Doug removed the empty chair, and, before seating himself with us, asked, "May I join you ladies? The preparation for this has been simply indescribable. I cannot stay on my feet another second." As Leah and I nodded and made room for him, he exclaimed, "Where is your tea? Where is Fyodor!"

"We've ordered. We haven't been here long," I said.

With an audible sigh of exasperation or exhaustion, Doug settled himself at our table. *"Pink,"* he said, fingering the heavy tablecloth. "This pink has *got* to go."

"It's pretty," I said.

He *tsk*ed. "Tacky, tacky. Pink! Morris wanted lamp shades. He wanted little lamps on the tables with *pink* shades. Pink! Well, I managed to talk him out of that, thank God. Can you imagine? Pink lamp shades? 'Morris, it'll look like a boudoir,' I said, and *that* convinced him, finally, but when it came to the linens, he would not give in, and here we are. Pink! But I haven't even welcomed you! This whole thing has been exhausting. *Where* is your tea?"

As if in response to Doug's rhetorical question, Fyodor appeared. He rapidly covered the tiny table with pink-rimmed crockery, my pot of tea, and a dainty little triple-tiered glass contraption, each layer of which was piled with miniature pastries, crustless sandwiches, and squares of frosted cake interspersed here and there with whole strawberries, clusters of green and purple grapes, and slices of orange and melon. Food makes me feel mothered.

"This is just like a birthday party," I said to Doug, who flushed with pleasure, but then interrupted Leah's praise by seizing her spoon, examining it closely, grimacing, and summoning Fyodor to replace it.

"It looked fine to me," Leah said. "Everything does. Everything is perfect." Before serving herself, she tried to cajole Doug into sharing the cakes and sandwiches with us, but Doug insisted that he couldn't possibly touch a thing.

Leah and I helped ourselves. Partly to divert Doug from his scrutiny of the food, china, silver, and linen for any minute deviations from perfection, I said that I'd been happy to meet his father. How was Mr. Winer? I asked. And the Bedlingtons?

Nelson and Jennie, Doug said, were a godsend. The family had been futilely trying to persuade Mr. Winer to wear an identification bracelet on his long daily walks, or else to limit himself to repetitive perambulations of the block in front of his own house. The dogs had solved the ID tag problem without hurting Mr. Winer's pride: Their tags bore his address.

I swallowed a tiny cream puff and said, "I thought your parents might be here today. Because of . . ." I caught myself. I'd been about to say something about celebrating the launch of the Sunday teas, but the word *celebrating* stuck to my vocal cords. I coughed lightly. Today was the twenty-eighth of June. Morris had been dead less than two months. Wasn't it a little soon for Doug to *celebrate* anything? "Or Stephanie," I added to cover my embarrassment.

"Holly, Stephanie —" Leah began.

Before Leah could blurt anything out, I said, "Oh, that's right. She had something at her church. That's too bad."

"Isn't she a love?" Doug said. "And her little dog, too?" The phrase sounded familiar. I remembered it as a croaking threat. *The Wizard of Oz*, that was it: "And your little dog, too." Then the evil cackle of the Wicked Witch of the West. I used to have nightmares about that movie. I didn't care all that much whether Dorothy got back to Kansas, but I was scared silly that something bad would happen to Toto. I glanced sharply at Doug, picked up a fork, and started on a little cube of multilayered cake filled with chocolate and fruit. While I worked my way through a watercress sandwich, a raspberry tartlet, and a bite-size butterscotch eclair, Doug chatted with Leah without making even the most oblique reference to her beautiful red hair. Leah, in turn, somehow succeeded in conversing for four or five minutes without once permitting Bernie Brown's name to pass her lips. At the end of this near conversational triumph, however, Doug once again began to grumble about the waiters and then moved from the burden of running a business to the horrendous responsibility of being a landlord.

"I had no idea!" he exclaimed. "But what choice did I have? What was I going to do with Morris's things? As it is I had to rush half of them into storage, and I don't have the slightest idea what's where, and it's all going to have to be sorted through, but Stephanie was desperate, and she is my cousin Sheila's oldest friend, so what could I tell her? Stephanie moved here very precipitously, you know, and the apartment she was in, well, it was a perfect dump, if you want to know the truth, and the miserable landlord was giving her a dreadful time about Ruffly."

"That's illegal," I said. "That dog isn't —"

"I know! I know! But Stephanie is not a disputatious person, and the place was *not* suitable for her. The neighborhood was . . . Well, I won't say what the neighborhood was like, but it was completely unsuitable, and I was far from satisfied that it was safe to leave Morris's house sitting there empty. And talk about depressing! And Morris would just have hated that. So I had mountains of Morris's things thrown into boxes and carted away or stashed out of sight, and *in* Stephanie went, and, in all fairness to myself, I did warn her that there was a neighbor with a perfect *phobia* about dogs —"

"Alice Savery," I said.

"Morris adored her, of course."

I found that hard to believe. "He did?"

"Because she was such a perfect *type*," Doug explained. "I never could stand Alice, but Morris would egg her on and get her to perform. Do you know that she used to address him in *Latin?* Morris adored it."

"Like Professor Finley," Leah said.

"What?" I asked.

"My father told me. It's a sort of famous Harvard story. Professor Finley . . . He was a professor of classics, and one morning he was taking a walk by the river, and there were some men fishing there, and he greeted them in Latin: *'Salvete piscatores'* — Hail, fishermen — and then supposedly one of the guys yelled out, 'Hey, piss on you, too, buddy!' " Leah had kept her voice low, and when she finished, she glanced around as if to assure herself that no parental figure had overheard her uttering the word *piss* in public.

Doug certainly wasn't offended. He laughed and said something about town and gown that reminded me of Kevin Dennehy.

"Doug?" I began. "Uh, Morris may have thought Alice Savery was sort of the quintessential Cambridge eccentric, but Doug, did you know that she's actually gone to the police? About Ruffly? They don't take her seriously or anything."

"Oh, she hasn't! The harridan! She never . . . She calls me incessantly!" He switched to a wickedly accurate mockery of Alice Savery's Brattle Street pseudo-British. " 'Mr. Winer, that dog has been in my trash again,' and then she goes into the most revolting details about saliva and the rabies virus, and I don't have the patience with her that Morris did. The last time she called me, I said to her, 'Miss Savery, what's tearing up your trash bags are the raccoons living in *your* carriage house' — it's a fright, and it's positively infested with animals — 'and,' I told her, 'if you'd have it torn down or repaired, you'd have no more problems with your precious *refuse!*' "

"Raccoons are more likely to carry rabies than a dog is," I said. "And rabies actually is spreading in Massachusetts. The biggest problem is that people are getting panicky."

"Oh, Morris wanted to get the poor things all vaccinated," Doug said. "He was reading about Alpine foxes. He had some grand plan about feeding the raccoons some kind of Swiss rabies vaccine. . . ."

Silence fell at our table. Leah had the tact not to break it. Doug and I shared what seemed to me a moment of mourning. For all Morris's frivolity, he cared about other living creatures, and he acted on his concern. It sounds corny to say that he'd risked his life to save a stranger, but the time he'd plunged into the Charles, that's precisely what he'd done. Lots of animal lovers were worried that public panic about the spread of rabies would result in senseless efforts to eradicate raccoons, opossums, bats, and even properly vaccinated cats and dogs. Morris hadn't merely felt sorry for the wild animals; he'd intended to protect the helpless raccoons in his own neighborhood.

162

Maybe the grief for Morris was more than Doug could tolerate. "My staff!" He shot to his feet. "I have to see what they're up to. If I don't keep an eye on them every second," he confided to Leah, "they do the most unbelievable things. Last week I caught Fyodor exiting the kitchen with a tray, and something about it looked peculiar to me, and I reached out and flipped open one of the sandwiches, and you'll never believe what was in it! I almost passed out. Garbage! Some stupid boy in the kitchen had mixed it up with the *crab salad!* And Fyodor has been told a hundred thousand times to check every order just as if he were going to consume it himself, but with Fyodor, everything goes in one ear and out the other without tarrying in between. A garbage sandwich!"

"The customer might not even have noticed," Leah pointed out. Entirely ignorant of the circumstances and stories surrounding Morris Lamb's death, she added innocently, "Some people don't even notice. They'll eat absolutely anything."

17

Playing the dog show game without bragging is like passing Go without bothering to collect your two hundred dollars; if you give it a miss, you aren't really playing at all. Everyone passes Go, of course, but not everyone has the good fortune to be the first to land on Boardwalk, and if you happen to be the lucky one, you're not merely expected to snap it up, but considered a hopeless fool unless you promptly invest your all to up the rent from that token fifty dollars. If you've got a shot at Park Place? Buy! Add houses! Buy a hotel! Buy two! Monopoly is not some New Age game.

Neither are dog shows. When American and Canadian Champion Malopoly's Boardwalk Beauty, C.D., T.T., W.P.D., goes Best of Breed at the Atlantic City Area Specialty, at a minimum you're expected to send in the win to your area editor so it can appear in the "Something to Howl About" column of the *Alaskan Malamute Club of America News-letter*. And when she's linebred to Ch. Monolith's Park Place? Or when you're just so proud of her that a mere gratis newsletter howl won't do? Well, what you do then is to take out a full-page ad in *The Malamute Quarterly*, which, like every other self-respecting breed-specific publication, provides its subscribers with an unparalleled opportunity to brag, brag, brag about their dogs in unbridled and endlessly satisfactory detail, an opportunity, I might add, completely denied to human parents.

Really. Flip open an issue of *The Malamute Quarterly*, and what do you find? Right at the top of the page: Am/Can Ch. Malalong Cassidy, C.D.X., R.O.M., then a gorgeous show photo, and, underneath it, the dog's OFA number and rating (excellent), CHD probability (almost zero), and the information that he's CERF clear, then a four-generation pedigree, and maybe a list of his own impressive wins and achievements and those of his get, and then something like, "The foundation sire of Malalong Kennels, Cass is so ideal that he makes the standard look un-typey. This dog has everything — beauty, brains, movement. . . ." Brag, brag, brag! Check out *The Borzoi Quarterly*, *The Irish Wolfhound Quarterly*, *Doberman World*, *The Corgi Cryer*, any breed publication you like.

With one exception. Which one? The one

that doesn't exist. Where, O where is *The Human Being Quarterly*? *Baby World*? Where is *The Infant Cryer*? Where are the wonderful advertisements, the gorgeous photos, and the strings of letters and numbers attesting to health, intelligence, and temperament? Where, where, where are the *brags*? Nowhere. Why? The answer, sad and obvious: The game of human children is Monopoly with no Go and no two hundred dollars, nothing to brag of at all.

Or so I assumed until I met Ivan, whose last name was not, in fact, The Terrible, but Flynn-Isaacson. This boy seemed to me definitely to merit a costly spread in *Kiddy Kennel Review*. I'd observed Ivan's foray into Alice Savery's territory, but the date of our first real encounter was Wednesday, July 1. The place was the Avon Hill Summer Program. The occasion was a hands-on grooming workshop. The *hands* were those of Leah's eight students. The *on* was Rowdy, who'd been drafted into service because he was both big enough to go around and sucker enough to tolerate what I imagined would be the inept swipes and yanks of sixteen brush-and-comb wielding juvenile fists.

Perhaps I should say outright that especially since I got involved with Malamute Rescue, I have come to resent young children. I don't have anything against them *per se* or *in vacuo,* as one not only says in Cambridge, but says aloud, preferably in the hearing of other people. No, what I increasingly have against little children is the same thing I have against cats, a species I unequivocally like, *per se* and *in vacuo.* I keep getting all these phone calls from people who would make great adoptive owners of rescued Malamutes if only, only, only they didn't have those damned babies. Or toddlers. The policy laid down by Betty Burley, the coordinator of our local rescue effort, is that we don't place rescue dogs in families with young children. Period. If you ask Betty why, she'll explain that we don't know the entire life histories of the dogs. The truth is that Betty doesn't trust parents. Neither do I, and with good reason: How far can you trust people ashamed to brag and too cheap to advertise?

Back to Ivan. By ten-thirty on Wednesday morning, my portable grooming table was set up on the grass adjacent to Leah's classroom at AHSP, and all eight of Leah's little beasts, five girls and three boys, were simultaneously practicing their rudimentary grooming skills on what was undoubtedly the happiest Alaskan malamute ever to grace a Goodrich nonskid easy-clean vinyl surface, and that's saying something. Rowdy is crazy about children, and if you avoid water to the extent of not even whispering the word, he loves to be groomed. Once Leah's campers, if you'll pardon the gross expression, started carefully parting and brushing out their assigned sections of Rowdy's coat, he would've been content to stand patiently, his feet firmly planted, for as long as they'd continue to stroke him.

Leah had wisely assigned Rowdy's head to the tallest child, a round-faced Asian girl named Mee Lee, who had a trace of an accent and the deft and gentle touch you'd expect in a professional groomer with ten years' experience. Mee Lee was dressed in brand-new pink Oshkosh overalls and a matching flowered jersey; and the tiny red-haired girl dutifully working on Rowdy's left foreleg foot wore a lavender shorts-and-top outfit with appliquéd butterflies that might as well have been arranged to spell out "I'm from the suburbs." The remaining six were scruffy Cambridge whiz kids with rumpled unisex clothes and uncombed hair. A golden-eyed boy with coffee-colored skin and a plump, yellow-haired girl discovered that each had accompanied a parent to Cuba the previous winter. He went with his mother, she with her father. Neither child seemed even slightly surprised to learn that the other, too, had met

Castro. Was I impressed? Not at all. Whenever I find myself in Havana, I always pop in for a nice gossip, of course, but I'd always supposed that adulthood had its privileges.

Ivan, who'd been handed the vital but ignominious assignment of brushing Rowdy's tail and anal area, didn't mention any recent hobnobbing with Fidel. He made quite a powerful impression on me nonetheless. Except for those big, round violet-blue eyes, he wasn't much to look at, a scrawny, wiry kid whose brown hair still stuck up in the clumps and tufts I'd noticed the first time I'd seen him and evidently hadn't been shampooed since. But as soon as I began to talk with him, I finally understood how he'd quickly become the focus of Leah and Matthew's attention. Planted at Rowdy's heavily-furred rear end, Ivan carefully grasped the dog's tail in his left hand, raised it, pointed an undercoat rake straight ahead, caught my eye, and demanded to know, first, whether the anal sacs were vestigial organs and second, whether Rowdy would mind having them emptied.

I shot a protective hand toward Rowdy. "Yes! He certainly would mind. And they don't need emptying. They're not full."

"Do they ever explode?" Ivan asked eagerly.

"Not that I've noticed." I sounded casual,

as if such an event might entirely fail to blow my superb sangfroid.

"I read that in a book," Ivan explained. "It said that sometimes if dogs are, like, in stressful situations, they'll explode. All of a sudden, they'll just empty their anal sacs."

"I guess that sounded pretty interesting," I murmured.

"It did." His reedy little-boy voice was serious, but those eyes gave him away. "I wondered if it made a noise."

"What it makes is a mess," I said firmly. "And it doesn't smell very good, either. But if you're worried about having it happen while you're working on his tail, don't, because it isn't going to. His anal sacs aren't full, and that's not how he reacts to stress. Besides, he likes being groomed, and he likes being the center of attention. He's having a good time." Then, either because I'm slow to catch on or because Ivan looked like a little kid and, damn it, *was* one, I put on a high-pitched talking-to-dopes voice and inquired, "Do you know what kind of a dog Rowdy is?"

"Kotzebue," Ivan said, "but not pure Kotzebue. Is that how you pronounce it?"

Kotzebue? About one adult in five hundred thousand can recognize an Alaskan malamute, never mind tell a Kotzebue from a M'Loot. To malamute fanciers, the distinction between the two principal lines is sharp and clear, but practically no one else even knows that it exists.

"Does your family breed malamutes?" I asked. If so, Ivan would have known how to pronounce *Kotzebue,* and, besides, Leah would certainly have told me, but I was so surprised that I didn't think.

By now, Ivan was ineffectually running a porcupine brush over the top layer of guard hair on Rowdy's tail. "My father's dead," he said.

"I'm sorry." For Ivan. For asking.

"He died a long time ago. In Cameroon."

I struggled to remember where Cameroon was. "Oh," I said feebly.

Ivan looked up and stared at me. "Men don't live as long as women," he informed me. "Most men don't. On the average. It's a matter of probabilities."

"I guess that's true."

"It is," he said decisively.

I wondered whether to assure Ivan that his mother would live a long time. Leah had mentioned her, so I knew she was alive, but I was afraid that she might have some terminal illness I hadn't heard about or that Ivan would inform me that one in every nine American women gets breast cancer or that he'd produce some other argument I'd be unable to rebut.

171

I wished Rita were there to advise me. I was forced to follow my instincts. "Do you have a dog at home?" I asked.

He switched to Rowdy's left rear leg, someone else's territory, and began to brush vigorously. "No," he mumbled.

"A cat?"

"We don't have anything." He made *home* sound like a vast empty space.

"Then how come you know what a Kotzebue is?" I asked a little too brightly.

"Because I read it in a book. My mother got it for me. It's called *This Is the Alaskan Malamute.* It's a pretty good book."

"Yes, it is. It has good pictures." The remark wasn't as condescending as it probably sounds. The book *does* have good photos, including an extraordinary number of the legendary Floyd, Inuit's Wooly Bully, my favorite of which isn't one of the show-win shots but a snap of that gorgeous dog in the ring at Westminster in 1968. The handler isn't even looking at the dog — he's bending over to set him up for judging — but the great showman, the pretty boy, is glowing and grinning. That picture captures the independent show-off joy of the dog and of the whole breed. The photo also happens to highlight Rowdy's almost uncanny resemblance to this extraordinary creature, but that's incidental.

So I said that I too liked the pictures, and Leah, who was leaning over to supervise the application of grooming spray to Rowdy's left side, overheard and interjected, "Ivan's a little beyond picture books. Aren't you, Ivan? He just finished *The Call of the Wild.* And not the abridged version, either."

Critics complain about Jack London's anthropomorphism or claim that he portrayed dogs not as they are, but as we wish they were. I disagree. I love Jack London. What's more, I know the secret of his power. Jack London *did* write about dogs as they are: In their hearts, they are exactly as we wish them to be. No other writer has ever captured that identity with London's passion.

"My mother says that it's an example of anthropomorphism," Ivan said, "because Buck thinks and remembers and everything, so he isn't really a dog. He's more like a person."

"What do *you* think?" I asked.

"I think he's a dog," Ivan said.

"I do, too. And I always cry at the end."

"I didn't," said Ivan, stiff-jawed.

"You did so, Ivan," one of the girls told him. "I saw you."

"Everybody has feelings." Leah spoke in the sanctimonious tone of progressive education. "So everybody gets to cry. Everybody feels sad sometimes, so everybody gets to cry. It's all right."

In lieu of responding to Leah, at least directly, Ivan trained those violet-blues on me and demanded, "Did you know that people have only twenty-three pairs of chromosomes? But dogs have thirty-nine."

"I did know that," I said. "Impressive, huh?"

"The chromosomes are in pairs, and so are the genes *on* the chromosomes, and if both the genes are just the same, in a pair, then that's homozygous, and if they . . . if the genes are both recessive . . . if they're homozygous recessive, then you see it! Like blue eyes, at least in people. And the way you remember that is easy, and that's that it takes two to tango! And if one of the genes is dominant and the other's recessive, then all you see is the dominant, like brown eyes, in people, but the gene for blue is still there! You just can't see it. And the way you remember that is because nobody's asked it to dance! It just has to sit there, because —"

"Because it takes two to tango," I said. "I've never thought of it that way before."

"Neither did Matthew," Ivan said, shaking his head. "Until I explained it to him," he added.

"Ivan, you aren't getting to the undercoat." I handed him a wire slicker. "What you need

174

to do is sort of part the hair, like this. You're right-handed, so you hold back a section with your left hand, and then you just brush out a little bit at a time. Okay? Only be careful not to scratch Rowdy's skin or your hand with the wire bristles. Good! That's it!"

"This isn't very fascinating," Ivan said morosely.

"Well, it doesn't have to be done all that often," I told him. "And maybe you'd like it better if you'd got one of Rowdy's sides or something. Maybe you can get someone to swap with you."

"No one's going to trade something good. Mee Lee got the head." He glared at her. "She sucks up to everyone."

"Mee Lee is doing a very good job, and she's tall enough to reach. But you're right. She is lucky. Almost anyone would rather get the head than —"

"Than a stupid dog bottom." Ivan transferred the glare from Mee Lee to me. *"Anyone,"* he said, "would really rather get the whole dog."

A kid worth a full-page spread. I'm afraid you'll have to imagine the photo, but otherwise?

Ivy League Kennels
("Bred To Think/Born To Talk")

Proudly Introduces
IVAN FLYNN-ISAACSON
Eyes Clear Violet-Blue Prelim.
IQ (9 years) Staggering

"The Terrible" is pictured taking Best Junior Mind at the Avon Hill Summer Specialty under respected judge Holly Winter. Already pointed, Ivan exhibits quality, type, soundness, and creativity — he has it all! And he's a personality-plus kid, too! Watch for him! He's a winner!

Exclusively Handled By:
Harvard University Kennels
Cambridge, Massachusetts 02138
"Registered Professor's Brats Since 1636"

18

"So for once," Rita conceded, "a dog is probably not a bad idea."

Every child deserves a dog, but a child worth a full-page ad? A boy who's lost his father? And who's getting himself in trouble instead of getting himself in the ribbons for junior handling? I'd arrived home from the grooming demo at Avon Hill convinced that Ivan was a kid worth not just any dog, either, but worth a stellar representative of the breed of breeds, the dog of dogs, dog to the nth, the incomparable Alaskan malamute. I pay no higher compliment. Was Ivan ready, though? And which sex? I was leaning toward a bitch small enough for Ivan to control. Also, I had a hunch that it might do Ivan some good to discover that there was one creature on earth smarter than he was, and for raw IQ, the odds are in favor of the bitches. (Yes, in malamutes, too.) On the other hand, for a boy without a father, a male might be a better choice. So I'd asked Rita, who, for the first time since she'd got the damned hearing aids, had shown up at dinnertime with a collection of gourmet take-outs for us to share. By the time I'd finished telling her about Ivan, my kitchen table was littered with empty and half-empty plastic containers, and I was pouring boiling water onto freshly ground French roast Swiss-water-process decaf, which is what Cambridge psychotherapists drink except when they're due to see really boring patients and want to be sure of staying awake. Mostly, though, therapists find their patients interesting and thus avoid what they consider to be the perils of caffeine. Writers love caffeine, of course. I, for example, regularly dose myself with the stuff. Tea is my usual drug of choice for the sustained release effect needed to turn out free-lance articles and stories, but when my column is overdue, I switch to coffee, and when I'm up against a serious deadline, I hit my nervous system with a Puerto Rican wonder drug called Café Bustelo, and if you think that café is nothing more than the Spanish word for coffee, that's only because you've never tried Bustelo, *siempre fresco, puro y aromatico,* the greatest writing tool since the invention of the stylus.

"For *once?*" I demanded.

"If dogs were the panacea you think they are . . ." To display the aid in her right ear, Rita lifted the hair that had grown almost long enough to give her a choice about whether to go public about her hearing loss. That's how she explained it, anyway. It seemed to me that what really gave her a choice were the aids, not her hair. If she couldn't hear whispered conversations or the turn signals on her car or a million other everyday sounds, it was perfectly obvious that she had a hearing loss, wasn't it? How could she possibly keep it a secret? Only one way, right? Hearing aids.

"As a matter of fact," I said, thumping Rita's coffee mug onto the table in front of her, "Willie would make a not-bad hearing dog." As such, he'd have to accompany Rita everywhere, thus ridding me and my third-floor tenants of those damned home-alone barking fits, but I didn't say so. "Willie is very sound-oriented, and he could hardly be any more alert. And Rita, they do that, you know. Sometimes you really can have your own dog trained to assist you. And if Willie doesn't shape up —"

"Do me a favor," Rita said sharply. "For once, for once, Holly, please do *not* rationalize. I know it works for you. Boom! Your hearing goes to hell, and what's the first thing you say? 'Hallelujah! The perfect excuse to get another dog! And now if I'd only go blind. . . .' Or that's what you'd like to think. But the fact is that just like everyone else —"

"Could I remind you of something?" I took my place at the table and sipped some coffee. It wasn't bad — not show quality like Bustelo, but good pet quality and altered, of course: no caffeine. "Rita, this is something you're always saying, okay? Try assuming that we're all doing the best we can. I am trying, and maybe I'm not succeeding, but I *am* trying, all right? So go easy."

"I'm sorry." She held the coffee mug in both hands as if she were about to offer it to me as an apologetic libation. "Holly, look. Sometimes it just doesn't help to have you take things so . . . so lightly. Maybe eventually I'll be ready for that, but I'm not now. It's like . . . You remember that thing I got through the mail? That, uh, pamphlet on alien abduction. And all you thought . . ."

A month or two earlier, Rita had received a booklet designed to inform mental health professionals that zillions of people who might appear simply to have lost their minds had actually been abducted by beings from outer space. The booklet explains how I happened to become a repository of esoteric bits of information on the topic of alien abduction. Before reading it, for example, I'd always assumed that little green men were *green,* but they aren't — they're gray — and I would have sworn that *dreams* about

UFOs were just that, dreams, whereas, according to the experts, alien abduction dreams, in marked contrast to all other dreams ever dreamt by human beings since the first time Adam fell asleep, aren't really dreams at all, but accurate memories of real events. And while we're on the topic of that report, let me warn you that if anyone ever asks whether you've heard or seen the word *trondant* and whether you know that it has a special meaning for you, just say no! It's a trick question. Answer yes, and you'll be dismissed as some joker who's trying to claim credit for a UFO abduction, but who's never actually gone farther from home than the suburbs of Cleveland, okay?

"So I didn't take it seriously," I admitted to Rita. "But neither did you! That's why you showed it to me in the first place, because —"

"Because, if you really want to know, because it roused a lot of anxiety, and the reason it did was —"

"I know! You've told me a million times. Because the introduction was written by some famous professor of psychiatry at Harvard Medical School, so you showed it to me so I could make some kind of crack about it, and I did, right on cue! And I said that what *that* proved was that if you were looking for signs of intelligent life in the universe, Harvard probably wasn't the place to start, and I also said that if *people* were being kidnapped, all that proved was that the alien beings weren't too bright, because —" As perhaps you've surmised, at precisely four o'clock that afternoon, I'd consumed one large cup of Bustelo.

"Enough!" Rita jerked her manicured right hand up and then sharply down in unintended imitation of beginning dog trainers who've read about the drop signal in a book but haven't yet figured out exactly what it's supposed to look like. "But the other part is that those people's suffering is real. You don't believe — and I don't believe — that they've been abducted by aliens, but these people have had terrible experiences, right here on earth, way too close to home, in most cases, and to make fun of —"

"Rita, I made fun of the pamphlet, the report. I thought it was stupid. So did you. But I never said the people were stupid, any more than you did. Look, feeling as if you've been in contact with any kind of Other, capital *O*, is horrible. Even just the ordinary sense of not really being yourself . . . Rita? Are you still not . . . ?"

"More than I was," she said quietly.

My own voice matched hers, soft, low-pitched. "Have you talked to Stephanie Benson?"

Rita nodded stiffly. "She's an interesting woman. Among other things . . . Anyway, Stephanie said this obvious thing, and it's so . . . What she picked up on was actually this same theme, and she pointed out . . . I don't know why I didn't think of it. *Alienist.* It's British, and it's out of date, but it's not a bad word for therapist, and I never made the connection. For that matter, neither did Lang." Rita's analyst, of course, Norris Lang, who also, I might add, either hadn't noticed her hearing loss or hadn't insisted that she do something about it. If I were a shrink, first of all, I'd make all my patients have their vision and hearing tested, and I'd make sure they had jobs they liked, and I'd refer them all to purebred rescue groups to adopt wonderful dogs, and I'd enroll them in dog training classes. And before long, the handful who weren't promptly cured would be too busy with dogs and clubs and shows to worry about their sanity, and I'd have no patients left, all of which explains why psychotherapy concentrates on dreams, impulses, memories, and wishes instead of on the primary life force we *can* control, namely, the dog. And if you don't believe me, just try bringing your dreams to heel or teaching your memories to drop on recall. And even after years of therapy, what have you really got, at best, but a slightly improved version of your same old self? No matter how wonderful you've become, don't you need someone *else* to love? Someone who'll love you more than you could ever love yourself, someone with an undeniable reality infinitely more powerful than all the shadowy chimeras of mere mental life? Even after all those years of fifty-minute hours, don't you still need a *dog?*

"Alienist," I said. "I like that. And I'm glad you met Stephanie. I just wrote an article about her." Ruffly played a considerably more prominent role in my prose than Stephanie did, but I didn't want to disappoint Rita, who's a mother hen about my career. In particular, she persists in trying to incubate the infertile hope that one of these days I'll transfer my membership in the Dog Writers' Association of America to the People Writers' Association, and I haven't yet broken the news to her that whereas the former crows and cackles in merry unison, the latter consists of dozens of broken eggs.

"Did I thank you?" Rita asked. "I didn't even thank you. And I'm sorry I snapped at you. And, really, Ruffly is remarkable."

"All hearing dogs are." They're merely a special case in point, but when I say things like that, Rita worries about me. Unnecessarily, of course, but she does. "Did Stephanie say anything to you about this problem with Ruffly?"

"She mentioned something about all the transitions."

"Maybe she's decided that's all it is."

"What did you . . . ?"

"Seizures, maybe. Some kind of neurological thing. He's having weird attacks, she says. Maybe he's hearing something. I didn't see a thing."

While I was warming the coffee to refill our mugs, Leah and Matthew showed up with two quarts of Toscanini's ice cream, a frozen confection so vastly superior to all others that it practically deserves an entirely different name. They also had a video they'd just rented, the remake of *The Invasion of the Body Snatchers*. Matthew's selection, no doubt. The title, I was certain, represented the precise nature of his intentions toward Leah, who, on her own, would have been content to review *The No-Force Method of Dog Training* or would have chosen an undubbed French film and stuck a strip of masking tape over the bottom of the TV screen to blot out the subtitles.

"Leah," I said as she dished out ice cream, "what do you know about Ivan's mother?"

"She's nice," Leah said unhelpfully.

I clarified my request. "Would she let him have a dog?"

Leah and Matthew exchanged glances. Leah suppressed a grin.

"What's that about?" I asked. "Is there something wrong with . . . ?"

Leah interpreted. "There's nothing wrong with her. It's just that she might not even notice. She's really nice. She's just kind of oblivious." Leah fished spoons out of the drawer and stuck them in the ice cream. She and Matthew distributed the bowls.

"How oblivious can she be?" I said. "She's a professor of something, isn't she? And she's raising Ivan. If she manages to work and —"

"I don't know." Leah shrugged. "You just always have the sense that her mind is somewhere else. On the rain forests or something. But with Ivan, she really tries. She just doesn't understand much about kids, and she never really expected . . . The thing is that she and Ivan's father had a prenuptial agreement that he was supposed to be responsible for, like, seventy-five percent of the child-rearing, and then —"

"When did his father die?" I asked.

Leah looked toward Matthew. "When was it? A while ago."

"Two years ago," Matthew said confidently.

186

"In Cameroon," I said. "What did he die of?"

Matthew answered. "Septicemia. He was there doing research, and by the time they decided to evacuate him, it was too late."

I wondered exactly how Ivan's father had managed to abide by the prenuptial agreement to do most of the child care while simultaneously conducting research on the other side of the globe. Then a possibility occurred to me. "Was Ivan there? Was Ivan with him in Cameroon?"

Matthew shook his head.

"No," Leah said, "I know he wasn't. Ivan's been at Avon Hill since kindergarten."

"So Ivan never got a chance to say good-bye to his father," said Rita, who'd accepted one small scoop of vanilla and was slowly feeding herself minute lumps of it.

Matthew nodded politely — he really did have meticulously correct manners — but his face looked blank.

"Does that matter a lot?" Leah asked. Before Rita could respond, she added, "I wondered, because Ivan . . . He'll tell you his father died — He'll kind of drop it like a bomb, especially with people he doesn't know — but other than that, he doesn't talk about it at all, and it's kind of hard just to go up to him and say, 'Hey, Ivan, how do you feel about . . . ?' because, obviously, you *know* how he must feel, more or less."

"But does *Ivan* know?" Rita asked.

"How could he not?" Leah said.

"What I'm asking," said Rita, sounding like her old self, "is whether this little boy had any help in dealing with this profound loss. Did anyone help him to articulate his feelings? Was anyone *there* for him? *Is* anyone?"

"His mother spends time with him, if that's what you mean." Leah helped herself to more ice cream and generously added another scoop to Matthew's bowl. "She gets books for him, and they read together all the time. Ivan reads . . . Well, he probably reads as well as I do, but they read aloud together. Plays and things."

"That's, uh, a mixed blessing," Matthew commented.

"*Midsummer Night's Dream,*" said Leah, smiling.

"How is that — ?" I started to ask.

"Ivan identifies with Puck," Leah told me.

Matthew elaborated. "In the Avon Hill play, it's . . . It's their own play. They write it, they produce it, they do everything, and the idea is that they write their own parts, and we're there strictly as advisors, backup —"

" 'Not censors,' " Leah said censoriously. She was obviously quoting someone.

188

"So Ivan is creating some kind of dilemma?" I asked.

"The feeling is," Leah said, "that he ought to be encouraged to be more creative, because what he's doing now is basically just copying Shakespeare."

"Robin Badfellow," Matthew added.

"He must say it a hundred times a day," Leah said. "What he says is, 'Robin *B-a-d* Badfellow is my name.' And the director — the director of AHSP, not the director of the play — she's a kid — anyway, the director tried to have this sort of tactful talk with Ivan, because he's also borrowed a lot of the dialogue and stuff, but she didn't get anywhere."

"Because," Matthew explained, "Ivan told her that if it was all right for Shakespeare to borrow plots from other people, then it was all right for him to borrow from Shakespeare."

"That's hard to argue with," I said.

"Ivan is always hard to argue with," said Leah, "which is one reason this leave-him-free-to-express-himself method —"

"That's not —" Matthew began.

"Oh, yes, it is," Leah said. "And what's wrong with it is, you give Ivan a choice, and he'll always screw things up, and then what are you supposed to tell him? 'Great job, Ivan!' How could you? I keep telling you, what we need to do is to set him up so he *has* no choice. Like with that woman next door to you, Matthew."

"Alice Savery?" I asked.

Leah ignored me. She went on lecturing Matthew. "You know what's going to happen? In fact, it's happening now. First of all, someone ought to drive Ivan home from the program or walk him home or whatever, because, now, he's like a dog running loose; he's just invited to get into trouble. And then when she shows up at the program and tells us we have to tell Ivan to quit sneaking into her carriage house, all that's really happening is that we're not just giving him a choice, but we're showing him what the wrong choice is. And, you know, Matthew, it's really dangerous, because —"

"The carriage house is a firetrap," Matthew agreed, "and he does go in there. I saw him there the other day. But that story about the kids sneaking in there to smoke, that's . . . if they did it, they would've burned it down by now, and —"

"Why doesn't she just have it torn down?" Leah demanded.

"Leah," Matthew said firmly, "the point is that you can't safety-proof the whole world."

"You don't have to," Leah said, "because not all of it's relevant."

"Leah, you're not being rational. Here's
. . . Take my mother, for instance." Matthew
spoke with unusual animation. "In theory, one
could redesign the environment so that deaf
people receive the sensory input they need
exclusively through visual channels — no
more telephones, just TTYs; every film has
subtitles; and so forth and so on — but in
practice —"

"I think that's a wonderful idea," Leah said.

"It's cost-ineffective," Matthew told her
sourly. "And no one could reasonably suggest depriving most people of telephones because —"

"But everyone could have a TTY," said
Leah. Turning to Rita and me, she added,
"You type instead of talking, and instead of
hearing, you —"

"We know," I said.

"Stephanie has one," Leah said. "And, Matthew, you know what? Why doesn't she just
quit answering the phone and use the TTY
instead?"

Matthew was exasperated. "Because most
people don't, and the reason they don't is that
they don't need them, and it makes more sense
for the small number of deaf people there are
to use hearing aids and amplifiers than it does
for everyone else to change everything just
for them. And that's the point about Ivan.

You can't reshape the world so that he can't get in trouble, because, even if you changed everything, he'd just discover something new."

While Matthew and Leah scrapped about whether the world should be changed to accommodate people who couldn't hear, I kept a protective eye on Rita, but I couldn't tell how she was responding. Then she suddenly addressed Matthew: "One in ten," she told him defiantly. "That's the incidence of hearing loss in this country. One person in ten. That's *not* a small number."

Matthew's beautiful manners and his disbelief did battle on his face. I felt so sorry for him that I said, "Rita, is that right?"

"Yes," she said. "It's more common than all other disabilities combined."

"Damn it, I wish I'd known. I would've put it in the article about Stephanie and Ruffly."

In an effort to lighten the tone of the conversation, I spoke a little frivolously and must've ended up sounding outright delighted that there were a whole lot more deaf people around than I'd ever imagined.

And, in a strange way, I was. I was delighted. In case you don't have malamutes, maybe I'd better explain that the apparent callousness of my response was Rowdy and

Kimi's fault. Back when I had golden retrievers, I was a nice, normal person with conventional thoughts and feelings. In those days, for instance, when my friends got promoted or won the lottery or inherited substantial legacies, I experienced heartfelt pleasure for them and did not concoct silent schemes to divert the money into the treasury of Yankee Golden Retriever Rescue. A simple creature of the here and now, I saw things merely as they were. Now I've been taught always to envision possibilities. Simply to survive, I've had to learn to view the world from the malamute angle as well as from my own. Sometimes I fear that my two once-radically-divergent points of view may eventually merge into one; even now, I find myself regarding road kill less and less as senseless highway slaughter and more and more as potential dinner. When squashed animals on the roadside actually make me salivate, I'll know that the dogs and I have finally become one.

But my transformation from decent human being to shameless opportunist was as yet incomplete. Although I knew all the statistics on the millions of abandoned dogs killed by needle and gas all over the United States each year — millions of wonderful would-be hearing dogs — I wouldn't actually have deafened anyone to save them. But one in ten? One person in ten *already* hearing-impaired? A beautiful prospect arose. During the previous year, the Bureau of Animal Regulation and Care of the City of Houston, Texas — *one* city — had euthanized 1,909 dogs, which, in case you wondered, meant thirty-one tons of canine carcass dumped in the Houston landfill. So call me callous if you want, but, while we're at it, what about all those other people with special needs? If you're in a wheelchair, it's hard to reach light switches high on the wall, but it's easy for your dog; and it's a lot of work to wheel that chair, but pulling it along is your dog's idea of fun. So in Houston alone, it seemed to me, there must be at least 1,909 people with special needs that those thirty-one tons of dog could have met beautifully. Not just people who had trouble hearing and seeing and walking, either, but solitary people who simply needed a friend. Loneliness, too, might be much more prevalent than I'd ever dared to hope.

Elation. Jubilation.

19

What taints the pure capitalism of my investment in my house is not only the color I painted it — red — but the ideologically suspect planning I've devoted to it. Like the old Soviet five-year plans and ten-year plans, my short-term projects always require revision or renewal. Take the one-year plan to build a window seat in my bedroom, which had its target date postponed a couple of times and then got totally fouled up when Rowdy began sleeping in the spot where the window seat is supposed to go. Now, if I had the cash to implement the ten-year plan to replace the leaky old storm windows with tight-fitting new ones, Rowdy would relocate to colder turf in the winter, and the immediate success of the five-year plan to scrap the rattly old air-conditioner and have a new model set in the wall would dislodge him in the summer, but, as it is, the grain harvest has been a little disappointing, and even if I could afford the window seat, I'd have to stage a forcible invasion of Rowdy's little satellite republic to grab it from the dogs and reclaim it for the people. So much for Soviet communism.

In contrast, consider the benefits of Japanese industrial long-term, think-big capitalism with its fifty-year plans, hundred-year plans, two-hundred-year plans perfectly designed to achieve a desirable arrangement of affairs in the distant future and to avoid disappointments and embarrassing failures in the near future as well. Take my fifty-year plan to buy the little, long, supernarrow spite building, as it's called, that occupies the corner of my lot at the intersection of Appleton and Concord. *Spite?* Two people had a property dispute. One got even. Or so I assume. Anyway, one of the long brick sides of the spite building runs along my yard and helps to fence it in, but — here comes the plan — it would be no trouble at all to knock a door in that wall, get my plumber-friend Ron to install a tub, move in a few odds and ends, put up some sturdy partitions, and presto! The cold-weather grooming area I need, and kennel space for Malamute Rescue. I could use both now, of course; I wish that the spite building would come up for sale and that I had the money to buy and renovate it. But do I actively *covet* it? No. Why? It's a fifty-year plan, that's why. I have lots of time left.

But back to the immediate future, the plans

196

for which had originally included, in addition to the installation of the long-deferred window seat, the purchase of two comfortable chairs to flank the fireplace in the living room and the acquisition of a microwave oven that was supposed to pay for itself in no time by enabling me to produce almost-no-cost-as-if-freeze-dried liver treats that the dogs wouldn't be able to tell from Redi-Liver. Then Leah got into Harvard, and my plans . . . Well, not that I expected her to *live* here, of course. If the dogs had known, they might have. I did not. What I did expect was that she'd spend some time here, and I wanted to make it comfortable for her. My misguidedly girlish redecoration of the guest room and the installation of the extension phone hadn't cost much. The real money had gone into the TV, the VCR, and the cabinet that hid them from view when they weren't in use.

At that moment, however, they were. How anyone could even think about watching *Invasion of the Body Snatchers* on a full stomach was beyond me, but as soon as Matthew and Leah had finished their ice cream, Leah brought the dogs in from the yard, and she and Matthew took the video to the living room and started watching it. Then the phone rang. It's not just my plans that get changed; it's everyone's. I answered. The caller was Stephanie Benson. She startled me by almost shouting: "Hello? Can you hear me?"

"Perfectly!" I yelled. "Can you hear me?" To Rita, I mouthed: "Stephanie Benson."

After Stephanie and I had exchanged another couple of bellows and concluded that each could hear the other just fine, Stephanie apologized for bothering me. I felt alarmed. Had one of Ruffly's episodes culminated in coma? Had he injured himself? I was relieved when Stephanie explained that she'd thought there might be something wrong with her phone. Then she paused and said that maybe the trouble was with her hearing aids. They'd been malfunctioning lately, she thought. She wasn't sure what the problem was. That was why she'd called. Could she speak to Matthew?

When I summoned her son to the kitchen phone, he showed no sign of being irked at the interruption. He just took the receiver and said, "Mom?" Then he listened and said, "It's probably a wrong number." He asked Stephanie some questions and gave her some instructions. Had she put new batteries in her aids? Was she positive they were fresh? She should check to make sure that the phone connections were tight. Was the volume control working? He made her experiment with it. Then, evidently at her suggestion, he hung up and, after politely requesting my permission, called her back. She must have answered on the first ring.

Although Rita and I made a pretense of chatting while Matthew used the phone, we couldn't help overhearing, of course, but then Steve arrived, and I actually missed the rest of what Matthew said to his mother. By then, Leah had stopped the video, and she and Rowdy and Kimi had come into the kitchen to find out what was going on and to greet Steve. By the time Matthew's call ended, he had a small audience for his explanation, the gist of which was that he couldn't tell what was going on — probably nothing — but — with a glance toward Leah — would it be all right to watch the rest of the video at his house? His mother had insisted that there was no need for him to return home, but he couldn't diagnose the problem from a distance. Besides, he suspected that his mother might be getting crank calls. If so, she'd feel better if he were there.

Everyone agreed that, of course, Matthew should go home.

"Leah," I said, "you're welcome to go watch the video at Matthew's, but this is definitely not a good time to take Kimi there. If something is going on and —"

"It's kind of late, anyway," said Leah, who,

I might add, could listen to music, read, and talk on the phone until one A.M. or maybe even later, for all I knew, and then arise at seven and get to AHSP on time looking and acting as if she'd had ten hours' sleep. I wasn't sure whether she actually enjoyed staying up late or whether she simply wanted to be someone who did enjoy it. "I think I'll go to bed early," she added. To Matthew she said, "We can watch the rest tomorrow. Or another time."

With apologies and thanks to Leah and me, and mannerly departure noises to Steve and Rita — but not a word to Rowdy and Kimi — Matthew departed. Then Steve — Have you actually met Steve? My God, maybe I'm starting to take him for granted. Well, in case you haven't been introduced, he's tall and lean, and when his brown hair is long enough to wave, it does; and if you don't view him from the rear, his eyes are his best feature. They change from green to blue depending, in part, on what color he's wearing. A vet with chameleon eyes. And he doesn't even specialize in reptiles.

Steve had arrived with a six-pack of Geary's pale ale, which I happen to hate, but drink anyway out of loyalty to my home state, where it's brewed and bottled. Rita loathes Geary's even more than I do and has no reason to consume it, so I fixed her a gin and tonic. Meanwhile, Steve poured ale into two pewter mugs presented by the Cambridge Dog Training Club to Rowdy and Kimi in honor of their official AKC Canine Good Citizenship. Then he filled a glass tumbler that Vinnie, my glorious last golden retriever, had won years before at a fun match. (Short on drinking vessels? Show your dogs.) He handed one mug to me and, despite my intense glare, gave the other to Leah, who'd taken a seat at the kitchen table. A true gentleman, Steve reserved the mere fun-match trophy for himself.

With a shrug toward the door through which Matthew had departed, Steve asked, "So what's going on?"

I told him about Stephanie's call. Then Leah took over. As I hadn't realized until Leah spelled it out, Stephanie had more difficulty with phones than she usually let people know about, especially when callers used speaker phones or, worse yet, those cordless contraptions acquired as bonuses for subscribing to cheap magazines.

To my surprise, Rita spoke up vehemently. "Those things! And you know who always uses them? Mumblers." If the word had been *murderers,* Rita's tone wouldn't have been any more damning than it already was.

Leah was cradling the mug of ale in her

hands. It seemed to me that she disliked the taste of alcohol. What she enjoyed was holding adulthood in her hands. "So," she said, "if someone calls and Stephanie can't hear right, she gets sort of upset, because she can't tell whether it's someone she knows, so she doesn't want to just hang up, or whether it's a wrong number or the person's already hung up. Also she doesn't totally trust the phone lines in their house because she found out that the phone company didn't do the wiring."

"*Morris* did?" I tried to envision Morris Lamb crawling along baseboards, running lines through walls, and installing jacks. What came to me was an image of the two Bedlingtons in a tangled heap of telephone paraphernalia and Morris wired to his dogs and laughing gleefully at himself. "Are you sure?" I added. "Morris wasn't exactly a home-repair type."

"Doug Winer put in the phones," Leah said, "and he was just there, and he checked everything. And Matthew says there's nothing wrong with the phone system, but —" Leah eyed me.

You don't have to be very handy to put in an extension, and I *am* a home-repair type, but we'd ended up with a trivial problem. Either the phone in my kitchen or the one in Leah's room worked fine alone, but when we tried to use both at once, the line went dead.

"I'll fix it," I assured her. "I just haven't had time."

"And Stephanie also keeps saying that there's something wrong with her hearing aids," Leah told Steve, "and when she moved here, from New York, she had to start going to this new audiologist, and the one here says there's nothing wrong, not that she can find."

Steve looked as if he wanted to say something, but he just drank Geary's.

"Steve, you saw Ruffly, right?" I asked. "Weren't you supposed to see him today?" All he did was nod. Veterinarians aren't schooled to blab about their patients' illnesses, but they aren't required to take a vow of silence, either. "So did you see him or not?" I demanded.

"Yeah. She brought him in." As usual, Steve spoke evenly and slowly.

Sometimes his calm exasperates me. Sometimes it scares me. I've repeatedly explained to Steve that it's only bad news you have to break; good news you can just blurt out.

He still doesn't get it. "A brain tumor," I said. "Ruffly has a brain tumor. It's an early neurological sign, isn't it? Steve, would you *please* —" I broke off. He seemed to examine his thoughts. After that, I guess, he paused to organize them. The man is a human Casablanca — all that waiting and waiting and waiting.

Eventually, he cleared his throat. "I can't find a thing. It's probably some stimulus he's picking up on. We're going to pursue it, to be on the safe side. We're going to be real cautious, real thorough."

"Seizures?" I asked.

"It's a remote possibility. Some unusual kind of petit mal seizures. But it's real remote. Or maybe what's going on is that this is a dog that's zeroed in on the owner, hyper-attuned, and, at the same time, he's hyper-attuned to the environment, and they've moved twice in a few months. So what's impinging on him is her stress and his own stress. These assistance dogs are prone to stress. They've got a lot of responsibility. If that's his problem, once she settles down and the new sounds start to get familiar to him, he'll be back to normal."

"But Steve, what about these, uh, episodes? Attacks. That's what Stephanie calls them. That's not generalized stress."

"A stimulus. Possibly a seizure. Or she jumps, the dog jumps," Steve said. "We'll look for other things, but that's probably what we're going to find. Stephanie adapts, Ruffly'll adapt. End of problem."

Before he'd finished speaking, Rita's eyes were narrow with rage. "I have really had it with both of you," she said coldly, "and with Leah and Matthew and this audiologist of Stephanie's and everyone else who's so busy trying to drive her crazy."

Rita rose, and stood behind her chair with her trembling hands resting on its back. "Here you have an intelligent, cogent, superbly self-possessed, highly-developed, and articulate woman who makes certain observations of two subjects with which she is intimately familiar — *her* hearing and *her* dog — subjects about which she understands infinitely more than you do, and when she reports these observations, how do you people respond? You tell her she's wrong. You tell her that what she knows is happening is *not* happening. And you know what that does to people?" Rita slammed the chair forward against the table. "It drives them nuts, that's what. I'm going upstairs, and I'm going to take out my hearing aids, because I've heard all I really want to hear from people today. For once, I'm going to really enjoy being deaf." She stomped out. The door slammed shut behind her.

Steve looked stunned. "Did I say something?"

"Yes," I told him. "The word *adapt*. Steve,

when you said that to Rita, you said the wrong thing."

In the silence that followed, I worried more about Ruffly than about Rita. Any veterinary problem that puzzled Steve terrified me.

20

No matter how tropical the temperature in India, the faithful continue to make way for the cow, but here in Cambridge, the hellish summer climate turns our sanctuary into Bombay in August, and Thursday night dog worship at the Cambridge Armory takes a two-month summer recess. Thus at seven o'clock on the evening of Thursday, July 2, I stood dogless on Stephanie Benson's doorstep. When I rang Morris's chimes, Ruffly barked, but by the time Stephanie opened the door, he was playing canine good citizen at her side. As I followed them into the entrance hall — no falls this time — and through the living room and dining room, I kept a close eye on Ruffly for a sign of something amiss, but, as on my previous visit, he was lively, friendly, and alert. When we reached the kitchen, I bent down to pat him.

In contrast to the living and dining rooms, the kitchen still contained some of Morris's belongings, including an entire wall of floor-to-ceiling shelves packed with cookbooks.

The mail-order kennel-supply catalogs stacked on one of the shelves could have been Stephanie's, but the pastel premium lists and entry blanks for AKC shows that lay on top of the R.C. Steele catalog had certainly belonged to Morris.

The rest of the house, or at least the rooms I'd seen, had oversize casement windows with those cranks that never work and the kinds of sliding glass doors that can be lifted right out of their tracks and safely rested against a wall while the burglar's busy inside. In the kitchen, though, what looked to me like new Andersen windows gave a view of Alice Savery's house. Better yet, the wall that faced the backyard consisted of natural-wood-and-glass panels alternating with hinged doors that opened onto a big redwood deck thick with patio furniture and equipped with a gas grill. The stove, refrigerator, and dishwasher were of some strange German-sounding brand, but everything else was standard expensive new American kitchen — polyurethaned wood floor, granite-topped island with built-in cutting boards, handsome cherry table with Windsor chairs, and those cabinets with glass-paned doors favored by people with the money to hire others to keep the interiors fit for public display.

The last time I'd been in this room, Morris

had been in the midst of inventing some Mediterranean-inspired fish stew. Every surface had been covered with fresh plum tomatoes, bunches of parsley, fish heads, fish frames, salmon chunks, swordfish steaks, and lumps of what may have been monkfish. Bowls of bivalves were disgorging sand into water, and live lobsters were crawling around in the sink. The floor was thick with dog toys and Bedlingtons, the air with anise, wine, and basil. Morris was drinking amaretto and singing snatches of "Ave Maria."

The cookbooks on the lower shelves still showed the same old dog-gnawed spines, and Nelson and Jennie had left permanent tooth marks on the legs of the table and chairs. But the counters were now almost bare, and there wasn't a Nylabone or a ball in sight. No one was singing, and the smell was so unpromising of dinner that if I'd been blindfolded, I'd have been unable to guess which room I was in. On a counter under the bracket that had held Morris's wall phone sat an answering machine and a big white phone with oversize buttons.

The light from the windows and doors and from recessed spots set everywhere in the ceiling was as bright as ever, and when I knelt down to say hello to Ruffly, I got a good look at him. I didn't really expect to find some diagnostic clue that Steve had missed, but if

Ruffly happened to be showing one, I wasn't about to forego the chance to observe it, either. My close-up inspection revealed only that Stephanie took beautiful care of her dog. Ruffly's black-and-tan coat felt as smooth, clean, and healthy as it looked. His eyes were clear, his nails neatly clipped, his teeth free of tartar. His giant ears had been recently swabbed. I ran my hands over the dog, talking softly to him as I did so.

"Doug's out back planting things." Stephanie was uncorking a bottle of wine. She paused to gesture toward the deck.

I smiled. "I saw his car out front."

"I asked him to stay for dinner — I thought you wouldn't mind? — but he says he can't."

"That's too bad."

"Wine *is* all right, isn't it? White. But if you'd prefer something else . . ."

"It's fine," I assured her.

Stephanie wore a loose dress of some unbleached homespun material. When she raised her arm to pour the wine, the dress looked like the ceremonial costume of some ancient religion. To my surprise, she said, "Doug is still *so* guilt-ridden."

"He's very conscientious. He fusses about details. But I wouldn't say he's —"

"It's the garden." She spoke very softly. "You *do* know about Morris?"

Answer yes to a question like that, and you already know as much as you're ever going to. "Sort of," I said.

"Well, it was Doug who . . . I'll show you later." Stephanie handed me a goblet of wine. "Now probably isn't the best time. Doug . . . Well, the garden is . . . It's a box, really, with the dirt inside. A raised bed. He built a whole elaborate little miniature garden. There are hoops that go over it, and there's plastic that goes over the hoops, so you can turn it into a little greenhouse, and there's some kind of underground heating and watering system. But the point is, Doug built this little garden as a gift for Morris. And they planted . . . I don't know a thing about gardening — and not much more about cooking! But all sorts of edible flowers and exotic greens, salad greens, and that's where Morris must have begun gathering — But what a thing to start talking about! We're having a salad! I don't . . ." She faltered.

"That's fine," I assured her. "I'm not —"

"I *bought* everything. After, uh, after what happened, Doug tore out everything in the raised bed. That's what he's out there doing now, planting it with lettuce and something or other. He bought little lettuce plants. It was just an empty box of dirt, rather depressing, not that there was any real danger, but,

211

even so, he's so guilt-ridden . . ."

Whatever the true cause of Morris's death, Stephanie clearly accepted Doug's account. I was about to say something about Mr. Winer, Doug's father, when Doug tapped lightly on one of the open glass doors of the deck and walked in. The tapping set Ruffly to work, but as soon as Stephanie reminded him that Doug was a welcome visitor, Ruffly calmed down.

At Stephanie's insistence, Doug accepted a small glass of wine, and the three of us moved outdoors to the deck, taking seats on the tan pipe-and-canvas lawn chairs that had been torn and scratched by Morris's dogs. The raised garden, located a few yards beyond the deck, was clearly visible to all of us. As soon as Stephanie caught sight of the rows of lettuce and some orange marigolds that Doug had just planted, she said a polite and appropriately subdued thanks. Although the lettuce would immediately bolt and turn bitter in the July heat, I should probably have added a quiet word of admiration, but after a quick glance, I averted my eyes. Mounds of earth are what they are; one pine box looks pretty much like another; and Morris Lamb really was dead. What threw me into near tachycardia was that, at first glance, the elements suggested the grave site of a giant recently interred by a lazy undertaker who'd only half buried the coffin, but had piled the raw earth with flowers nonetheless.

When I recovered, Stephanie was inquiring about how things were going at Winer & Lamb, and Doug was telling her all about the expansion of the mail-order side of the business and the preparation of the new catalog. "Our *old* ones!" he exclaimed in disgust. "Did you ever . . . ? No, of course not, why would you? You don't really cook, do you? Either of you? Not to speak of? Or collect? Well, you wouldn't have had any reason to see our old catalogs — it's a very specialized clientele — and, frankly, the way I felt when I looked through our last catalog was, well . . . I wished they'd all been lost in the mail! That nasty, cheap paper and the typographical errors! No sense of design whatsoever — nothing but a horrid little list. It was so amateurish that it made me sick."

Stephanie pointed out that knowledgeable collectors were probably satisfied with a simple list, and I added that the dealers who specialized in used and rare dog books relied on catalogs that were far from color glossy, but Doug said that we both sounded just like Morris, who hadn't understood that to survive the threat posed by the megabookstores, they had to expand the mail-order business. Morris hadn't wanted to be bothered with the tremendous work required to turn out a thoroughly professional product — speaking of which, he must fly! In taking leave, Doug thanked his hostess, told me what a pleasure it had been to see me again, and otherwise displayed an updated version of Mr. Winer's gentlemanly manners.

After Doug left, Stephanie and I returned to the kitchen, where she overbroiled two salmon filets and prepared a big salad that we eventually ate at the big glass-topped table on the deck. Dessert was a pastry cream and fresh fruit tart from the combination bakery, cheese shop, and gourmet take-out on Huron near the corner of Appleton. Instead of blurting out something like, "Oh, I've bought this, too!" I tactfully limited myself to exclaiming about how wonderful the concoction looked and tasted, but, to her credit, Stephanie made no effort to pass it off as her own and immediately told me where it had come from. After dinner, she made the inevitable French decaf. As we sat on the deck drinking the coffee and talking, Stephanie amazed me by asking whether I'd mind if she smoked.

"Not at all," I assured her.

"Matthew has forbidden me to smoke in the house, but every once in a while, I give in to the old urge," she explained. "You're sure?"

"Really," I said.

She went indoors and returned with an ashtray, cigarettes, and a big red lighter. I honestly didn't mind. I was merely surprised. Wine, sure, but tobacco? Not exactly Biblical. Also, if Stephanie had been a lawyer or a professor instead of a priest, smoking would still have seemed out of character.

Throughout the preparations for dinner and the meal itself, as Stephanie and I spoke lightly about Cambridge, Doug, and Winer & Lamb — and rather heavily about Rita and Ivan the Terrible — Ruffly had been a model hearing dog. When Stephanie had put the salmon under the broiler, she'd set a timer, and Ruffly had performed his sounding-working dance in response to the buzzer. While we ate, he lay peacefully under the table at Stephanie's feet. By the time we'd both emptied our coffee cups and she'd finished her cigarette, I was convinced that Ruffly was the most problem-free dog I'd ever met. Stephanie had graciously turned my dog-watching visit into a social occasion, and dinner had been a success, but my real purpose had been to witness one of Ruffly's odd episodes, and, in that, I'd once again failed completely. As I was helping Stephanie clear the table, I wondered whether

Ruffly's problems, far from being serious, were nonexistent, entirely imaginary, the product of the human mind. In referring a psychotherapist *to* Ruffly's owner, maybe I'd done things the wrong way around. On the other hand, maybe Steve and I were both missing something — maybe there was something terribly wrong with the wonderful little dog.

21

Rita's audiologist had presented her with a self-help book about hearing loss that Rita and I agreed was largely a sales pitch for hearing aids. Both the audiologist and Rita's ear-nose-and-throat specialist had sold Rita on the benefits of wearing two hearing aids, and the book offered the same arguments about the joys of binaural hearing. Having paid for both aids, Rita insisted on wearing both. According to the experts and the book, two aids produced sharp stereo sound that one little amplifier couldn't even begin to match. Rita didn't dispute the claim. Far from it. The unbearable racket was precisely what bothered her most. Mainly, however, Rita hated the book because it reminded her that she had a hearing loss.

My complaint was different from hers. Let me say that I like to read. I enjoy every volume published by Denlinger's, Howell, and T.F.H. If I had the money, I'd own every item in the catalogs of 4-M Enterprises and Direct Book Service. I like James Herriot and Donald McCaig. After *The Call of the Wild*, my favorite novel is *Flush*. I'm convinced that *Love on a Leash* is the funniest story ever written and that Helen Thayer's *Polar Dream* is the most thrilling. Strictly between us, though, my opinion of almost every other book I've ever opened, from *The Brothers Karamazov* to Roget's Thesaurus, is that it would have been all right if only it had had a little more to say about dogs. So my objection to the hearing loss guide was nothing new.

But can you imagine? Close to two hundred pages about how to deal with hearing loss? And not so much as a single sentence stating that hearing dogs even exist. Dostoyevsky was pushing it, but, look: What choice did he have? Mitya buys a Cherrybrook franchise, becomes the first authorized Bil Jac distributor in Moscow, and eventually adds a successful U-Wash-Em pet grooming facility. Ivan Fyodorovitch breeds borzois, pursues lure coursing, and cheers up. Alyosha, D.V.M., joins a lucrative upper-crust small-animal practice. Happy family of real dog people. Nothing to moon or bicker about. Ergo, no plot. But this hearing-loss expert? What was his excuse?

The deceitful book was, however, where I learned to make sure that Stephanie was looking at me when I began talking to her. For instance, instead of addressing Stephanie while she was stowing the leftover fruit tart in the depths of the refrigerator, I transferred my attention to Ruffly — not that it ever wanders far from the nearest dog — and had just begun to move toward him when, WHAM — all at once, his big ears folded flat, and he jerked his head as if he'd been walloped. What I saw looked exactly like hand shyness.

But where was the invisible hand from which Ruffly shied? Alien spacecraft hovering over Highland? And, no, Morris Lamb's house had *not* been built on the site of an ancient pet cemetery. To judge from the way Morris's glass cube was awkwardly jammed against Alice Savery's yard, it had probably been erected on the site of nothing more ominous than a delphinium border, so relax. Holly Winter, not Stephen King. And in case you've forgotten — or maybe never knew before — dogs really do hallucinate. A particularly weird form of the disorder occurs in the King Charles spaniel; the affected animals persist in trying to catch imaginary flies. Isn't it interesting to be a dog writer? And you thought Stephen King was strange. But does Stephen King know about hallucinatory fly chomping in the King Charles spaniel? Probably not. Stephen King is strictly make-believe. If you're after the truly freakish, check out reality.

That's where I started. As I've mentioned,

Ruffly looked like a mix of lot of different breeds, but the King Charles spaniel wasn't one of them, and Ruffly just didn't strike me as a dog who'd had a momentary brainstorm. Canine distemper can produce a fly-biting syndrome, but the immunized Ruffly had just passed one of Steve Delaney's exhaustive neurological exams. Besides, Ruffly was wincing, not snapping at insects.

The episode lasted only a few seconds. When it ended, Ruffly's head returned to its normal position, but he kept his ears pinned flat, and he acted vaguely contused or disoriented. He moved first toward one of the glass-paneled doors, then scuttled to Stephanie, who was closing the refrigerator door. When he reached her, he trained huge, puzzled eyes on her face and pawed at the skirt of her dress as if he wanted to tell her something.

I shouted, just the way the book said not to. "Stephanie, it happened! Ruffly . . . Stephanie, this dog is reacting to *something*." During the episode, I'd had my eyes exclusively on Ruffly. If I remembered correctly, he'd been watching Stephanie. But I wasn't positive. And I might have missed some stimulus that had triggered that dramatic response. "I'm going to look outside," I said hurriedly. "It's possible . . ."

With that, I went tearing out to the deck and down the stairs to the backyard, where I paused a second to get my bearings. Floodlights illuminated the lawn and the raised bed, but the rhododendrons and azaleas at the sides and the rear of the property were big, dark lumps that could have been anything. I held still and listened. A car passed on Highland. I tried to remember whether I even knew the layout of Morris's yard. What separated his cube from Alice Savery's colonial wedding cake, it seemed to me, was, first, a narrow walk that led to his yard and deck, then a thin row of tall bushes — lilacs, maybe — and then, beyond the bushes, perhaps ten feet of grass and flowers that belonged to Miss Savery. Just as I headed for the walkway, bright floods suddenly came on; a motion detector had sensed my presence.

Faith in the crime-deterrent powers of light always amazes me. If you were a burglar, a mugger, or a murderer, would a little harmless illumination send chills down your spine? Does a stupid little light bulb really calm your fears? Of course not. So if you're scared, quit assuming that every criminal is Count Dracula! Get a dog! Get a great big dog!

Still unconvinced? The motion sensor did for me precisely what it would have done for an intruder — lighted my way and sped my progress. As I dashed down the walk, I heard nothing but the slap of Reebok soles on concrete, but when I reached the street and slammed to a halt, Highland suddenly burst into sound. From somewhere between Alice Savery's house and her prize fence, a childish imitation of a rebel yell rang out, followed almost immediately by whoops, giggles, and a rapid-fire series of firecracker pops that emanated, it seemed to me, from the far side of her property. Simultaneously, Alice Savery's front door opened, and Stephanie and Ruffly emerged from Morris's house. Despite the recent slap by the invisible hand, Ruffly began to bark, and I suppose that he must have run toward the source of one of the sounds, too, but I didn't watch him. Instead, I sprinted after the little boy who'd just dashed out of Alice Savery's yard and was heading down Highland, away from Morris's house and toward his whooping and giggling companions, who'd set off the cherry bombs and promptly fled.

When I reached the end of Alice Savery's fence, Ivan — unmistakably, inevitably Ivan — was briefly visible under a streetlight ahead of me, but by the time I'd passed the next two houses, I'd lost him. I jog with Rowdy and Kimi, but I'm no real runner, especially by comparison with a pack of adrenaline-powered little boys who knew every twist and turn in the maze of driveways, paths, and through-the-yard shortcuts of Highland Street. On the street and sidewalks ahead, I saw nothing, and the only sound I heard came from behind me: women's voices. Showing Alaskan malamutes in obedience has forced me to become a good sport. I hate losing as much as ever, of course; all I've really learned is to behave myself.

The path of humility led back to Alice Savery's house, where Stephanie Benson and Miss Savery stood about a yard apart in the pool of light thrown by a globe over the front door. Alice Savery held herself rigid. With her arms tightly folded across her chest and her fingers digging into her biceps, she reminded me of a petrified first-time Novice A handler during the Long Sit and Down. A steel beam planted near Miss Savery would have looked comparatively warm and relaxed, but Stephanie's posture and manner conveyed solicitousness as well as ease. In trying to calm Miss Savery's fears, she was engaged in what seemed to be a familiar task. When Stephanie presented me to Miss Savery, I stretched out a polite hand. Miss Savery responded with nothing but a cursory nod. Mostly because I needed something to do with my rejected right hand, I quickly crossed my arms. In the absence of a malamute, I'm a confident handler. Besides, I'd shown under judges a lot meaner than Alice Savery. Neither she nor I acknowledged that we'd met before.

"The kids have vanished," I reported.

"They've left a little something behind." Stephanie held up an object so anomalous that for a moment I didn't even recognize what it was: a canister of iodized table salt.

"What . . . ?"

"It kills grass, apparently," Stephanie explained.

At the end of October, I would've caught on immediately, but this was the beginning of July. Once I understood, I wondered whether I needed to explain. I decided that I did, for Stephanie's sake, anyway. People from Manhattan are capable of not knowing the most astoundingly ordinary things. The first time Rita saw a raccoon in Cambridge, she honestly did not know what it was, and when I told her, she assumed that it must have escaped from a zoo.

"It's an old Halloween trick," I said. "Is the box empty?"

"Yes," Stephanie said, "and there's at least one other empty one on the lawn."

"Usually they write things." I felt oddly embarrassed, as if my explanation of the details of the childish prank somehow made me a participant. "Swear words. Then when the salt kills the grass . . ." I stopped. The rest was obvious.

Stephanie was outraged. "What a cruel thing to do! And how incredibly silly! But, really, they couldn't possibly have understood how hard Miss Savery works in her garden, or they'd never have done such a terrible thing." Stretching out a robed arm toward Miss Savery, she continued. "I am *so* sorry that —"

"Gypsum!" Alice Savery's loud, dictatorial tone made the noun sound like an imperative verb.

Stephanie looked bewildered.

"Gypsum," I interjected. "It helps undo salt damage. It's worth a try."

Alice Savery's icy gaze was wandering somewhere in back of us, but I assumed that she was listening, because she snorted. Before that, I'd always thought that snorters pursued their hobby strictly in private, but Alice Savery actually managed to agitate the air in her nose in some way that produced a remarkably loud and scornful noise. If Stephanie hadn't been there, I might even have asked her to teach me how she'd done it, just out of curiosity, of course. Scorn isn't a reaction I often need to express, and when the occasion arises, words suffice.

"Well," said Stephanie, "if you have any

of this, uh, gypsum, I'm sure that Matthew would be glad to help do whatever one does with it, Miss Savery. He isn't home right now, but when he gets home, I'm sure he'd be happy to help. Maybe he could . . . Is it any use to dig up the affected area?"

Alice Savery said nothing — it's possible that the sight of Ruffly squatting on the lawn rendered her speechless. I touched Stephanie's arm to get her attention. "Stephanie, uh, where do you keep your pooper-scooper? I'll run over and get it."

"Oh, don't bother," Stephanie said.

Alice Savery's eyes narrowed. Mine probably did, too. Cleaning up after your dog is one of the basics. I wasn't familiar with the program that had trained Ruffly and placed him with Stephanie, but the particular program didn't matter. Every hearing dog organization drills its human students in the fundamentals of responsible ownership and emphasizes that every hearing dog is an ambassador for all hearing dogs. How could Stephanie possibly . . . ?

She redeemed herself. Pulling a plastic bag from a side pocket of her dress, she said casually, "I'll take care of it."

While Stephanie was heading across the lawn, Alice Savery grumbled audibly. Her piercing eyes moved back and forth as if scan-

ning for the presence of a sinister eaves-
dropper. When she spoke, her voice was rank
with suspicion. "One sees what one sees." The
woman had the air of reluctantly granting me
a glimpse into some vast store of secret knowledge. "One hears what one hears."

People who watch and listen often do, I
thought.

22

Existentialism died this year. Or, maybe, yesteryear; I can't be sure. Its trappings survive. Take Leah: Camus and black. But the essence perished, and what killed it was the normalization of the absurd. I must be behind the times, or, maybe, unbeknownst to me, I'm stuck in some crucial stage of the grieving process. I'm working on it, though. I've practiced the sentence until I can get it out fine. All I can't do is utter it with a straight face. "Hi, I'm Holly," I say, "and this is my swine, Luigi."

Not that I have anything against pigs — or against any of the other pitifully inadequate dog substitutes with which the spiritually impoverished attempt to enrich their bleak, allergic lives. On the contrary, I've always been a fan of the theater of the absurd, and if you doubt me, consider the *angst* that's plagued me ever since a neighbor of mine, Frank, acquired Leo, a Vietnamese potbellied pig. Not that there's anything wrong with Leo. Far from it. He's hideous, and his hoofs require rather frequent trimming, but he's perfectly friendly. There's nothing wrong with Frank, either. No, the sick individual in the family isn't Leo or Frank, but Frank's wife, a frigid woman with whom poor Frank endured five unspeakably frustrating years of sham marriage, sixty maddening months of abstinence with a so-called partner who denied him the most basic marital right of all: the right to a family dog. Her excuse? Not headaches. Sneezing. Painful, watery eyes. Asthma, I think. And when she was desperate to get out of it, hives, too. Frank's dilemma? Roman Catholic. And, in fact, the Church is what saved his marriage: It was Father Leo Bianci, S.J., who proposed the solution — the pig. Hence, the name.

My anguish? When I told Steve Delaney about Leo, I casually added something like, "Gee, I wonder what Rowdy and Kimi will make of a pig," and, instead of pausing to mull over the situation the way he usually does, Steve had an instant reply: "Pork chops."

So when I arrived home from Stephanie Benson's, I was glad to find Steve there, not only because I'm always happy to see him, but also because, ever since Leo's arrival, I hate walking Rowdy and Kimi alone at night. In the daytime, I can always spot Leo from a distance and do a swift about-turn, but, after dark, I'm always afraid that we'll come upon the pig suddenly and that the dogs will lunge before I can stop them. So Steve is always a good dog-walking companion, but if, God forbid, one of the dogs somehow managed to get loose and attack Leo, a veterinarian would obviously be the perfect person to have on hand.

Steve had let himself in and was sitting at the kitchen table idly fooling around with Rowdy and Kimi while simultaneously drinking Geary's and studying an article on salivary cysts. Anyone with a delicate stomach does well to avoid veterinary medicine and, for that matter, dogs altogether, but, so far as I know, nothing actually compels vets to crave spaghetti whenever they're reading up on tapeworms. Salivary cysts? Press on them and what you get is brownish fluid, but don't tell Geary's I said so. Maine needs all the business it can get.

The evening was cool for Cambridge in early July, and pig-free, too, at least on the route we took, Concord to Fayerweather, then across Huron and up the sociogeographic hill toward Governor Weld's house and Brattle Street. Steve walked Kimi, and I took Rowdy, who suddenly becomes a one-person dog whenever he decides that Kimi is edging him out in their rivalry for my affection. As we walked, I told Steve about everything that had happened at Stephanie Benson's, with particular emphasis on Ruffly, of course.

"What he did was very, very sudden," I said. "One second, he was standing there, and the next second, he'd jerked his head to the side and flattened his ears. Steve, it was exactly as if someone had slapped him."

"And what was he doing just before that?"

"Standing there, I think."

"Alert?"

"He's always alert. His ears were up. And if I remember it right, his tail was wagging a little. But he wasn't reacting to one of his sounds, if that's what you mean, and the doorbell wasn't ringing or anything like that. I don't know! He was just *there*."

"Any trembling?"

"I don't think so. He did seem frightened, I guess, but I don't think he was shaking."

"And after? Anything about his gait?"

"Nothing. Why? When you saw him, did you . . . ?"

"No."

"You look as if there's something . . ."

"I'd better get a neurological consult. Treating these assistance dogs —"

"Steve, I am telling you, it didn't look neurological. You should've seen it! It just did not look medical."

"That's a real risky assumption, Holly. I wish I'd seen it. One of the things about treating these dogs is that the owners depend on them, so you're real reluctant to bring the animal in for observation. If Mrs. Benson's open to it, I'm going to stop by this weekend."

"I'm sure she will be, and she understands about tonight." Steve trains with Cambridge, too. Since we don't meet in the summer, he'd assumed he'd have that Thursday evening free and had volunteered to do a rabies immunization clinic at a local shelter.

We paused to let the dogs sniff an overgrown privet hedge. Rowdy made a couple of passes at it, cocked his leg, lowered it, turned around, and hit the spot again. Then Kimi checked it out and, not to be outdone, squeezed her hindquarters against the privet and executed a full rear-end bounce. Steve laughed. A man who admires the sight of a bitch lifting both legs at once? And a vet, too? The man for me. Ah, love.

After this romantic little interlude, we returned to the topic of Ruffly, and Steve said, "Tell me about the environment."

"What?" The request threw me for a second. Sure, that hyperintellectual Off-Brattle coldness is toxic. But enough to sicken a dog?

"Anything that could serve as a stimulus,"

Steve explained patiently.

"I just had a thought. If there is a stimulus, then wouldn't Morris's dogs have shown some response to it, too?"

"It's worth finding out," Steve said.

"I'll ask Doug Winer. He has Morris's dogs. He'll know. Also after it happened, I went outside to see if there was anything there, and there wasn't, really, except that Ivan, the little boy Leah's always talking about, was right in the middle of the next-door neighbor's lawn dumping a lot of salt there."

"That old trick."

"Well, with this woman, it really was meaner than it sounds, because her garden is incredible. She must work on it all the time. So it's not like killing plants in my yard. It's more like doing something to one of my dogs, except that the grass doesn't actually suffer. But from her point of view, Miss Savery's, that's more or less what it's like. Really, the garden *is* her dog! And Ivan had some friends with him, and they set off cherry bombs. Anyhow, Stephanie and Ruffly came out, and then while Stephanie was talking to Alice Savery, Ruffly messed on her lawn, and the sort of strange thing was, that's one of the things she complains about — she actually went to the police about it; Kevin told me — but Stephanie has no idea. Stephanie had a plastic bag

233

with her, and she cleaned up after Ruffly right away, but Alice Savery didn't say anything to her about it."

We reached Huron, and Steve and I fell silent until we'd crossed. Huron's a fairly busy street, even at night, and my wolf gray dogs are so effectively camouflaged for night predation that I'm always afraid that a driver will see me, overlook Rowdy and Kimi, and inadvertently head toward them. I like to imagine that if that ever happens, I'll hurl myself between the dogs and the car, but some dreadful survival instinct would probably make me chicken out, and for the rest of my life, I'd have to live with the knowledge that I'd failed to save the best part of myself.

When we reached the posh side of Huron, Steve asked, "You told Stephanie about the neighbor's complaints?"

"No. I thought about it, but I decided, why worry her? Anyway, what just occurred to me was that if Ruffly *is* ever loose, which I don't believe he is, then he could be getting into something, plants or weed killer or lawn chemicals or whatever, and maybe that's what's causing his odd behavior. But I really don't think he is. Stephanie is the model dog owner, super-responsible, and even if she weren't, she needs Ruffly. There's just no way . . ."

"Since we're —" Steve broke off. "Holly, any chance this is hand-shyness?"

"*Stephanie?*"

"Yeah, Stephanie," he said. "Or someone else?"

"No! No one could, really. Ruffly is with Stephanie twenty-four hours a day. And Stephanie would just *not* hit him, and I can't imagine that she'd let anyone hit him, either." I was indignant.

"When this, uh, attack occurred, exactly where were the two of them?"

"In the kitchen. She was putting something in the refrigerator. Ruffly was . . . Well, he wasn't sticking his nose in the refrigerator. He was maybe, I don't know, two yards away?"

"And you were watching . . . ?"

"Ruffly. In fact, I even remember what I was thinking. I was thinking that he must definitely have some Papillon in him. Because of the big ears."

"Possible." Steve nodded. "But what I'm asking is whether you could see Stephanie or whether the refrigerator door was blocking your view of her."

I thought back. "Yeah. It was. That's how it opens. So, no, I guess I could see part of her, her back or whatever. But, mostly, the door was in the way."

"So, in theory, it is possible that she —"

"Physically, yes, she could've done something; she could've given him a signal or made some kind of gesture."

"Someone outside?"

"Someone walking through the yard? I'm not sure. If that happens, he ought do *something* — go to the window, point toward it, show some kind of reaction. I suppose Ivan could've been there. Also, look. As far as I know, Matthew was with Leah. But Matthew isn't a stranger, so maybe when it's just Matthew coming home . . . I don't know. Maybe whatever Ruffly does then is very low-key."

"This neighbor?"

"Alice Savery. Well, Ruffly must be used to her, because Morris's house — Stephanie's, now — is right next to hers, and Miss Savery's outside all the time, working in her garden, so, to a hearing dog, she must be background noise. Except . . . No, it couldn't have been, I think, because I went out only a minute or two after it happened, and by then Ivan was on her front lawn. So if she'd been outside a few minutes earlier, she'd have noticed him. That's one of her chronic complaints, kids in her yard. If she'd been outside, she'd have seen him, and she'd have done something, believe me."

"Huh. And then we're back to what the stimulus was."

"Rolled-up newspaper! Steve, I just thought of it. *That's* how you make a dog hand-shy from a distance. Or some other object. Those dogs don't cringe when you reach toward them. What terrifies them is when you stand back and raise your arm."

"That's a point. So who . . . ? The son could've, in theory. He lives there; he has access to the animal. And the owner. She does."

"And if Ruffly ran loose, Alice Savery, too. But I don't believe her; I don't think he's ever loose. Ivan? Steve, I really don't think he'd hit a dog. He gets himself in a lot of trouble, and, admittedly, he does hang around Alice Savery's, but probably not as much as she thinks he does."

"Enough to become background noise?"

"I don't know."

"Me, neither," Steve said.

"If we cut down here on Reservoir, we'll go right by there," I suggested. "You want to see the house?"

Neither of us expected Morris Lamb's house to tell us anything, and, in fact, it didn't. When we reached the little path that led to the backyard, the motion sensor detected us, and the floodlights came on. If Ruffly barked, I didn't hear him. Alice Savery's house was

237

entirely dark, and, except in one upstairs room — Matthew's, I guess — so was Stephanie's. Even so, Steve and I lingered for a few minutes to ponder the question of whether a dog writer and a veterinarian could find happiness in a neighborhood that neither could afford, even pooling resources.

In front of Alice Savery's, I deliberately edged Rowdy toward the famous fence. "Rowdy, lift your leg!" I urged him. All he did was sniff.

Class traitor.

23

"Fyodor! *Not* with your fingers! And if you'd stop wiggling, the avocado garnish wouldn't slip, would it?" Doug's distant scolding was barely audible over the lunchtime clatter in what must have been the kitchen at Winer & Lamb. His voice suddenly boomed in my ear: "Doug Winer. How may I help you?"

"Doug, it's Holly Winter. I'm sorry to bother you."

"It's *bedlam* here," Doug exclaimed happily, "and the decorators are insisting on closing us down so the painters can get in, and, well, it's a perfect madhouse!" Doug's elation in the face of self-created chaos was weirdly and uniquely Morris Lamb's.

"You're redecorating?"

"*Long*, long overdue." Doug sounded like an especially grim bill collector. "The competition is ferocious. If we neglect the café, we'll go under."

As I'd done dozens of times before, I assured Doug that everything at Winer & Lamb was always wonderful. Then I got to the point.

Had Morris's Bedlingtons shown any behavior that even remotely resembled Ruffly's episodes? Had Morris's dogs had any mysterious ailments? Had there ever been anything . . . ?

Nelson, Doug promptly reported, had once eaten forty-three dollars in cash, but it hadn't done him any harm. Was that what I meant?

No, not really, I said. I thanked Doug, anyway. While I had him on the phone, I asked about Ivan, but Doug didn't recognize the name. He certainly knew that the neighborhood children plagued Alice Savery, but, according to Doug, Morris had never had a problem with them, and they never bothered the other neighbors, either.

"Good God! They're not after Stephanie, are they?" Doug sounded serious and alarmed.

"No, I really don't think so. It's just that we're trying to find some explanation of what's going on with Ruffly." I used a phrase of Steve's. "We're casting a wide net."

"She's not making herself *interesting*, is she?"

"Stephanie?"

"Because that's positively the worst thing to do. Morris kept trying to persuade Miss Savery that if she'd stop making herself *interesting*, then the children would find someone else to torment, but, of course, Miss

240

Savery wouldn't listen."

Morris seemed a wildly improbable source of that good advice. Making himself interesting was one of Morris Lamb's great pleasures. With me, at least, he'd always succeeded. The reflection and, in fact, my entire conversation with Doug Winer, left me in a peculiar mood that interfered with my work. Even at my most productive, I'd have found it difficult to get serious about a talking dog collar ("Pat me! Pat me!" "Clip my nails? Just try it!") or a kitchen utensil specially designed to get every last glob of pet food out of the can, and the prospect of advising the readers of *Dog's Life* to buy an aerosol pet repeller was ludicrous.

My mail didn't help. In addition to the electric bill and a bunch of dog magazines, it brought an envelope from *Dog's Life* containing a letter from some guy who must have read my column without understanding a word I'd ever written. *"Dear Holly,"* it said. *"My last dog died about four months ago, and I'm starting to think about a new one. What I want is a dog that can wander around the neighborhood and make friends and not get into trouble. What kind of dog can you let run loose?"*

I grabbed some stationery and scrawled the only honest answer: *"Any dog you don't love."*

Truthful, yes. Helpful, no. I tore up my

letter. How could one of my readers possibly ask such a question? Like every other member of my profession, I'd already answered it hundreds of times: The free-Rover makes so many enemies that when he's finally hit by a car, the neighbors want to dance in the streets. As if to confirm my sense that any further dispensing of advice would be useless, noise broke out overhead: Willie began yet one more of the prolonged fits of senseless barking that I'd repeatedly told Rita how to cure. Until that afternoon, I'd limited myself to lecturing Rita. Now I took action — and, no, not with one of those damned no-bark shock collars and not with ultrasound, either. The radical remedy? My landlady key admitted me to Rita's apartment, where I set up a portable crate, into which I locked the protesting Scottie, one pressed-rawhide bone, and one Gumabone Plaque Attacker, its hollow middle filled with freshly melted cheese. Then I stomped downstairs and muffled the yapping with the cotton I use to clean the dogs' ears. Instant magic? No. Willie wasn't a tough case. It took twenty minutes for him to fall silent.

My sense of professional competence restored, I made a big cup of Bustelo and whipped off a column that began with the letter I'd just received, moved to phony expressions of regret that the days of the free-range neighborhood dog were over, and ended with an analysis of the anthropomorphism inherent in the romantic idealization of the loose dog as a symbol of spiritual freedom, which, by the way, is just what the roaming dog symbolizes. So does death.

By the time I'd finished, I was drenched in caffeine sweat, and Rowdy and Kimi were pleading for their overdue dinner, so I fed them, put them in the yard, took a shower, and, of all things, got so dressed up that when Steve arrived, he decided that I must have forgotten that we were going out to dinner. Whenever he sees me wearing anything fancier than kennel clothes, he assumes that I'm on my way to or from a show.

We ate at a little Indian restaurant on Beacon Street in Brookline. My main course was a mild spinach concoction, *palak paneer* (evidently meaning *baby food,* not bad), but Steve ordered three kinds of bread, a dish of fiery citrus pickles, a salad that tasted like glowing embers, and a curry that would've done as the penultimate test in the Bombay licensing exam for flame swallowers. After a few bites, he started mopping his head and face, and all through the meal, he kept pouring down beer and exclaiming about how great everything tasted. Even so, I drove us home along a circuitous route that happened to lead us to Toscanini's in Central Square, where we stocked up on mouth-burn remedies to take back to Appleton Street.

When we arrived, Leah and Matthew were at the kitchen table consuming ramen noodles, Leah with evident satisfaction, Matthew with the expression of a dog given a half-cup of low-cal chunks in place of his usual bowlful of Joy Demand laced with safflower oil to make his coat shine. I decided that with a person as inexpressive as Matthew, any show of anything resembling emotion was preferable to the usual watered-down, no-cal, no-taste, invalid-bland affective diet that he seemed to self-prescribe as a preventive antidote for human feelings.

But, of course, Leah's friends are always welcome in my house.

In even sharper than usual contrast to Matthew, Leah was radiant with excitement tonight. She couldn't wait for Matthew to conclude his rise-when-a-lady-enters jack-in-the-box trick to begin spilling out her news, which, in characteristic Leah fashion, wasn't even her own, but Matthew's, except, I suppose, to the extent that it concerned a dog. Despite the sticky city heat of a gusty July evening doomed to end in a night of thunder, Leah wore black tights topped by swathes of black jersey. She'd tried to subdue the unsophisticated exuberance of her red-gold curls, too, but the humidity had betrayed her. On the crown of her head, an elasticized black velvet ribbon was losing the struggle to retain its grip on a thick mass of hair. A cloudlike halo of escaped bronze tendrils framed her flushed, eager face. (*Cloudlike.* You noticed? Indeed, the ad copy for Wonder Fluff dog shampoo. There's an off-chance that Leah had actually used it.)

"Ruffly *saved* Matthew's mother!" she exclaimed. "You have to hear all about it!"

Most of the time, I manage to ignore Leah's resemblance to my own mother — the voice, the astonishing hair, the remarkable way with dogs — but once in a while, when Leah catches me off-guard, I feel as if I've encountered Marissa's ghost. With my mother, too, no one ever had much choice about hearing all about everything. On this occasion I really was eager to hear all about Ruffly. The piece about him had turned out pretty well, but, after mailing it, I'd realized that something was missing: a good rescue story. If it hadn't been Friday night, I might even have dashed to the phone to tell my editor to put the article on hold. Monday morning would be soon enough. I'll also confess something: As a *person,* I genuinely hoped that Leah's news was about some trivial incident that hadn't even alarmed

Stephanie. As a *dog writer?* Well, I prayed that little Ruffly hadn't merely nudged Stephanie away from a slow-moving vehicle or warned her about a minor grease fire, but had heroically dragged his large-framed and bosomy mistress from the brink of some major, eminently publishable, and preferably ecclesiastical disaster.

"Oh," I said, disguising these warring emotions. "What happened?"

By now, Steve had dished up and distributed the ice cream, and Matthew seemed more intent on working away at his bowl of vanilla than on enriching my forthcoming contribution to canine, ahem, literature, but maybe he simply accepted the inevitable. When Leah is bent on holding the floor, it's useless to compete.

"It just happened! Right after Stephanie got home, she went out to the deck, and you know how there's a big gas grill there?" The question was one in intonation only; Leah didn't pause long enough for me to nod, but went breathlessly on. "There's one of those built-in grills, and she'd been out to dinner, and after she got home, she made some coffee and went out to the deck because Matthew won't let her smoke in the house."

Stephanie had mentioned the ban. I remember how surprised I'd been to learn that she smoked at all. I still was. I glanced at Matthew, who was almost frowning. It occurred to me that I might be misjudging him. Maybe he was just hard to read, like a tailless shaggy dog with a curtain of hair permanently drawn over his face.

Leah was gesturing enthusiastically with a spoonful of ice cream. "And Stephanie sat down, and there was . . . You know how windy it is? And she sat where the wind was blowing away from the grill, and she was just about to light her cigarette, but Ruffly bumped her arm, and then he just stood there staring at the grill, practically like a statue, and then Stephanie got up, and when she got really close to the grill, she could smell the gas. The valve wasn't all the way off, and if it hadn't been for Ruffly, especially if the wind had changed, she'd have been blown up!"

"How did Ruffly know?" I asked.

"You can hear it," Matthew answered. "My mother can't hear it, but the gas hisses a little. And if she'd been paying any attention, she would've smelled it."

"No, she wouldn't," Leah said firmly. "Not with the wind blowing away, would she?"

"Well, it wouldn't make much difference," I said. "What she should've noticed wouldn't really matter. Steve, would Ruffly have responded to the gas? To the smell?"

He shrugged. "More likely the sound. Those dogs are all ears." He asked Matthew how the gas happened to have been left on, but Matthew said he didn't know — maybe the valve was faulty. His mother had used the grill a couple of times. He'd had to turn it off and on for her; she didn't understand how it worked, and it made her nervous.

It seemed to me that any woman capable of getting herself ordained should be able to overcome a sense of female helplessness about gas grills. If the Church gives you the power to look God more or less in the eye and yank souls from the flames of hell, why go all fluttery in the face of a backyard barbecue? But I didn't say so; I didn't know much about priests. Or gas grills. What Leah and I both said was the obvious: how fortunate that Ruffly had been there.

But Matthew wasn't impressed; he didn't give Ruffly much credit at all. If there'd been a serious accident? A fire? An explosion? If his mother had been injured? Well, rationally speaking, it would have been her own fault. After all, he said, Stephanie knew she shouldn't smoke.

24

What stands between me and a darling black-and-white malamute puppy named Bernadette is a biological impossibility that's entirely the fault of a woman once secularly known as Susan Cloer who joined the Holy Order of Breed Rescue; started combing the streets and animal shelters of Houston, Texas; encountered temptation; resisted it; and thus earned the only half-facetious title of Mother Teresa of the Malamute. The Temptation? Bernard. Starved down to fifty-nine pounds, the black of his coat bleached auburn by the Texas sun, Bernard was nonetheless recognizable as a better-looking Alaskan malamute than many of those seen in the ring. Equally evident — temptation, temptation — was this beautiful dog's potential to sire the would-have-been Bernadette, to whom Bernard would doubtless have passed along not just the white tip on the end of his tail, but the incredibly striking diamond-shaped black markings on his white face, too — if only it hadn't been for that damned Susan Cloer, as she was then. Texas.

Tough. Stood right up to Satan. "Satan," Susan announced, "haven't you heard? All rescue dogs get spayed or neutered. *All.*"

And there went Bernadette, which turned out, by chance or by cosmic design, depending on your faith, to be the name of Ivan's mother. Bernadette Flynn-Isaacson lacked black diamonds on her cheeks, of course, but she had a highly distinctive feature nonetheless, namely, the saucer-shaped blue-violet eyes she'd obviously bequeathed to her son, who was currently seated at the Flynn-Isaacson kitchen table surrounded by library books about dog care and mail-order kennel-supply catalogs — Cherrybrook, R.C. Steele, and a couple of others — that Leah must have given him. While studying *This Is the Alaskan Malamute*, Ivan was eating the kind of lunch that educated Cambridge parents feed their offspring, a nutritionally balanced and ethnically diverse combination plate consisting of fried squid, a slice of leftover pizza, and three marinated artichoke hearts spread with peanut butter and decorated with little mounds of raisins, an inventive twist on ants on a log, I decided. But was I disgusted? No. Curious. Interested. See what dogs will do for you? B.D., Before Dogs, you witness a little boy digging his oversize, still-ridged grown-up teeth into a marinated artichoke heart topped with peanut butter and raisins, and you're gripped by nausea or repulsion, but A.D., After Dogs, post-conversion, the negative made positive, your soul drool-scoured and restored to perfect acceptance of Nature in all her once loathsome guises, you greet life eagerly and harmoniously as a fascinating series of equally informative encounters with the Divine. I came close to asking Ivan for a sample to take home. Marinated artichoke hearts plus peanut butter and raisins? Discovered by Holly Winter in Cambridge, Massachusetts, on Saturday, July 4: the only food the Alaskan malamute has ever been known to refuse. Glory, hallelujah!

"Would you like something?" Bernadette asked. "Shall I fix you a plate, too?"

Is there one clean? I wanted to reply. *And, if so, how could you possibly find it?* The mess was incredible — discarded pieces of clothing, half-empty jelly glasses, a bowl of rotting fruit, food-encrusted bowls, used tea bags, and, even by local standards, an extraordinary amount of printed material. On two long unfinished boards tenuously supported by wall brackets, I spotted two one-volume editions of the complete works of Shakespeare; a Danish-English dictionary; *The Chicago Manual of Style*; Alice Childress's *Like One of the Family*; a collection of Simenon mys-

251

teries not in translation, either (around here, escapism goes just so far); and, in what I suspected was a vestige of some abandoned cataloging scheme, a few dozen biographies of people who didn't have much in common. Alice James, Joe DiMaggio, and Virginia Woolf rubbed spines with Roger Tory Peterson, George Sand, Wagner, and Billie Burke. Imagine the pillow talk. Kitchen or no kitchen, the battered copy of *The Joy of Cooking* looked out of place. The books were the least of it. Edging one wall in what looked like a primitive effort at insulation were high stacks of *The New York Times* (Sunday in one pile, daily in another) and what must have been a complete five-year collection of *The New York Review of Books*. Magazines? On the countertops. *Nature, Science, Harvard Magazine, Bird Watcher's Digest,* and, inexplicably, *Gourmet.*

"Sit down! Tea?" Bernadette withdrew her hands from a salad spinner full of water and greens, made a token swipe at a rust-stained dish towel, and began to clear a space at the table, which served mainly as a repository for Xeroxed articles with notes scrawled in the margins and a few dozen yellow pads that looked as if they'd been used in some foolish attempt to take the toe prints of a couple of million chickens.

I'm no stranger here; I knew the signs.

Bernadette's pale brown hair had been cut short about four months earlier, probably the last time she'd noticed it. She wore jeans, a red T-shirt, and old running shoes. I was willing to bet that if she'd been forced to close her eyes and guess what she had on, she'd have had no idea whatsoever. Although she probably told herself that the kitchen was untidy, I was positive that she didn't care. Why do housework? She was happy already. It also occurred to me that since Bernadette was — what was it? — a socioecologist, maybe some of what struck me as junk was material saved for recycling. In Cambridge, you always have to remind yourself that absolutely anything — the height of the stacks of old newspapers in the kitchen, the length of the hair on any given body part — may well represent a carefully thought-out political decision.

I accepted the offer of tea and stated the Cantabrigian obvious: "You're writing a book."

"Two!" As if to remind herself of the reality, she repeated, "Two! But I'm on sabbatical this fall."

Since moving to Cambridge, I've concluded that all professors are permanently on sabbatical or about to go on sabbatical, and I'd previously felt outraged that all those academics were getting paid to loll around recuperating from the rigors of teaching four hours a week, if that, while I was pursuing my no-work-no-check occupation. This time, however, I was delighted. On sabbatical? Writing *two* books? Here in this cheerful mess? Although Malamute Rescue doesn't require applicants to develop instant agoraphobia, the presence of someone at home doesn't exactly prejudice us against a prospective adopter, either.

Having failed to locate a teakettle, Bernadette managed to find a saucepan that she filled with bottled water. The gas stove was one of those practically antique white enamel models you still find in Cambridge apartments, the kind with a built-in space heater as well as burners and an oven. After she'd twisted a knob a few times and tried blowing on the pilot light, Ivan finally stopped reading, went to the stove, and somehow persuaded the burner to produce a thin blue circle of flame. His mother set the pan on to heat. Then she dragged a chair to the sink, climbed on it, and began to rummage in a cupboard.

Ivan returned to his seat and said, "Really, she is writing two books, but they're about the same thing, only one of them is popular, and maybe she's going to publish it under another name so her department doesn't find out." So young yet so jaded.

"Oh," I said.

"Because if a lot of people buy the book, the other people in her department might get jealous and not give her tenure."

Bernadette's laugh was a beautiful, prolonged peal of glee. "Well spoken, Ivan! Straight to the point. Holly, would coffee do?"

"Fine. Anything."

"Coffee appears to be what we have," she said, "and I know we have milk."

Ivan evidently felt the need to explain his mother's unexpected knowledge of the contents of her own kitchen. "We have a milkman."

"I do, too," I said. "In fact, we have the same milkman, I think. Jim, right? I saw the box on your porch. Pleasant Valley Farms."

"He's your milkman?"

"You know, Ivan," Bernadette said, "women can deliver milk, too."

Ivan corrected himself. *"Milk person."* He scowled. "That sounds stupid. It sounds like somebody nursing a baby." Ivan licked some peanut butter off his fingers, wiped them on his Avon Hill shirt, and said, "Creamery . . . creamery . . . creamery representative!"

"Excellent," his mother told him, climbing down from the chair.

Ivan lost interest in the word game. With

a look of impatience, he demanded, "Could we talk about the dog now?"

Bernadette laughed and ran her hands through her shaggy hair.

"Of course," I said.

Ivan was eager. "Do you want to see the yard? The fence is five feet, eleven and three-quarters inches high."

"He measured it," Bernadette told me.

"Uh, we need to slow down a little," I said reluctantly. "You know, Ivan, it's important to make sure that this is a good time for you to get a dog at all, a good time for both of you, you and your mother."

"We had a dog before," Ivan said.

"Oh, you did?" In case you're not involved in rescue, I should explain that if a prospective adopter's last dog lived to fifteen, I'm impressed. But if the last dog got hit by car? Or died of heartworm because the people were too stingy to pay for preventive medication? Sobbing means nothing, by the way. People will go out their way to guarantee that Rover gets run over or dies of parvo or lepto, and then, once he's not going to cost them anything, they get choked up and teary-eyed while telling you how much they loved the dog they murdered.

"Oh," I said. "What was your dog's name?" Ivan was dry-eyed, but I wasn't about to ask a kid who'd lost his father to talk about the death of his dog.

"Ivan —" Bernadette began.

But Ivan got in ahead of her. "American Canadian Bermudian Champion Inuit's Wooly Bully." He even managed to get it out with a straight face. I've mentioned the pretty boy before. International Ch. Inuit's Wooly Bully, ROM — three countries. International; ROM, Register of Merit, sired five or more champions — was an Alaskan malamute bred and owned by Sheila Balch, not Ivan Flynn-Isaacson, who hadn't even been born when Floyd died. Floyd. Call name. Pretty boy. Get it?

Bernadette had finished slopping the boiling water into a Melitta cone precariously balanced on a hand-painted pottery pitcher. When she poured the coffee, it spilled on her hand and all around the dime-store mugs. She didn't seem to mind. She gave me mine and said gently, "Ivan, our dog was named Hector." To me she said, "Hector died when Ivan was only two."

"I remember him!" Ivan insisted belligerently.

"Maybe you do," Bernadette said. "And you've seen a lot of pictures of him."

I drank some coffee. It was surprisingly good. "What kind of dog was Hector?" I asked.

"A mutt," Bernadette said. "A little brown dog. He belonged to an old man we knew, and when the man had to go into a nursing home, we took Hector, and he was already seven by then, and he lived another ten years. To seventeen."

"Hector did tricks," Ivan added.

"He did," Bernadette agreed, smiling. "That's true. We didn't teach him; he knew them when we got him. He was like a little circus dog. He could dance on his hind legs, and before he got old, he could walk on his front legs, too. He was a wonderful dog."

Hector sounded wonderful to me. He also sounded nothing whatsoever like an Alaskan malamute. I was feeling guilty and rotten. With Rowdy's inadvertent help, Leah and I had roused Ivan's longing for a malamute. We'd built up his hope of actually getting one. From a malamute's point of view, there was nothing wrong with the home that Ivan and Bernadette could provide — fenced yard, someone at home a lot — but no matter how interested the child, the real dog owner is always the parent, and I was far from sure that Bernadette shared Ivan's eagerness. And if she'd raised a mere child to become as trouble-prone as Ivan, what could she do with a malamute? My other concern was Ivan's size. A wiry, strong-looking kid, he was nonetheless too small to control a dog with the bulk and power of the average malamute, and it made no sense to get him a dog that was too big for him.

"Ivan," I said, "your mother and I need to have a private talk. Is there somewhere you can go?"

"No," he said.

"Ivan! Of course there is," Bernadette told him. "Why don't you take your books to your room?"

"Because —"

"Please just do it!"

When Ivan had reluctantly gathered up his dog books and departed, I bluntly told Bernadette that I was afraid that all of us had set Ivan up for disappointment. Most malamutes outweighed him, and, regardless of size, they were all born to pull. No child could take full responsibility for a dog, and children's initial enthusiasm sometimes vanished rapidly.

As I started to say more, Bernadette cut in. "You don't understand. You're worried that, with Ivan, this is some kind of passing fad. What you don't know is that Ivan doesn't *have* passing fads. Ask him to show you his collections."

"What does he collect?"

"Wildflowers. Feathers. Bird feathers. He's

been doing that since he was three. They're all in scrapbooks, all catalogued. And if you think he's just looking at the pictures in the dog books —"

"No —"

"He's been reading since he was four. He taught himself."

"He's very gifted. That's not the issue. One issue . . . Look, it seems to me that we both need a little time to think this over. I'm going to leave some things for you to read, about malamutes and about adopting adult dogs, okay? For *you*. Not just for Ivan. And you think about whether this is something you really want to do. And in the meantime, I'm going to ask around about the dogs we have available." Then I lightened up and said that I hoped we could work something out. I meant it. We desperately need good homes. (Interested? Alaskan Malamute Protection League, P.O. Box 170, Cedar Crest, NM 87008.)

Bernadette said that she hoped we could work something out, too. After that, she insisted that I have lunch. To my relief, she brought out a big loaf of Italian bread and four kinds of French cheese, and made a salad of the fancy baby greens she'd been washing. When Ivan rejoined us, I tactfully suggested a few breeds other than the malamute that might interest him.

"But I'm not really interested in keeeshonden," he replied solemnly, with an emphasis on the correct plural. "What I'm interested in is Alaskan malamutes."

"Besides, Ivan doesn't get *interested*," Bernadette said cheerfully. "What he gets is *obsessed*."

25

On the assumption that the godly, like the dogly, are early risers, I'd been tempted to phone the twice-blessed Stephanie Benson at seven that morning, but I'd waited until nine o'clock, an hour before I'd considered it civil to call Bernadette, especially on a Saturday that was also a holiday, the Fourth of July. When I reached Stephanie, however, she cheerfully assured me that she'd been up for hours and had, in fact, just returned from the Star Market, where she'd impulsively decided to celebrate Ruffly's symbolic birthday — Independence Day? Did I remember? — and her renewed faith in him by having a little barbecue. Could I come?

"Steve and I —" I started to say.

"Oh, Steve's invited, too. After all, it's a celebration of Ruffly." Stephanie sounded so elated that I had to accept.

My reluctance? I'll confess to a prejudice against dog parties, which aren't very popular in New England, but are a growing trend in other parts of the country, especially Halloween costume parties to raise funds for humane societies and breed rescue groups. I don't object to wearing a costume, but I'm so averse to making my dogs look ridiculous that the one time I simply had to attend one of these affairs, I compromised by going as Sergeant Preston and putting red harnesses on Rowdy and Kimi. Unfortunately, everyone saw through my ruse, and we didn't get a prize. Also, the dogs hated what was supposed to be the main canine fun event, bobbing for hot dogs. They kept trying to filch splintery chicken bones that could have punctured their intestinal tracts, so I spent most of the so-called party sticking my hand down Rowdy and Kimi's throats to fish for dangerous objects, and ended up eating what I tried to think of as dog-person chicken salad, cold drumsticks coated in fresh saliva.

But this wasn't October 31, costumes were out of the question, and Rowdy and Kimi weren't invited. Besides, Stephanie had a good reason to celebrate. Her account of the gas grill incident agreed with Leah's. Stephanie hadn't smelled the gas because the wind was blowing it away from her. It made only a faint hiss that she might well have missed. It was also possible that her aids had cut out, she said; they were still giving her trouble. And Matthew was right: She shouldn't smoke.

Even so, if it hadn't been for Ruffly? Well, no matter what else was going on with him, he'd demonstrated his complete reliability.

As I've said, from a dog writer's point of view, the rescue would have been a lot better if Ruffly had dramatically saved Stephanie's life about two seconds before it was otherwise doomed to end. As it was, Stephanie might have smelled the gas in time to put away her lighter and turn the valve off. Also, even if she'd used her lighter, she'd might well have survived. In reality, a bad burn would have been terrible, but it seemed to me that, given the happy outcome, Ruffly would have done well to save his mistress from certain death, not just from uncertain injury. Furthermore, I would have preferred that Stephanie not smoke. For *Dog's Life*, Ruffly should have been perfectly heroic; Stephanie, absolutely blameless. In toying with the idea of a few touch-ups — inevitable fatality, no cigarettes — I found myself irked at both Ruffly and Stephanie for forcing me to choose between deceiving our readers and disappointing them.

I could hardly expect Stephanie to share my discontent; she was a priest, not a dog writer. Her faith in Ruffly fully restored, she was unequivocally delighted. Just before my visit to Ivan and Bernadette, I'd reached Steve, and he'd agreed that to refuse the invitation would have been mean and sour.

"This is a barbecue?" he asked.

"That's what she said."

He got what I'd missed. "On the *same* gas grill?" He sounded more amused than worried.

I wasn't really worried, either. In fact, when I was driving home from Ivan and Bernadette's, I heard a story on the radio about the holiday crowds already packing the Esplanade, and according to the weather report, the temperature was eighty-five and rising, so I was glad that Steve and I weren't going to the Hatch Shell after all and equally glad that we had some kind of July Fourth event to attend instead, even a dog party at a rectory. Wild times.

When I got home, I had to ease myself into the back hallway because the crate in which I'd incarcerated Willie yesterday took up most of the floor space. It was an ordinary collapsible wire cage designed for easy carrying and storage, but Rita hadn't folded it correctly and must have had a tough time just getting it down the stairs. To stow it away properly, I had to set it up and then break it down and latch it, and the metal-on-metal noise of the wire sides hitting the floor pan must've alerted Rita to my return. One floor up, her door opened. I listened. Willie barked. Rita didn't give even a low growl. The door closed.

About twenty minutes later, after I'd stored the crate in the cellar and put the dogs out to doze in the shade of the yard, Rita rapped so sharply on my kitchen door that her rings must have bruised her knuckles. When I opened up, though, what she thrust at me wasn't the battered hand of friendship, but the cheese-improved Plaque Attacker I'd freely and generously given to Willie a mere twenty-four hours earlier. Before leaving the toy in the crate, however, I certainly hadn't encased it in a clear plastic bag.

"Look!" I said happily. "He's been chewing it already. See? It's kind of rough around the pointy end."

Standing there in the hallway glaring at me, Rita looked like a long-suffering tenant driven at last to confront a slumlord with irrefutable evidence of the presence of rats. As if she could hardly bear to touch the plastic bag, she extended it far from her body, pinched between the thumb and first finger of her right hand. She honestly looked as if she were proffering a plastic-encased rodent carcass.

"Oh, how horrible," I said. "But I couldn't use poison, could I? Not with the dogs around."

Rita finally opened her mouth, but she hadn't softened any. "What?"

266

"The trap." I suppressed a grin. "It's not very humane, I know, but Rita, I got desperate. Dog toys? Those things *really* breed. Two today, ten tomorrow, a hundred thousand next week. So yesterday afternoon, as soon I heard that telltale scurrying, I ran and got out the trap. I'm terribly sorry about the dead Plaque Attacker, but —"

"Oh, for Christ's sake," Rita snapped. "And stop smirking!"

"Rita, is something *wrong?* No, don't tell me. Rita, this is entirely my fault. A terrier? Bred to go after vermin. Willie went right after that nasty little dog toy, didn't he? And got inadvertently caught in the trap." I eyed Rita. She said nothing. "Brave little fellow," I added. "Who would've thought he had it in him?"

The Plaque Attacker still dangling from her hand, Rita said, "Your key is for emergencies *only*. Isn't that our agreement?"

"Rita, I've just —"

"And cut the rodent crap."

I reached out and took the plastic bag. "Here, let me dispose of that for you. Phew! I'm afraid it's already beginning to —"

"Holly, when I am not home, you stay the hell out of my apartment, and, furthermore, if *I* want to hire someone to train *my* dog —"

"It probably won't be me. After all, *I* just might be effective."

"Do *not* shout at me," Rita said with dignity.

"Do *not* shout in my hallway. You're *not* my only tenant, you know, and I will *not* have the Donovans disturbed by people squabbling in the hallway any more than I'll have them driven out by a dog on the floor below that never shuts up. So come in!"

The Donovans, who rent my third floor, have two Persian cats and no dog, but, in all other respects, they're ideal tenants. They never complain about anything, even the washing-machine-rehydrated dog treats that kept clogging up the coin-op dryer in the basement, but it honestly wasn't fair to inflict Willie's barking on them. Lawrence, the husband, is an ordinary-looking, slightly plump Harvard M.B.A. with skin a few shades lighter than his wife's cinnamon, and he's less colorful than Ceci in most other respects, too. He dresses drably and is quite self-effacing, but Ceci wears dress-for-success clothes and has the air of authority that originally led me to believe that in renting to the Donovans, I'd scored a major dog-world coup. Much to my original disappointment, though, Ceci turned out not to be a real judge; all she does is sit on some circuit court of appeals. But, as I've said, they're excellent tenants, anyway, and I didn't want Willie driving them away.

Once Rita had deigned to cross my threshold and I'd closed the door, we lowered our voices, but increased the intensity of the dispute. Rita hit me with two of the dirtiest epithets in the verbal cesspool that passes as the psychotherapeutic lexicon — *intrusive* and *passive-aggressive* — and I accused her of using her hearing loss to justify her selfish disregard for other people's needs.

That got to her. "Selfish! I don't believe it! Holly, have you ever wondered why I am wearing these hearing aids? Is this really something I'm doing exclusively for *me?* Well, you know what? It damned well is not, because the fact is, I don't really enjoy hearing. And you know why? Because the world is a screaming mess! I'm used to a nice, quiet world, and that's how I like it, and the main so-called benefit I get from these things is that everything is clattering and banging all the time, and I hate it! Turn on the faucet, and instead of a nice, peaceful nothing, I get snap, crackle, and pop, like breakfast cereal, for God's sake, and —"

"Rita, why you are wearing the aids, if I might remind you, is so that you don't keep going to the wrong funeral. Remember Morris Lamb?"

Strangely enough, Rita and I had drifted toward our usual seats at my kitchen table, but instead of actually sitting down, we'd stationed ourselves behind the chairs almost as if we intended to use them as shields or as weapons against each other.

"Well, let me remind you, Miss Know-It-All," Rita said, tightening her grip on the chair, "that there happen to be a hell of a lot of people who don't hear a damned thing, for all practical purposes, and who manage just fine, thank you, by signing instead of —"

"Absolutely right," I interrupted. "But *you* aren't one of them, and why you aren't one of them is that you don't know a thing about deaf culture, and you're probably not going to learn anything about it, either, because, for a start, not only do you not sign, but you aren't actually deaf, either. All you are is —"

"Don't say it! Hard of hearing. Politically correct stance: Being deaf is not an illness, so it's not something that needs to be *cured*. Hearing loss is no loss at all." Rita spat out the words. "But just having a hard time hearing? Walking around with these hideous fake-flesh radios jammed in my ears so nobody has to bother to speak up? Well, that's a whole other matter."

"Poor little Rita," I said brusquely, "caught

between two worlds, rejected by the truly deaf —"

"Oh, shut up! You simply do not understand —"

"What I understand perfectly is that my second-floor tenant has carefully trained her dog to become a nuisance barker, and I, for God's sake, am a *dog writer*, but that much atmosphere I really don't need."

"Fine," Rita said. "Fair enough. But how about coming to me directly and —"

"Because I have already done it! And meanwhile Willie's gotten steadily worse, and you haven't made the slightest move to do a thing about it, that's why, and yesterday, I finally ran out of patience —"

"And took it upon yourself, knowing full well how I feel about people intruding in my private space and also knowing full well exactly how I feel about *imprisoning* dogs in *cages* —"

"Damn it, Rita, I did not imprison Willie. All I did was crate him temporarily with not just one but two very attractive chew toys so that he'd learn a socially acceptable way to entertain himself when you're not home." I broke off. "Speaking of which, since you disapprove so strongly of my vicious methods, and since you're so busy returning my instruments of torture, where's the rawhide?"

Rita shifted her feet and pursed her lips, but she said nothing.

"You tried to get it away from him, didn't you?" I said vindictively. "But Willie wouldn't give it up, would he?" Although I knew I was right, gloating was entirely unnecessary and unsporting, and I am thoroughly ashamed of it. But I *was* right. If Willie had rejected the rawhide or if she'd simply forgotten it, she wouldn't have been half so furious at me.

Instead of yelling, Rita took a deep breath, held it, and exhaled slowly. I had the impression that she wasn't merely respirating, but was performing some kind of mind-body or, worse yet, mindbody — one word — exercise she'd learned in the eight-session stress-reduction workshop she'd taken the previous winter. Eight sessions. Sound familiar? Basic beginners' dog training. Eight sessions. World's most effective stress reduction. And Rita's silly, pointless breathe-your-way-to-inner-peace beginners' human soul training had even met on Thursday nights. But not at the armory. Not where my friends and I are training our dogs. Those charlatan gurus are smart enough to shield their clients from a clear view of the genuine secret of cosmic harmony.

"Rita, look. I probably shouldn't have used my key," I conceded, "but what choice did

I have? I have tried to talk to you about the barking, and you have not done a damn thing about it, and the reason is, I think, because you don't get how big the problem is. Look. Willie is suffering from bored dog syndrome. And when you're home, he isn't bored, so he doesn't do it, so you don't hear how bad it is. But you *do* know that the Donovans aren't complainers, and it isn't too hard to guess that if Willie keeps it up, what they're going to do is just nicely and politely find another apartment. And what am *I* supposed to do? And what about Kevin? And Mrs. Dennehy? And the other —"

"All right! Did I say there wasn't a problem? There's a problem."

"And all I did, Rita, was to do exactly what any other reasonable, contemporary dog trainer would've done. Modern methods. No pain, no discomfort, no force. Lock him up in a safe place for a short time, and —"

"Holly, at the risk of repeating myself, I do *not* like to see dogs in cages, and, furthermore, this high-handed —"

"Fine," I said. "We'll have it your way, then. You don't like positive methods? Great. There are plenty of others, and Willie's your dog." I switched to my most obsequious salesperson voice. "Now what would you prefer, madam? I don't happen to have any shock

273

collars in stock right now, but I can certainly order one for you, or . . . Let's check what's on hand. I'll be right back."

I dashed to my study, rummaged around in the boxes Beryl had sent, and hustled back to the kitchen with a dog-silencing device in each hand. In my absence, Rita had taken her usual seat at the table. At first glance, I was tempted to hope that the move signaled the beginning of a return to the comfort of our friendship. Then I realized that I had caught Rita's habit of overpsychologizing everything. Rita sat down only because her feet hurt. Moral: If you intend to stand your ground, don't wear high heels.

"Here," I announced, raising my left hand, "is your simple old low-tech no-bark, no-bite Velcro-fastened muzzle. Just clamp Willie's jaws together, slap it on, and there you go! No noise. Or not much, anyway. Of course, he won't be able to eat or drink anything while he's got it on, and he'll probably manage to claw it off before long, and it won't *teach* him a thing, but, hey, no cage!" I tossed the muzzle on the table, then held up the little red plastic box in my right hand. "So now we move on to high tech, namely, the automatic bark-activated Yap Zapper with optional manual operation at a simple touch of this button." I pointed the device straight at Rita and pressed. The Yap Zapper made an almost inaudible click, and its tiny red light flashed off and on. "And there you go! You can't hear it, I can't hear it, but any dog within —"

Rita sat straight up, grabbed for her ears, and exclaimed, "What was that?"

As I've said, from the human standpoint, or at least from my human standpoint, the Yap Zapper had done practically nothing. The click was as soft as the tap of a fingernail, and you had to look at the gadget to notice the little light that showed that the device was working.

"Ultrasound," I said. "It's called a Yap Zapper. It gives a one-second burst of sound that's —"

"Do it again," said Rita, all curiosity, her anger and defensiveness suddenly gone. "Or wait . . . The dogs . . . ?"

"They're too far away," I told her. "The range is ten or twelve feet. It's —"

"This is so weird," Rita said. "Press it again."

Once again, I aimed the Yap Zapper and pushed the button. Rita jerked her head as if she'd just climbed out of a swimming pool and was trying to shake the water out of her ears.

"Rita, are you hearing it? Because, supposedly, it's . . . It's supposed to be out of the range of human hearing. We — people — only hear up to whatever it is, but dogs can hear sounds way, way above what we can. Rita, can you *hear* this thing?"

"Not exactly," Rita said. "That's what's so freakish. What I *hear* is total silence."

26

"Maybe you're quicker than we were; maybe you got it right away. Rita and I, however, had to hit the books. Back in graduate school, Rita had taken a course that touched briefly on human hearing, and sometime thereafter she'd refreshed her knowledge by cramming for the psychology licensing exam, but she'd soon forgotten everything except some psychoanalytic gobbledygook about the erotic significance of orifices, and in her recent reading about hearing loss and hearing aids, she'd ignored the technicalities and concentrated on what she called the socioaffective aspects of — believe it or not — *dialoguing* and their implications for — I swear to God — *languaging*. Therapists!

I wasn't much help, either. I knew that dogs could hear sounds pitched too high for human ears. To illustrate the point, I immediately produced the example of the so-called silent dog whistle inaudible to people but audible to dogs. My knowledge of the details, however, was as scanty as Rita's.

Before long, though, we'd strewn my kitchen table with what was, even for Cambridge, an oddly assorted collection of reference materials, and, soon thereafter, we understood almost everything, which is to say, everything except the trivial matter of *who*.

But the *how?* Rita's deceitful no-hearing-dogs self-help guide informed us that human beings don't hear sounds above 20,000 cycles per second. According to the canine authorities, dogs are vastly superior to people in this regard. (So what else is new?) Just how vastly superior? A couple of my books said that dogs hear sounds up to about 40,000 cycles per second, but Rita came across the suggestion that dogs may even hear some sounds within the range of 70,000 to 100,000 cycles per second. Are you with me? Cycles per second is frequency — pitch — as opposed to volume in decibels, which brings us to the hearing aids and the Yap Zapper. The operating instructions for Rita's aids assured us that since an aid with a maximum sound pressure level greater than 132 decibels may impair hearing, this model safeguarded the user by cutting off sounds louder than 113 decibels. And the Yap Zapper promotion material? The bursts of sound were, as I'd known, high-pitched, and, as I hadn't known, 120 decibels loud. In other words, the bursts were too high-pitched for a person to hear, but, nonetheless, loud enough to make Rita's hearing aids momentarily and automatically quit working.

Just like Stephanie's. Rita and I reasoned that, far from malfunctioning, Stephanie's aids were cutting out, as she described it, by responding to high volume, regardless of pitch. And Ruffly's episodes? I hadn't been too far off. "Sound shyness," I said to Rita, shying away from painful slaps of loud sound pitched too high for human ears but not too high for Ruffly's.

Not that I get off on diagnosing a veterinary problem that's baffled Steve Delaney, D.V.M., but by the time Rita and I had worked it out, I was wired. Also, our friendship restored, we were drinking coffee, and although Rita had insisted on decaf, I was fine-tuning my nervous system with genuine Puerto Rican formula three-tablespoons-per-cup Bustelo, so I was eager to zip over to Stephanie Benson's, where I'd modestly announce my diagnostic triumph and gracefully accept the eternal gratitude not only of the rector but of her Principal Employer, too, I assumed. I could see and hear it all. That Companion Dog Excellent title? Rowdy's C.D.X.? Fair and square, no cheating, of course, and, yes, I know it by heart. Chapter 2, Section 7 of the Good Book, the ban on "any assistance, interference, or attempts to control a dog from outside the ring." But if God is *inside* the ring? Preferably with a good grip on Rowdy's collar and on his soul, too. Well, according to my reading of the regulations, divine intervention does not count as double handling. C.D.X., here we come!

Rita interrupted this beatific vision. "Holly? Holly, there's a hitch."

Naturally, I thought, coming to earth abruptly, *there always is.* For instance, take the time Rowdy ended up next to that Kees bitch on the sits and downs. The hitch? She absolutely must have been starting to come in season, or Rowdy'd never, ever have behaved like that. And the Retrieve on Flat? Rowdy never refuses the command. He retrieves anything, anytime, anywhere. The hitch? A silly technicality, an arbitrary rule. To qualify, the dumbbell he brings back has to be his *own.*

"What hitch is that?"

Rita picked up the Yap Zapper and fingered it lightly. "The maximum range is what? Twelve feet? That's —"

"That's not a hitch," I said. "There must be a dozen of these things on the market, probably more, and they're not all the same. The idea of this one is that you just put it in the dog's kennel with him or else you put it in

280

the room with him, and then when he barks, it goes off automatically; or else, if you're there, you press the button yourself. But they're all different. Some of them aren't even all that high frequency. You can hear them; they're perfectly audible to people; they're just really loud. All they do is substitute for someone standing there and screaming at the dog whenever he barks. On some of them, you can adjust the sensitivity so that if the dog just whines or whatever, nothing happens. Some of them react only to barking, not to whining or howling. There's a really big one that's meant for kennels, which is really unfair, I think, because it blasts all the dogs even if it's only one dog that barks. Some of them aren't even for barking; they're for any behavior you don't want. They're in all the catalogs. I'll show you."

Which catalogs? Are you serious? No, not J. Crew and not L.L. Bean. Victoria's Secret? Well, if your OFA excellent, CERF clear champion bitch is proving totally impossible to breed, anything's worth a try, I guess, but if you honestly don't know what I mean by *the* catalogs, I am now about to save you thousands of dollars in pet supplies. No kidding. R.C. Steele, color glossy catalog, fifty-dollar minimum order: 800-872-3773 or if you use a TDD, 800-468-8776. Cherrybrook, no illustrations, just a price list, but no minimum order, and a portion of each sale is donated to the Morris Animal Foundation: 800-524-0820. Tell 'em Holly sent you. And, no, I don't receive a commission. So why am I revealing the inner secrets of the Sacred Brotherhood and Sisterhood of The Fancy? So you'll stay out of pet shops that sell dogs. Why do that? Puppy mills. But that's a whole other story.

The Cherrybrook and R.C. Steele catalogs are the essential First Books of the Kennel Supply Testament, our Deep Discount Torah, so to speak, but before long, Rita and I were also leafing through Foster & Smith, UPCO, Master Animal Care, New England Serum, and eight or ten others, including at least two apocrypha, which is to say, yuppie-targeted, reverse-discount (double-markup) catalogs. After Rita finally quit ridiculing such everyday items as plastic-lined polka-dot lace-trimmed canine sanitary panties and a fluoride-impregnated rawhide chew in the form of a plate of spaghetti and meatballs, she got herself under control, turned to the right pages, and verified what I'd been saying. In brief, if you wanted to explode auditory dynamite in your dog's ears, there were a lot of ways to do it — audible or inaudible to people, bark activated, manually operated, with or without adjustable sensitivity, and with or without a lot of other options, too: waterproof cases, happy tunes to reward the dog for good behavior, a maximum effective range varying all the way from a mere ten feet up to a whopping seventy-five feet.

I picked up the Yap Zapper again. "This would probably do it, if you stood right outside the window. Except, for all we know, I guess, it could be inside — one of those big kennel models? It could be *any* of the ones that people can't hear. The point is, this *is* what's doing it, something like this. It has to be."

Rita looked sad and tired. "That isn't really the point, is it? The real point is, Holly, what a vicious, vile thing for someone to do. And to a *hearing* dog!"

"Ruffly's kept right on working," I said, "but, yeah, it could've gone the other way, and, Rita, Stephanie's had Ruffly for over a year, and, by now, she takes it for granted that he'll do the listening. So besides being really hard on him, it could've been . . . But, Rita, we don't necessarily know. . . . It *is* possible that it's all a mistake."

"I don't see how."

I hesitated to raise the topic, but it had to be said. "In one of the catalogs? Maybe in more than one, there's one of these ultrasound things that's actually marketed as, uh . . ." As my voice dropped, my gaze rose involuntarily upward. "As, uh, the simple solution to the problem of your neighbor's noisy dog. . . ."

"Oh," Rita said flatly.

"The idea is, uh, no direct confrontation. Or what to do when you've asked the people a million times, and the dog is still driving you crazy."

"Yes, I *get* the idea."

"So it's possible that it isn't even aimed at Ruffly. Ruffly can't be the only dog around there, and he barks now and then, but he's not a nuisance barker. As I said, those gadgets aren't selective. If they get triggered, they just blast away. Any dog in the vicinity gets hit, not just the one making the noise. Also, whoever's doing it doesn't necessarily . . ." I didn't finish the sentence aloud. The salt on Alice Savery's lawn? Ivan had known that the salt would kill the grass, of course, but he was simply too young to grasp Alice Savery's devotion to what struck me as her companion vegetables. "Rita, it's even remotely possible that Morris Lamb *owned* one of those things and that it's still in the house. Maybe if the batteries are weak . . . like smoke detectors? You know how they go off when the batteries are low?"

"That's a very benign hypothesis."

"It is," I agreed. "And Doug . . . Well, I'm not sure, but Doug . . . Doug Winer was Morris's partner, and it's his house now, and he'd probably know if Morris had bought one of those things. And, of course, Doug would know exactly what something like that could do to a hearing dog, and he's such a hovery landlord, and he knows about Ruffly's episodes, so even if he'd forgotten that Morris had one of these gadgets, he certainly would've remembered by now."

Rita smiled sourly. "Or he's hit on a strange way to deliver an eviction notice."

"Oh, evicting Stephanie is probably the last thing Doug wants to do," I said. "It's true that Doug's cousin, who's an old friend of Stephanie's, did pressure him to rent to her, but why would he want her out? She's got to be a great tenant —"

"Don't remind me. Hard to find."

"Hard to find," I agreed. "And Doug lives with his elderly parents, and if he'd wanted to move the whole family to Highland Street, he had the chance, right after Morris died. And he didn't. He stayed in Brookline with his parents, and he rented Morris's house to Stephanie. Besides, I met his father at a show, a while ago, and I really don't think that this would be a great time to move him anywhere.

He — Mr. Winer — is . . . I guess he's in the early stages of Alzheimer's, and it seems to me it would be pretty disorienting for him to move from where he is. But that's . . . You don't know Doug. If he wanted Stephanie out, he'd just . . . Come to think of it, I'm not sure what he'd do. He wouldn't just order her out. He'd be very polite about it, I think. He'd keep apologizing, and he'd fuss about where she was going to go, and he'd give her all the time she needed, that kind of thing."

Rita looked skeptical. My friendship with Doug Winer was a mere acquaintanceship, but Rita didn't know him at all. "Holly, tell me something." She took the Yap Zapper from my hand. "Just how accessible are these things?"

"Well, you just saw. They're in the catalogs."

"Have you ever seen one anywhere else? In a store?"

I tried to remember. "Not that I can think of. Maybe at shows, but I don't think so. As far as I know, they're mainly a catalog item."

Thus accessible to . . . ? I remembered the stack of kennel supply catalogs on the cookbook shelves in Morris Lamb's kitchen, catalogs available to Morris, of course, and to Doug Winer and to his tenants, Stephanie and, of course, Matthew. And only a few hours earlier, I'd seen Ivan with the same catalogs.

Rita patted the R.C. Steele catalog, which sat on top of the pile on my table. "Holly, does Stephanie order from these?"

"She might. But Morris Lamb did, I'm sure — Morris was a dog person — and his catalogs are still there, at his house. At least I assume they were Morris's. But Stephanie wouldn't . . . Rita, why would Stephanie . . . ?"

"I wasn't thinking of her," Rita said. "I was wondering about the son."

"Matthew?"

"Matthew. Didn't you or Leah tell me that it came as something of a surprise to him, having his mother move here with him?"

"Yes." I hesitated. "On the other hand, Rita, he seems quite devoted to Stephanie. That's how he talks about her, and, before she got Ruffly, apparently, Matthew rigged up gadgets to help her, and he's still the one who checks her phones, stuff like that."

Rita made one of those noncommittal therapist noises.

"He's too polite to go around bad-mouthing his mother," I argued, "but the sense I have, honestly, is that he's, if anything, more devoted to her than most kids that age are to their parents. Like tonight? Stephanie is having this little barbecue."

"I know. She invited me. I'm going."

"Good. Well, Matthew and Leah are going to be there, and a lot of kids that age would refuse. It's the last thing they'd want to do. But, you know, I'm just guessing. It really is hard to tell how Matthew feels about anything. Except Leah. How he feels about her is pretty obvious." I thought for a second and added, "And dogs. You can't miss it. One thing that's perfectly obvious is that Matthew does *not* like dogs."

27

Stephanie Benson was a little too heavy of body and mind to approach cuteness, but when I aimed the Yap Zapper at her and said, "Okay, stick 'em up," her wide grin displayed those clean, square teeth, and she dutifully raised her hands. I pressed the button, the little red light blinked, and, instead of lowering her arms, Stephanie raised them high, waved her hands from the wrist, and made her fingers dance gleefully.

"The applause of the deaf," she explained.

Although science would also have had us aim the Yap Zapper at Ruffly, Stephanie and I agreed to assume that we'd found the cause of the dog's problems. Before trying the device, we'd banished Ruffly to the deck, where Doug Winer was puttering with the valve of the gas grill, and, to make doubly sure of sparing Ruffly any discomfort, we'd gone all the way to the living room, at the front of the house, before activating the Yap Zapper. When the experiment was successfully completed, we immediately returned to the kitchen, not only because Stephanie was in the middle of preparing food for what she persisted in calling Ruffly's birthday party, but also because she was determined to find out whether the Yap Zapper would explain her problems with the telephone as miraculously as it had demystified both Ruffly's episodes and the apparent malfunction of her aids.

"Stephanie, I honestly don't think —" I started to protest.

"What harm will it do? We'll give it a little try, and if the phone rings, there we are!"

"It's only this extension? The white phone?"

In Morris Lamb's day, as I've mentioned, the kitchen had been a cheerful jumble of great food and pretty dogs, but Stephanie kept the counters and the granite work island tidy. The only area that looked even slightly messy was what I suppose a decorator would have called the communication center. The mounting bracket for Morris's phone now held a couple of little plastic jacks from which sprouted a tangle of wires that led to a gray answering machine and to Stephanie's telephone on the counter, which also held a jar of tiny dog biscuits, a pad of bright pink While You Were Out message slips, and a tray of pens and pencils. The phone was one of those full-size, enhanced amplification, big-button AT&T white models with fire, police, and ambulance symbols on the top row of buttons, and immense numbers and slightly smaller letters on the buttons underneath, as if hearing loss put people in constant need of emergency aid and simultaneously impaired their vision and their manual dexterity.

"This is the only one I ever answer," Stephanie said. "It's the only one I can hear on. I'm getting another one just like it, but, in the meantime, either I answer this one, or I let the machine pick up. So let's try it!"

Stephanie wore an Easter-egg lavender homespun cotton dress that flowed around her as she made her way quickly to the deck, where she asked Doug to take Ruffly around to the front of the house for a minute or two. After they'd passed by the kitchen windows, I waited briefly, then aimed the Yap Zapper at the big white phone. I pressed the button. The little red light flashed on and off. The phone didn't ring. At Stephanie's insistence, I held the gadget right next to the phone and pressed the button. But, once again, the experiment failed.

"Oh, well," Stephanie said cheerfully, "maybe I was being greedy. I was hoping there'd be some sort of sympathetic vibration or something. I don't really understand these things. It's all those years being married to a physicist, I suppose, and then Matthew, too. Live with people who understand everything about something, and one winds up understanding nothing oneself. In any case, this other business is more within my own discipline, and I'll have to ponder the matter of precisely how to approach her about it. Loving one's neighbor as oneself is always particularly challenging when *neighbor* must be taken literally, I always think."

Stephanie was right: She did not have a scientific mind. When I'd first tried to explain what ultrasound was, I'd mentioned the gadget designed for use on a neighbor's dog. Unfortunately, Stephanie had latched onto the example, and I now had difficulty in convincing her that the sound reaching her house did not necessarily emanate from Alice Savery's and might even come from some long-untouched device of Morris Lamb's. Or maybe Stephanie simply didn't like the idea of having her house searched. Who would? And when I finally persuaded Stephanie of the need to look, she promised that she and Matthew would go over the place, but scrupulously pointed out that the cellar was packed with cartons of Morris Lamb's belongings, possessions and papers that no one but Doug had any right to examine. It seemed to me that my fondness for Morris Lamb was proof against whatever horrible secrets I might un-cover while searching for some hidden version of the Yap Zapper, but I felt embarrassed to say so. Also, since Doug Winer was right out-side, it made sense to question him first and, if necessary, to ask him to delve into Morris's cartons.

When Stephanie and I moved out to the deck, we found that Doug had returned from the front of the house. He was near the grill, bending over to fasten the latch on a small metal toolbox.

"Doug, where's Ruffly?" Stephanie asked. "Ruffly! Ruffly, come!"

"He was here a second ago," said Doug, rising to his feet. He wore an open-necked shirt, freshly pressed shorts, and athletic shoes so clean that they looked brand-new. The ten-nis whites highlighted the blackness of his hair, including the thick growth on his arms and legs, and the individual whiskers emerg-ing on his face after what I suspected was a recent shave. "The naughty boy, did he run off? Ruffly!"

Within seconds, however, Ruffly danced up the stairs to the deck, ran to Stephanie, stood on his hind legs, and balanced there. "Good boy," she told him warmly, and added, to Doug and me, "Compromise. He knows not to jump on people, so he gets his front paws within a half inch, and he stops right there."

The little paragon's contrast with my own dogs was beginning to grate on me. I almost wished that Ruffly had appeared with a dead squirrel in his mouth just to prove that he was a normal dog after all. When my envious surge abated, I took a good look at Ruffly and realized that I didn't entirely trust his consistent display of faultless behavior. In other words, I felt the way I usually do when I'm watching a poodle in the obedience ring. As a big fan of poodle antics, I'd become pretty good at predicting when an apricot mini was going to ruin a 200 score by leaping up into the handler's arms, or when a black standard heading for high in Open B was going to turn the Retrieve on Flat into tug-of-war by refusing to part with the dumbbell, but Ruffly didn't show the devilish glint in the eye or the little telltale wiggle in the gait. The tilt of his head? Although it was Ruffly who was Stephanie's Victrola, her canine ear trumpet, he might have copied the bewitching angle from the old RCA ad. Only when I'd worked my way down the full length of the dog did I finally spot the cue: Almost imperceptibly, the very tip of Ruffly's tail drummed a minibeat of deviltry.

Before I could decide what to make of that observation, however, Stephanie asked me to explain our discovery to Doug and announced that she was going to make a preliminary search of the kitchen, where the majority of Ruffly's episodes had occurred. Then she would examine her bedroom. In case the shots of ultrasound were fired from outside the house, she also wanted to close the windows and the big sliding glass doors. Ruffly, of course, followed her inside.

"A *crise* of some sort?" Doug asked.

"With luck, a resolved one." I went on to explain. Then I casually asked whether Morris had ever happened to buy anything like the Yap Zapper.

Although I'd tried to be tactful, Doug was insulted. Had I ever even heard Morris so much as raise his voice to his dogs? Had I already forgotten what Morris was like?

"Doug, I *had* to ask, just on the off chance, and ultrasound is really not an instrument of torture, but I'm sorry. And, no, I have not forgotten what Morris was like. Whenever I'm here, I keep half expecting to have Morris show up and tell me all about his wins, and then make me taste whatever he's been cooking, and the more different everything looks and sounds and smells here, the more I miss him, and —"

"God, it's awful," Doug said. "How I *loathe* being here. I can hardly *endure* walking up the stairs to the second floor. It's like going through it all over again, walking in that morning, and going up there, and *finding* him like that." The lilt in Doug's voice, the exaggerated emphases, the whole gay speech pattern sounded entirely unaffected; everything gay about Doug felt like a genuine expression of solidarity with Morris. "I have this *terrible* fear about being here." Doug pulled a terry cloth sweatband from one of the pockets of his white shorts and vigorously wiped the palms of his hands.

"Fear of — ?"

The July sun was beating down on the deck, and Doug's face was damp from the heat, but instead of mopping his forehead, he kept scrubbing his hands. It had been warm under the big striped tent at the Essex County show, and with Nelson about to enter the Bedlington ring, Doug had been keyed up. It's possible that the thick dog-show odors of grooming spray, canine perfume, and exhibitors' nerves had blunted my sense of smell or masked whatever odor came from Doug, but I hadn't caught so much as a whiff of after-shave. Now, though, the heat of the sun and the sweat of Doug's body activated Ivory soap and diffused it so effectively that I wondered whether Morris's backyard would ever again smell like fresh-cut grass.

Doug went through the motions of wringing out the sweatband, but no drops of moisture hit the wooden deck. He glanced around, and when he spoke, his voice was oddly flat. "Have you ever been afraid of seeing someone who wasn't there?"

I knew exactly what he meant. "My mother," I answered. "After she died." I'd been terrified of seeing her ghost. A somewhat similar phenomenon plagued me after Vinnie died. The difference was that I'd have welcomed even the most hazy, protoplasmic shade of Vinnie. I could have made this confession to Morris. To Doug? I didn't entirely trust him. Not everyone understands about being scared of seeing your mother, but feeling eager to greet the great obedience dog of your life in whatever form she chooses to materialize.

"It didn't start until I read about it," Doug said softly. He glanced anxiously toward the kitchen, as if there were a remote chance that Stephanie might hear him. "In a book Stephanie gave me," he added. "The book was supposed to, oh, allay one's fears, I suppose, but it was ghastly, the way it went out of its way to suggest new possibilities, and ever since then, I've been plagued by this terror that I'm doomed to start hallucinating visions of Morris. Every time I'm here and I hear sirens, well, I'm on the verge of a flashback, and I'm in the grip of a sort of compulsion to go dashing out to shoo all the police cars and the ambulances away."

I had to suppress a sudden, crazy urge to tell Doug about hallucinatory fly catching in King Charles spaniels. To my horror, anxious laughter welled in my throat. What suppressed it was a memory: Doug had gone to work at Winer & Lamb on the day of Morris's death as well as on the day of his funeral.

"They came in droves," Doug continued, his face ashen, "because I kept calling and calling 911. They sent dozens of policemen and two ambulances. It was horrible. First, there was no one, and then suddenly the house was filled with all these enormous men, and then they put me in the ambulance with him, and I wanted to clean him up — Morris would have despised being seen like that; he was a fright — and once we got to the emergency room, I had to wait and wait. And the absolute worst was when they started talking about a postmortem, and I couldn't understand a word they were saying until it hit me, and I was sick at the thought of these strangers cutting into Morris."

I was so confused and overwhelmed that I hadn't noticed Stephanie's reappearance on the deck. Without actually touching Doug, she reached toward his arm. She said gently, "Doug, please try to remember. That was not Morris. It was only his body."

A Christian priest seemed a peculiar source of those words, which Doug seemed to find oddly consoling. Or perhaps what helped was Stephanie's presence. Within a minute or two, he'd recovered. To my surprise, he told Stephanie how relieved he was that she was going to take the house off his hands. Neither of them lingered on the topic — the sale wasn't news to the buyer and the seller — and Stephanie graciously asked Doug whether he'd prefer to skip the party that evening. I expected Doug to take advantage of the opportunity, but he assured Stephanie that he was dying to come, and he apologized to both of us for having made a *scene* — Doug's word and his emphasis. His insistence on attending the barbecue puzzled me until I remembered his father's courtliness. Doug was now making amends for the unpardonable rudeness of having even suggested to his hostess that he felt like reneging on an invitation he'd previously accepted. Looking greatly restored, he picked up the metal toolbox, told Stephanie that there was nothing wrong with the valve on the grill, and launched into one of his normal fits of fussing about all the things he had to do at Winer & Lamb and at home before he'd have the pleasure of seeing us again.

When Doug finally left, I spoke bluntly to Stephanie. "Tell me something. It's none of my business, but a lot of people have been assuming that Morris died of AIDS."

Her surprise was unmistakable. "Whatever gave anyone that idea?"

"A lot of people still think of AIDS as a gay disease," I said, "and this story Doug keeps telling people about Morris being accidentally poisoned sounds so unlikely. In a way, it sounds just like Morris to go wandering around feeling creative and randomly gathering up things and then making a salad, but . . ." I faltered. "Maybe it sounds so much like Morris and at the same time so improbable that it feels trumped up, so people assume there's something to whitewash, something stigmatized, and then since Morris was gay, they think of AIDS."

"That's because Doug's not telling the whole story," Stephanie said. "What Doug is omitting is that he built the garden, the raised bed."

"I know he did."

"But Doug ordered the seeds, too. He had a catalog. It had a whole section on edible flowers, and Doug ordered some special collection, and he and Morris started the seeds. They planted them together, some of them indoors, some of them out here."

"That's harmless."

"In itself," Stephanie said. "In itself, it's harmless, but it's the source of Doug's terrible sense of guilt, as if he'd staged Morris's death. I've tried to help with that, but, unfortunately, it has some basis in reality. The garden is undoubtedly what gave Morris the idea. In effect, it is what killed him."

28

Imagine the cosmos as an Antarctica of infinite magnitude, cold, bleak, cheerless. The monotony is relieved once every three trillion light years by some tedious astronomical event. A boring mess of gas explodes. A few celestial epochs later, a black hole looms. Pity the poor aliens. Among other things, their kids must drive them crazy. Consider the possibilities of intergalactic whining: *When are we going to get there?* and *Ma, he hit me!* and *I have to go to the bathroom, and I have to go now!* And then the father, Ralph, yells, *Doris, can't you get those brats to shut up!* And Doris tries placating them: *Now, darlings, only another thirty zillion millennia to the next clean rest room, and in the meantime, let's see who can spot the first white asteroid. Aaron, you take the left, and Hazel, you take the right, and whoever finds it gets a lovely piece of green cheese. Won't that be fun!*

Now ponder the typical abduction story, which goes something like this: At nine o'clock on the evening of September 3, 1993, a woman we shall call Violet J. is driving her two-year-old tan Ford Escort from Hoboken to Hackensack when she experiences the first interesting event of her thirty-six years, the previous ten of which she's spent explaining the difference between universal and term insurance policies and selling both. After work, she watches television game shows while eating Rice-A-Roni. Her social life consists of occasional visits to discount shopping malls. Once in a while she treats herself to a wild fling by risking the price of a postage stamp to enter the Publishers' Clearinghouse Sweepstakes. She always promises herself that if she's ever the lucky winner of the Grand Prize, she won't change her life-style one iota.

Ah, but something will. Enter Ralph, Doris, and the kids. In the driver's seat of the Escort on the road to Hackensack, Violet has just reached forward and switched from a talk-radio discussion of household stain removal to a golden oldies station when a blinding burst of light appears, weird bells tinkle, and distant whistles sound. Some six hours later, a frightened and disoriented Violet finds herself in the passenger seat of the Ford Escort, which is inexplicably parked next to a foul-smelling Dumpster at the rear of the same pet shop where she once bought a gerbil that died three days later. At first Violet recalls nothing of the minutes immediately preceding those lost hours, but over the next few days, fragments return. She recalls that rubbing alcohol will remove ink from carpets and that Jerry Lee Lewis was singing "Great Balls of Fire." After that? Floating through space. Paralysis. Looming gray figures.

Hold it. Zillions of light years crammed in a flying saucer with whining kids for the sole purpose of spacenapping *Violet*? Come on! Sorry, Violet, but these beings don't want insurance, Rice-A-Roni, game shows, Ford Escorts, or anything else you have to offer. What's the one thing on earth worth that miserable trip through the great celestial three-dog everlasting night? Certainly not Violet. And not just any dog, either. After all, the cosmos is an infinite Antarctica. Of course. An Alaskan malamute.

But they won't get mine. Even co-owner-ship is out of the question. It's nothing but trouble. The last person I co-owned a dog with was my own mother, and I'll never do it again. My will weakens only when I watch Leah train Kimi. Leah is a great natural dog trainer, very charming, endlessly persistent, and so outrageously and implicitly bossy that she'd never undermine her authority by raising that sweet, rich, domineering voice.

At four-thirty on the afternoon of July 4,

about twenty minutes after I'd arrived home from Stephanie's, I was sprawled on the landing of the steps that lead down to my fenced yard. I was practicing the popular obedience training technique that consists of drinking coffee while your dog sleeps. The temperature had reached the high eighties. Rowdy was indoors snoozing under his air conditioner in my bedroom. I was reviving myself with iced Bustelo and supervising the spiritual development of that rank-novice postulant, my cousin Leah, who had yet to attain the elevated state of enlightenment that consists of knowing nothing whatsoever about your field of greatest expertise. Leah continued to harbor the illusion that in dog training, as in all other meditative endeavors, an objective truth exists out there somewhere and that revelation is reached by way of hard work. Novice that she was, she'd drenched herself and Kimi with the garden hose and was praying in the shade cast by the high brick wall of the luxury grooming spa and Malamute Rescue haven temporarily known as someone else's spite building.

The no-force technique Leah was applying — *binding* — consists of using a short lead to clamp the dog to your left side in perfect heel position while you simultaneously pour on praise for the flawless heeling you've set the dog up to execute. Leah was making cheerful noises to hold Kimi's attention, moving quickly enough to keep Kimi prancing happily along, murmuring heartfelt praise, and not giving Kimi a single opportunity to make a mistake. No force? No choice. I wished Bernie Brown were there to watch. As top handlers go, Bernie holds an unusually high opinion of Alaskan malamutes as competitive obedience dogs. His published view on the matter is that they make nice pets. I wonder, though, whether he understands that binding could have been designed for the breed. After all, Bernie Brown's approach is the only one to capitalize on the universal conviction of Alaskan malamutes that since they're smarter than everyone else, they're absolutely always right.

Hubris.

Well, yes. Hubris *is* one of the ten most popular dog names in Cambridge. But what I had in mind was the foundation bitch, so to speak: the arrogance of mortals who imagine themselves equal to the gods, the fatal flaw that stood between Oedipus and his Elysian OTCH. That was back in the old days, of course, before Bernie Brown. I'm serious. Take Oedipus. With Bernie Brown handling, the guy wouldn't even have *seen* his mother, never mind had the chance to you-know-what. And where would that have left Freud? In the absence of the name, in the absence of the event itself, would the concept have entirely eluded Freud? Does insight require the correct proper noun, which itself requires individuals to remain on their allotted continents in their assigned centuries instead of zipping around through space and time like Ralph and Doris on their pitiful whine-ridden excuse for what started as a happy family excursion, but turned into a galactic nightmare when Aaron and Hazel threw a conjoint celestial temper tantrum and, in an unprecedented moment of unanimity, refused to settle for the likes of Violet?

But what about Violet herself? Ralph's fault for getting lost? Doris's fault for misreading the map? Violet doesn't know, though. All that terror, all that suffering, and no explanation. No-fault divorce, no-fault car insurance, fine, but no-fault alien abduction? The hand of fate?

Violet might be persuaded to buy that explanation, but only because the sole companion animal she's had in thirty-six years is the gerbil that died. Violet does not own a dog. She does not train dogs. She knows nothing of the Brownian revolution. I am not Violet. I use Bernie Brown's methods as they suit me and my dogs, and as I understand it, that's exactly how he intends them to be used. I am no recent convert, I am not Leah, but I am convinced that the most effective way to train is to present no choice except the correct one, and, overall, I agree that the hand of fate is the hand of the handler, the voice of fate the handler's, the mistakes, the blame, the fault.

Leah has switched exercises. She's practicing what's called the come fore, the part of the recall that consists of having the dog position herself straight in front of the handler. With Kimi still on the twenty-one-inch lead, Leah moves forward and then calls "Kimi, come!" Simultaneously, Leah backs up, takes a seat in an invisible chair, and brings Kimi into the chute formed by her bent knees. Guaranteed perfection? Not quite. Kimi is not directly in front of Leah, but twists toward Leah's right side, all too ready to go around to heel position. Her forepaws are not even. The left rests on the grass a good inch ahead of the right. An *error!* Whose fault? Leah's. Notice her feet, the right toe an inch in front of the left. Peer into Leah's right hand. Fastidious adolescent, she dislikes the taste of Redi-Liver and shies from the dead-center, mouth-to-jaw spit. Kimi's error. Leah's fault.

Morris picked the greens, Morris made the salad, Morris ate it. How could he have been so stupid? Morris's fatal error. If the grill had exploded? In a way, Matthew was right. His mother knew she shouldn't smoke. Stephanie's fault. And Ruffly was charged with hearing for her. If he had failed to detect the gas? Then Ruffly's fault, too. But the grill hadn't exploded. Kimi had sat crooked, too.

Only a few minutes earlier, bound to Leah's side, Kimi had been deliberately set up to take credit for perfect heeling, and she had heeled perfectly, too. She'd had no choice. Any experienced dog trainer would have realized, however, that at this stage of training, most of the credit belonged not to the dog but to the handler. Old-fashioned trainers would have disapproved. They'd have told Leah to keep Kimi on a loose lead and to treat every error as the opportunity to get in a collar-jerk correction. In watching, they wouldn't really have understood what they were seeing. But an up-to-date trainer? Whether Leah succeeded or failed, any, absolutely any, contemporary trainer should have taken one look and said, "Oh, binding. Bernie Brown."

And a professional dog writer, trainer and handler of numerous consistently high-scoring golden retrievers, columnist for *Dog's Life*, member of the board of the Cambridge Dog Training Club, occasional contributor to *Off-Lead*, and every-word-of-every-issue front-to-finish reader of *Front and Finish?* An individual who continued to harbor the intense, if delusional, hope of putting a C.D.X. on an Alaskan malamute? A person who had spent the previous three weeks enduring her cousin's increasingly irksome proselytizing for the Bernie Brown method? Well, I'd have expected better. I could hardly believe how slow I'd been. I of all people should have spotted it: binding. The no-force method of murder.

29

By the time Steve arrived, I'd fed the dogs, taken a shower, and put on a black L.L. Bean tank-top dress with a wide jersey belt. Black may not seem like a festive choice for the Fourth of July, and it sure shows dog hair, but the weather was hot, the dress was cool, and, to my way of thinking, L.L. Bean's closest approximation to the rich and varied shades of Rowdy's coat was a perfectly patriotic choice. If I'd been Betsy Ross, the American Flag would display a head study of an Alaskan malamute against a field of stars and stripes, and our national colors would be red, white, blue, and dark wolf gray.

Steve turned up in a new white polo shirt and tan pants devoid of any particular canine or nationalist associations. Before he'd even entered the kitchen, Rita came pattering down the back stairs carrying a bottle of wine and wearing a red linen dress and red heels so high that it made my feet hurt just to look at them.

"Tah dah!" she announced. "Am I all right? Have I gone too far?"

"No," I said, "not at all. You look wonderful."

"Fetching," said Steve, D.V.M. and dog trainer, but not usually punster, at least not intentionally.

"*Fetching?*" Rita was delighted. "What higher compliment?"

Steve still didn't get it. While Rita explained, I called out, "Leah! Leah, you're due at the Bensons' at seven-thirty at the latest. Can you hear me?"

She was in the bathroom, but the shower wasn't yet running.

"Yes," she called out.

"Don't spend an hour on your hair, okay? And don't bring Kimi. Do you understand? There'll be food, and she'll steal everything, *and* there's a hearing dog in the house. I do *not* want you showing up with her. Is that clear?"

"Okay!" The shower started.

To console Rowdy and Kimi, who were prancing around depositing dog hair on our clothes and begging to go along, I doled out two Iams biscuits. Then I took two bottles of wine from the refrigerator, handed them to Steve, and picked up the present I'd wrapped for Ruffly, a squeaker-free polyester fleece toy in the form of a person — *great* toy, by the way, but if your dog chews, watch out for the ones with squeakers, and if you don't know why, ask your vet, unless, of course, your vet happens to be out of town enjoying a luxury vacation paid for by all those other dog owners who also didn't know why to watch out for squeaker toys until their dogs ended up in surgery and their vets ended up in Barbados. Got it?

Steve's van was parked in my driveway, and although Highland Street was only a few blocks away, I wanted to take it to Stephanie's. I hate hot weather. But Steve argued that it was a beautiful evening, and Rita agreed with him. Popping firecrackers volleyed like gunshots, and the heat, humidity, and air pollution had turned the evening sky a glowing orange-red that reminded me of an oil refinery fire I'd once witnessed on the outskirts of Philadelphia. Instead of whining about the heat and bragging about my privileged childhood on the cold Atlantic coast, I said that it certainly smelled and sounded like the Fourth of July, and it did, too, but I regretted my words as soon as I'd spoken. Mentioning the charcoal briquettes, lighter fluid, and charred chicken skin was fine, but the rat-a-tat-tat of the cherry bombs must have drilled through Rita's aids and into her ears like a sadistic dentist drilling into the unanesthetized nerve of an abscessed molar.

To avoid embarrassing Rita, I withheld an apology and changed the subject. I'd called Steve earlier to outline the ultrasound explanation of Ruffly's episodes. As we walked down Appleton Street, I began to fill in the details. Rita joined me. My ideas about the no-force method, though, I kept entirely to myself. Why, I'm not sure, except that I'd started to wonder whether I might be suffering from a psychiatric ailment that I'd previously dismissed as one of Rita's therapist jokes: reverse paranoia, the delusion that you're following someone. Sorry, but that's a direct quote.

As we crossed Huron Avenue, Steve said, "But you didn't find the source of the ultrasound."

"I checked outside and around the kitchen," I said, "but I couldn't go poking in Stephanie's closets, and, of course, I didn't know exactly what I was looking for. If it's one of the zappers meant for kennels, it would be a fairly big black box, I think. Or it could be a small one that Morris bought and tucked away somewhere."

Steve and I stride along at about the same big-dog pace. We kept glancing at Rita to make sure that we weren't going too fast for her. When she spoke, she sounded a little out of breath. "Holly, was Morris the kind of person who might have used one of those on his dogs?" She cleared her throat. "As we both have reason to know, and maybe the less said the better, not everyone feels comfortable . . ."

"Doug says no, but I'm not so sure. If the neighbors complained, Morris might have gotten all apologetic and ordered a Yap Zapper or something from one of the catalogs, and then never used it. He probably ordered chew toys and dog beds and stuff anyway, so it's possible that, while he was at it, he ordered some kind of ultrasound gadget, too. But Morris used professional handlers. Groomers. If he'd really decided that the dogs needed training, he'd probably have hired a trainer, although it's also possible that he would've been afraid that a trainer would be too hard on them." I avoided Rita's eyes. "I really don't know." What I knew for sure was that Morris Lamb would never deliberately have poisoned himself. Also, he couldn't have tampered with the valve of the gas grill; he died in early May, long before Stephanie's near accident.

"Could be a neighbor," Steve suggested. "That ad's in the catalogs. 'The ultimate solution to your neighbor's barking dog.' "

"There *is* this woman who lives next door," I said. "Alice Savery."

"Savery's sister," Rita said.

315

"Steve, you and I looked at her house? The really big rundown one next to Stephanie's. But the thing is, Alice Savery's very antidog, so she's not exactly likely to be on R.C. Steele's mailing list. And besides, what really gets to her is dogs in her yard, digging or leaving urine spots on the lawn, that kind of thing. If she uses any kind of dog repellant, it's probably . . . what's it called? That stuff that you sprinkle around."

Steve supplied the brand name: "Get Off My Garden."

"Yes. And *that's* in R.C. Steele, but it's in the gardening catalogs, too, which is probably what Miss Savery gets, and they also carry, oh, netting to keep birds off your fruit trees and maybe electric fences. But wait a minute. There *is* something to get rid of gophers, I think. I saw it in a catalog at my father's." Buck is no gardener. He stays on the mailing lists because every few years, he orders a couple of apple trees to replace the ones killed by deer. "I'm not sure, but I think maybe it uses sound. Would Miss Savery . . . Steve, are there even any gophers *in* Cambridge?"

"Not in my practice."

"Seriously."

"No. The only animal around here that's going to do any real damage to lawns is a skunk. They dig. But that's not what's going

316

on. Those pest repellers run constantly, or they're on a fixed schedule. Ruffly's only reacting every once in a while. Whatever the device is, it's malfunctioning and going off by itself every now and then, or something's triggering it. Barking. Someone pressing a button. Something."

"I didn't think of that." I shook my head. "But speaking of Miss Savery, I have wondered whether she might've noticed something. She must spend half her life outside in the yard, plus she's paranoid about kids touching her precious fence or running through her yard."

"Phobic," Rita said.

"Phobic. So if someone's been sneaking around Stephanie's using a Yap Zapper or something, it's not likely to have escaped Miss Savery."

"Someone like that's going to be the first person to call the cops," Steve said. "She isn't going to keep it to herself."

"Not necessarily," said Rita, trotting along breathlessly.

"Miss Savery calls them all the time," I said as we rounded the corner and started up Highland. "Kevin told me about her. She calls them about everything. So, damn, if she has called about someone hanging around Stephanie's house, they wouldn't've paid any attention, because she's cried wolf a million times. I should've asked Kevin to find out if she'd made any recent calls about anyone lurking around. Those nine-one-one calls *are* recorded. He ought to be able to look it up." As I talked, I found myself scanning the lush green yards. No matter how hard I stared, ultrasound wouldn't become visible, and a neighbor with a powerful, wide-range anti-bark machine wasn't apt to set it on a pedestal like a sundial or a birdbath. I looked, anyway.

"But even if she has called, what's that going to mean?" Rita gripped the bottle of wine. "It's going to mean that she called because she saw, (a) something that was there or (b) something she imagined was there, so —"

"Good point," Steve said.

"Damn!" I said softly.

"What?" Rita asked.

"Damn!"

"I *heard* you, I just —"

I caught Rita's eye, dipped my head, and stared pointedly. *"That,"* I said, "is Alice Savery, the gray-haired woman in the khaki dress, and she's coming straight down her front walk. Damn it, it never occurred to me, but it would be just like Stephanie to feel sorry for her and invite her tonight. She is *the* nastiest woman. If you didn't go to Harvard, she treats you like a dog that just messed on her rug, and she doesn't even like —"

"Class," Rita muttered, "the issue of the decade. She probably has a social mode that she switches into for occasions like this. Little anecdotes about her brother, that kind of thing."

"Right," I said sourly. "She'll keep us in stitches. If we have to spend an entire evening —"

"We don't," Steve said. "She's carrying a trowel and a bucket. She's weeding."

After marching down her front walk and peering up and down Highland Street without giving me even a nod of acknowledgement, Alice Savery headed back into her yard and then fell to her knees before a bed of what I thought were King Arthur delphiniums, the tall purple ones with little bits of white in the middle of the blossoms, white bees. Relieved as I was to be spared Alice Savery's condescension, something in the bend of her wiry spine and the sharp angle of her elbow aroused my sympathy. Cultivating the soil around her delphiniums, Alice Savery couldn't fail to see the arrival of guests next door. Alone with her flowers, she'd hear the greetings and the small talk, and, later, in her gracious, shabby house, the windows open to let in the night air, she'd have to smell the food cooking and listen to the ring of our wine bottles on the rims of glasses, the clatter of plates and silverware, the sounds of the party amplified by her own exclusion.

30

If I'd been allowed to choose my own spot on the deck, I'd have plunked myself down between Steve Delaney and the platter of jumbo shrimp. Stephanie, alas, was the kind of organized hostess who graciously prevents a guest from committing such transgressions as nuzzling up to her lover while stuffing herself with the premium appetizer and thereby weaseling out of the obligation to make polite conversation with people who have nothing to say. As it was, I found myself marooned on the opposite side of the deck from Steve and the shrimp, and right next to Matthew Benson and the equally voluble and charming gas grill. A low table in front of me held a round wooden cheese board with a dozen water biscuits and a fat rectangular chunk of what looked like the same cheddar I use to train the dogs.

Desperate for a topic, I asked Matthew how things were going at the Avon Hill Summer Program.

"Fine," he replied.

I waited for him to expand. He didn't. I reminded myself that he was a perfectly nice boy who probably froze up in the presence of adults. I should sympathize with him. His mother had probably raised him the way she did everything else: politely and efficiently. He'd been accepted at Stanford, his first choice, but Stephanie had insisted that he stay on the east coast. Then, when he'd turned down Stanford for Harvard, Stephanie had promptly accepted the job in Cambridge and ended up with exactly what she wanted: a son at Harvard, a prestigious parish, a house just off Brattle Street. I wondered precisely when she'd been offered the job at St. Margaret's and whether she'd kept her plans to herself until her son committed himself to Harvard. I tried to think out a rough schedule. Morris Lamb died on the night of May 8 or in the early hours of May 9. Stephanie had moved to Cambridge before then; she'd told me about visiting Morris. She'd been the rector of St. Margaret's when Morris died; she'd conducted his funeral service. When did college acceptances go out? The middle of April, I thought. By then, Stephanie must at least have applied to St. Margaret's. She probably knew that the job was hers. When Matthew turned Stanford down, he hadn't known that his mother would be in Cambridge; I was willing to bet that *she* had. The house on Highland, Morris's house? Here she was, her dark hair imperially swept back, the silver-and-turquoise Navajo necklace spread like a breastplate across the bodice of another robelike dress, white linen, spotless. Morris Lamb's death? Assistance dog organizations don't hand over meticulously and expensively educated dogs to untrained applicants. Anyone with a hearing dog has been through an intensive crash course on all aspects of responsible ownership. Stephanie knew not to let her dog eat houseplants, shrubs, or flowers. Any book on basic dog care would have given her a list of common poisonous plants: mountain laurel, azalea, foxglove, dozens of others that Stephanie could have bought at a local nursery. If she'd mixed the leaves of any one of those plants with real *mesclun* greens from our fancy local greengrocer and shown up at Morris's with a surprise gift? Morris would never have mistrusted her. Alternatively, she could have planted something directly in the raised bed. . . .

"Holly, are you with us?" Stephanie was cheerful and censorious.

"Yes! Sorry. The heat gets to me. I was daydreaming."

Doug stood up. "I'm proposing a toast to Stephanie and Ruffly." Doug must have shaved within the last hour; for once, his beard didn't show at all. He wore a blue-and-white pin-striped shirt that flattered his tennis-court tan, and a pair of navy trousers on which I was happy to observe a few white hairs. Bedlingtons don't blow coat, but all breeds shed at least a few hairs, thus loyally endowing their owners with the masonic rings of dog fancy. Doug raised his glass. "To Stephanie and Ruffly! Happy Birthday! Happy Independence Day!"

Ruffly had been reclining at Stephanie's feet, eyes open, ears up. At the sound of his name, or perhaps Stephanie's, he bounced to a sit.

We drank.

Stephanie lifted her glass. "And to Doug . . ." Her voice trailed off.

All of us waited for her to finish. Our wine glasses up, our mouths half open, our expressions increasingly puzzled, we must have looked awkward and silly. I finally spoke: "To Doug!"

What had Stephanie almost added? A tribute to Morris? Something about buying the house? In either case, it was a good thing she'd swallowed her words. Doug looked more relaxed than he had only a few hours earlier, but any mention of Morris would have thrown him into another panic, I thought.

I wished it weren't ill-bred to raise the question of what Stephanie was paying for Morris's house. Better yet, I wished that Doug and Stephanie were vulgar enough to answer it before it was asked. Steve and Rita didn't even know she was buying the house. Matthew, I decided, either knew the purchase price, could find out, or didn't care. I tried to work it out. The small size and passé-modern style of Morris's house made it worth less than the colonials, Victorians, and gigantic twentieth-century hodgepodges that surrounded it. For Off Brattle, the house must have been a bargain. Even so, a vacant lot in that location would have sold for enough to ease Doug's worries about the competition from the mammoth new bookstores. My thoughts wandered. The raised bed had been Doug's gift; Doug had built it. Having inherited Morris's estate, Doug had mourned his partner by immediately redecorating the café, instituting the Sunday teas, and expanding the mail-order business.

Doug's voice broke in. "Stephanie, I positively *forbid* you to lay a finger on that grill! I absolutely insist on charcoal."

Doug had brought a small portable Weber grill with him to supplement a giant Weber from Morris's cellar. He'd also contributed a bag of some kind of special charcoal, and he'd volunteered himself as chef. After delivering the rest of a lengthy scolding, Doug went down the steps to the yard. When Steve and Matthew joined him there, I got up and took Steve's seat next to Rita.

"Where on earth is Leah?" Rita murmured. I aimed my whisper at her ear. "French-braiding her hair. Ironing something black. I'll make some excuse and go in and call her." I turned so that Stephanie could see my face. "Is there something I can help you with?"

Rita seconded the offer, and Stephanie accepted. Before long, she had Rita and Matthew moving the chairs aside to make room for the glass-topped table that occupied a corner of the deck, and I was dispatched to the dining room to pick up a pile of table linen. Returning to the deck, I passed through the kitchen, where Stephanie was transferring romaine from a salad spinner to a big wooden bowl, next to which sat a package of croutons and a bottle of Caesar dressing. If Morris had been preparing a Caesar salad, he'd have tossed those croutons on the deck for the birds and poured the bottled dressing down the sink, and every surface in the kitchen would've ended up thick with the skins of garlic cloves, the crumbs of real French bread, the rinds of squeezed lemons, and the discarded bits of ten or twenty other ingredients that he'd have

326

impulsively decided to add to make the salad his own instead of Caesar's. I reminded myself that no one had any reason to poison all of us. Still, I was glad we weren't having *mesclun*. No one had any reason to blow us up or set the house on fire, either. Just the same, I was grateful to Doug for making sure that we'd barbecue over charcoal and not gas.

That's when my reverse paranoia started to double back on itself. The house had smoke detectors and a hearing dog who would sound an alert the second one of them went off. Any sensible arsonist would start a fire outside, probably by taking advantage of the gas grill on the wooden deck. And Doug Winer, of course, would collect the insurance money.

I'd finished spreading the white tablecloth over the glass table when Leah finally showed up, a half-hour late, with marigold-red curls blossoming from the Obsession-scented crown of her head. She wore a black blouse, a short black pleated skirt, and black stockings and shoes, too. Having ignored my injunction to arrive on time, she'd also disobeyed the spirit of my command to leave Kimi at home. At the end of Leah's leash, his gorgeous white tail flapping over his back as if to flag that perfect topline, his big pink tongue protruding from his showring smile, was, of course, Rowdy. He bore the delighted expression of a dog who knows that someone is getting away with something and suspects that *he* just might be the one. I scowled at Leah and Rowdy, and tried to predict the damage. As a food thief, Rowdy was almost Kimi's equal, but as a pouncer on small dogs, especially male terriers, he had an edge on her. Ruffly, however, would never have made it through the initial screening of hearing-dog candidates if he'd picked fights with other dogs. And Ruffly was neutered, too; Rowdy's sensitive nose wouldn't detect a belligerent hint of testosterone. Even so, I intended to make Leah take him home.

Then Stephanie came striding out of the kitchen. "Leah! And *this* must be the famous Rowdy! Isn't he beautiful! *What* a treat!"

As always, Ruffly was prancing off leash at Stephanie's side. He wagged his tail, folded those ridiculous wings of ears, and made the bold move of looking in Rowdy's direction. Leah, too busy giving Stephanie a warm smile and a charming apology for being late to pay attention to the uninvited guest she'd brought, held Rowdy's leather lead loosely in hand. Before I could grab it, Rowdy took a powerful step toward Ruffly, sniffed briefly, then veered to the side, bounded, tore the lead from Leah, dashed across the deck, and in one swift pass, grabbed the untouched chunk of cheddar and vanished beneath the half-set table.

Stephanie proved herself a real dog person. "He'll choke! Holly, if he tries to swallow all of that — Don't you think you should —"

"He's fine," I assured her. "If Rowdy had been Jonah, the whale would've ended up in *his* stomach, and he wouldn't have brought it up again, either."

No matter what God ordered. Gospel. Seriously. From the First Book of Rowdy, chapter 2, verse 10: *And the Lord spake and spake and spake unto the Alaskan malamute, but, as usual, it didn't listen to a single word She said.*

31

Stephanie would probably have made excuses for the whale, too. "Rowdy knew it was a party, didn't you, big dog? But no one offered *you* anything." The fiend sat in mock submission at my left side, his ears flattened against his head, his dark eyes at work on Stephanie. "So he made himself at home," she continued. "*What* a beautiful dog! Look at that face! You can see how sorry he is."

To understand a breed, understand its origins: *Alaskan* malamute, ultimate master of the *snow* job. Rowdy gently rested his right forepaw in Stephanie's outstretched hand. I couldn't actually see him tense the muscles to create the illusion of a human handshake, but I knew he was doing it.

"Sweetheart!" Stephanie gushed. "I am *so* sorry that we hurt your feelings."

By now, Leah had transformed the stiff gathering into a party. On the lawn just below the deck, where Doug had started the charcoal, Leah muttered something to the men, and Doug and Matthew's laughter and Steve's rumbling chuckle emerged from one of those gray clouds of barbecue smoke that reek of male bonding. Delegated to ferry food from kitchen to grill, Leah dashed up the stairs and across the deck. Rita, who'd been clearing away wine glasses, reappeared, followed by Leah, who carried a platter of raw steak.

"The rice must be almost done," Stephanie said. "Rita, Leah has forgotten the salmon. It's in a bowl in the refrigerator. Could you take it out? And Holly, maybe you could toss the salad."

While I was adding croutons and Stephanie was draining the rice, the phone rang. Rowdy, on a down-stay at my feet, ignored the soft burr, but Ruffly tore to the telephone, then dashed to Stephanie, who deposited the colander in the sink and made for the phone, clapping her hands. "Good boy, Ruffly! What a good dog!" Rita always removed the aid from her left ear before she used the phone, but Stephanie just answered. As she did, she reached into the jar on the counter, extracted a tiny dog biscuit, and tossed it to Ruffly, who sat expectantly on his haunches. He caught it neatly. Catching sight of Rowdy, whose drool was forming a slimy pool at my feet, Stephanie tucked the phone under her chin, reached back into the jar, sent a treat whizzing directly into Rowdy's mouth, and gave Ruffly unearned seconds. "My carpets do not need cleaning, and this *is* the Fourth of July," she told the caller, "but thank you." She hung up. "The phone is not Ruffly's favorite sound. After he does his work, all that happens is that he loses my attention, so we have to make sure there's a little something extra in it for him. Otherwise, he gets lazy."

Too moral to train with food? Consider that when a dog's performance really counts — hearing for someone, pulling a wheelchair, detecting arson by sniffing out hydrocarbons — the basis of training is virtually always food lures and food rewards. No food allowed in the obedience ring? In Open and Utility, no leash, either. Does that mean you shouldn't train with one? Of course not. So love your dog and get results. Train with food. Dog isn't interested? Nonsense. Any healthy, happy, hungry dog will work for food. Yours won't? Bake a slice of liver in sherry and garlic powder, cut it into little bits, and shazam! Billy Batson turns into Captain Marvel.

With Rowdy and Kimi, I don't have to fuss. I swear that either one would actually work for garbage. For steak, salmon, rice, peas, French bread, and salad — even with packaged croutons and bottled dressing — Rowdy would have instantly mastered the trick of flying through the air and landing smack in the middle of a glass-topped dinner table. Consequently, before I took my place, I hitched him to a deck post that was a little closer to the gas grill than I liked, but near my seat, where I could keep an eye on him. At the table, I again found myself stuck next to Matthew, who was on my left, but to his left was Leah, who'd talk so much that his silence wouldn't matter; and on my right were Doug and then Rita, so I didn't mind.

As I was spreading my napkin on my lap, I must have thrown a worried glance toward Rowdy and the grill. Doug leaned toward me. "There's *nothing* wrong with the valve. The entire grill is perfectly safe. I've half started to wonder if Stephanie didn't imagine the whole thing to begin with."

Like everyone else, I'd taken Stephanie's word that she'd found the valve open. Nothing else suggested that the gas had ever been left on.

"But then," I asked, "why not use the grill today?"

Doug's expression was wonderfully disgusted. "Phew! *Gas!* Sickening associations. Morris and I had terrible arguments about it." Doug politely turned his attention to Rita. "What lovely things Stephanie has!" He ran an appraising eye over the table. His voice dropped. "This is *Spode.*" The tone was reverent. "*Not* my favorite pattern," he murmured. "But Spode nonetheless."

Rita gave him a wry smile. "Indeed," she replied, "Spode nonetheless."

When their quiet laughter ended, Doug gallantly offered another toast to Stephanie. Serving dishes circulated. The talk became general. Stephanie asked Matthew and Leah how the Avon Hill play was progressing. Matthew complained that Ivan was messing it up by trying to add a new scene.

"But isn't that the idea?" Stephanie demanded. "Creative student participation and that sort of thing?"

"Yes," Leah answered, "except that it's so gory. It's all about hand washing and daggers."

Matthew explained the obvious: "*Macbeth.*"

"Ivan absorbs everything," Leah commented proudly.

"Defending him again," Matthew said. "He bought you off."

"With what?" I asked. I was serious.

Leah avoided my eye. Matthew answered. "Flowers."

"Ivan gave you flowers?" Stephanie beamed at Leah and then gave Matthew a knowing smile that he must have hated. "Leah, Ivan must have a mad crush on you. And how enterprising of him! To go out and buy flowers."

Matthew and Leah exchanged looks. Before Leah could stop him, Matthew said, "Yes, except that —"

Leah cut in. "Matthew!"

I couldn't stop myself. "Leah, let Matthew finish. Except what, Matthew?"

"Except that Ivan didn't, uh, buy them."

Doug spoke with deliberate drama: "Ah! The case of the purloined roses."

"Delphiniums," Matthew said.

"Ivan stole Miss Savery's flowers?" I said. "He raided her garden? He *didn't*."

"He did," Matthew said.

For the next few minutes, everyone caught everyone else up on Ivan, Ivan's pranks, Alice Savery, and Alice Savery's delphiniums.

"The classic dilemma of highly gifted children," Rita commented. "Peer relations. This, uh, shall we say mildly antisocial behavior, from an adult viewpoint, is probably an adaptive effort in the direction of normalizing himself in the eyes of his peers."

While Stephanie was adding something, I leaned in back of Matthew, tapped Leah's shoulder, and whispered, "Why didn't you tell me?"

Leah shrugged. "It was no big thing." She turned her attention to Rita and Stephanie. "It's true. Getting in trouble is probably the most normal thing Ivan can think of to do,

335

which is one of the reasons —"

Matthew groaned and finished her sentence: "— that Ivan needs a big dog. Leah —"

"Well, he does!" Leah's face flushed. "Ivan's problem is that he wants to be just like everyone else, just another normal, ordinary kid. A boy and his dog? What could possibly be more normal?"

I almost heard the answer: a girl and hers. In the all-seeing eyes of the American Kennel Club, Alaskan malamute Sno-Kist Qimissung, C.D., had one owner, Holly Winter, and Leah knew my opinion of co-ownership too well to ask directly to have her name added. In pleading for Ivan, Leah was also speaking for herself. I began to wonder how powerfully Leah's indirect pitch had shaped the picture she'd given me of Ivan. She knew how fussy I was in screening adopters of rescued malamutes. In Leah's accounts, Ivan's pranks were tricks without victims. I'd observed the salt-on-the-grass episode myself, and Leah hadn't intended to tell me about the stolen flowers. I remembered Ivan's easy mastery of the gas stove that had resisted Bernadette's efforts. Now I glanced first at the grill, then at Leah. "What else don't I know about Ivan?"

Leah was defiant. "So Ivan picked some flowers! In case you don't know, I like flowers. It was very nice of him. Besides, the blossoms were starting to fall off, anyway."

One of the summer gardening tasks Marissa used to assign me was cutting off delphinium stalks to encourage the plants to bloom again in the fall, but I didn't say so. Leah's infuriating habit of always being right needed no encouragement; it would produce a second bloom all on its own.

"I think it was lovely of Ivan," Stephanie pronounced genially. "Matthew, would you pass the rice to Holly, please? It seems to have bypassed her."

Like an overtrained dog — all obedience, no enthusiasm — Matthew immediately handed me the serving dish, and, ignoring Rita and Steve's tactless smirks, I made a show of helping myself to the rice, a food I hate. While I washed it down with swigs of Chardonnay, conversation among Stephanie's other guests grew animated. Matthew offered Leah a choice of the videos he'd rented for them to watch after dinner. Symbolically enough, it seemed to me, the one he plumped for was *Close Encounters*. I had a sudden flash to one of my dog-training friends who always comes to class with a hand towel looped through the belt of her jeans so she can keep mopping up the gallons of saliva that would otherwise mar the appearance of her beautiful Newfoundland, Thor. The image didn't quite fit.

For one thing, I liked Thor. For another, Thor was neutered.

In happy coincidence with my reflections on her son, Stephanie was telling Steve what a shame it was that Ruffly couldn't father any puppies. Ruffly, she proclaimed, was the ideal hearing dog; it was too bad there'd never be more just like him. I wanted to speak up and explain that if Ruffly were intact, his hormonal reek would provoke other males to pick fights with him, and instead of working his sounds, he'd work the perfumes of bitches in season, but I trusted Steve to make the same points — preferably not in those exact words.

In violation of my mother's dictates, I mashed a few flakes of salmon into the rice I hadn't yet choked down, forked a bit onto my tongue, and swallowed, but when I reached for more wine, my glass was empty. The closer of the two bottles on the table stood between Doug and Rita. I tuned into their conversation and decided to settle for water. Doug had discovered that Rita was a therapist. When people find out what I do, they're apt to ask for professional opinions, and I'm happy to advise either that Rover should be taught what he is supposed to do *(How do I get him to quit jumping, barking, leash-lunging . . . ?)* or that Rover should not be allowed to run loose in the first place *(How do I get him to quit chasing cars, running away . . . ?).*

Although the same two answers cover almost all dog-behavior questions, neither seemed even remotely relevant to the problem Doug was currently presenting to Rita. "Morris kept insisting, 'Oh, just *do* it! *Do* it, and you will feel so much better!' And his own parents were deceased, so it was easy for him, but, even so, I knew he was right, but then . . . I remember the moment so clearly, when this realization came tumbling down on me that it was absolutely impossible. It was Mother's birthday, and my father and I went to the florist, and we'd selected the most gorgeous arrangement for her, from both of us, and there was a little card to go with it." Doug paused. Rita waited. He sighed. "Instead of signing it first, for some reason, I handed it to him, and I gave him a pen."

"And?"

"And I'll never forget it. He wrote 'Albert J. Winer, C.P.A.' "

"Oh, God," Rita said.

"After that, what could I do? And Morris would not take it seriously. He kept making up letters for me to write. 'Dear Mr. Winer, Your son is gay. Love, Douglas S. Winer, A.B.' I was always half terrified that Morris would get carried away and let something slip when they were around."

"And now?" Rita asked gently.

"And now," Doug told her, "I'm half-terrified that *I* will. It would almost be better if Morris had gone ahead and done it for me." His voice had dropped to a whisper that would never have reached Rita's unaided ears.

"Seconds, anyone?" Stephanie asked briskly. "Thirds?"

Her human guests made noises about not having room for another thing, but as soon as we began to clear the table, Rowdy leaped to his big white paws and started to whine and *ah-roo*. Stephanie was all sympathy. Stephanie did not own a malamute. Give Rowdy an inch, and he'll take 196,950,000 square miles, which I should explain, in case you don't happen to live with a malamute and thus haven't been driven to find out exactly how far your dog will push you, is the surface area of the planet Earth.

"After Rowdy has settled down and behaved himself," I told Stephanie, "then he can have a treat, but not now."

"Well, then, Ruffly can wait, too," she said. "After we have his cake, the dogs can share the leftovers."

Rowdy was as likely to *share* food as he was to burst forth in fluent Mandarin. The doling out of treats, I decided, would be one situation that Stephanie would not control. With one of those aren't-you-a-stingy-mean-owner, poor-darling-sweet-big-doggie looks, Stephanie settled for depositing bits of steak and bone-free salmon in a little dish that she put in the refrigerator. Ruffly eyed her and danced expectantly around, but to my surprise she held firm. "Later! I promise. Later."

When the table had been cleared and reset for dessert, we resumed our places, but instead of resting quietly at Stephanie's feet, Ruffly now perched on her lap, his head winningly cocked to one side, ears akimbo. The sky had darkened to the color of pale smoke, and someone had turned on the outside lights to make the deck a bright stage. The indistinguishable mounds and lumps of the backyard shrubs became our invisible audience. One of the third-floor windows of Alice Savery's house glowed. I wondered whether she'd taken a loge seat. Stolid and expressionless, Matthew emerged from the kitchen, followed by Leah, who carried the cake, a white-iced rectangle heavily decorated with tiny American flags. The candle flames made hollows of Leah's bright eyes. Doug led the singing. His strong, true baritone miraculously kept everyone, even me, more or less on key.

By the time we were eating our cake, the floodlights had attracted a mass of hideous brown moths that kept hurtling themselves against the hot bulbs, and I was concentrating on not scratching the mosquito bites on my ankles. Although my rural childhood should have inured me to bugs, I still hate blackflies, but urban insects don't really bother me, and the temperature had finally dropped low enough to let me feel human again. From the way Stephanie and Rita acted, however, I concluded that Manhattan did not experience a black fly season. With Leah serving as his cheerful research assistant, Matthew took advantage of the opportunity to collect specimens for his flora and fauna unit, but the rest of us moved inside.

Stephanie had ended up with the kitchen in food-free order, so after carefully reassessing Rowdy's on-leash response to Ruffly, I gave in and let the big boy loose. As if to confirm Stephanie's obvious conviction that I was ridiculously mistrustful of my giant pussycat of a dog, Rowdy gave Ruffly a perfunctory sniff, ambled around, and then dashed to the living room, where people were gathering around the coffee table. Rowdy shook himself all over, fell to the floor at Stephanie's feet, and trained one almond-shaped eye on her and the other on the table, which held a sugar bowl, a pitcher of cream, and a plate of cookies, as well as a coffeepot and our cups. Rowdy prefers his with cream and sugar, but he'd happily have lapped up the cream, and he was a master sugar-bowl thief, too. Stephanie reached down to stroke him. "What a good boy Rowdy is. Why does she say such terrible things about you?" Without even a glance in my direction, Stephanie suddenly took a cookie from the plate, fed it to Rowdy, and nearly lost her fingers. My eyes darted to Ruffly. He was lying on the floor a yard or so away from Stephanie, his head resting rather forlornly on his forepaws, his immense ears as close to drooping as I'd ever seen them. I wondered whether he remembered the promised leftovers he hadn't received.

While Stephanie was still shaking the fingers of her hand and exclaiming happily, Ruffly abruptly jumped to his feet, barked, ran to Stephanie, pawed at her, fled through the dining room, and raced back, the perfect picture of the hearing dog at work.

"The phone," Stephanie explained. "Excuse me." Rising, she headed for the kitchen. Rita reached up to adjust the volume of her aids. Doug, Steve, Rita, and I looked at one another. Doug asked whether the phone had rung.

"It's very soft," I explained. "Before Stephanie got Ruffly, Matthew had had about all he could take of really loud phones, so now

they keep it just loud enough for Ruffly to
. . . Steve, where are you — ?"

He was taking big strides toward the
kitchen. "I'm going to see for myself." I didn't
understand his smile. Curiosity sent Rita,
Doug, and me after him.

Stephanie stood by the counter. Her left
hand clamped the receiver of the big white
phone to her ear, but she spoke to us. Her
voice was angry and frightened. "As usual.
Nothing but a dial tone." As she hung up,
she automatically reached into the jar of treats.
Steve moved in fast. He took the jar, put it
on the counter, knelt down, and gently
wrapped his big hands around Ruffly's little
head. Two pairs of intelligent eyes stared at
one another. "Gotcha," Steve told Ruffly.
"But no hard feelings. While it lasted, buddy,
it was a real good game."

And then Steve spelled it out: Consistently
rewarded with treats for working the sound
of a ringing phone, Ruffly had cleverly discovered that his performance yielded the same
happy result when the phone *didn't* ring.
Stephanie's perfect hearing dog had mastered
the trick of working a nonexistent sound.

32

In the next ten minutes, I decided that the Being who'd applied the no-force method to Morris and Stephanie was the Supreme Trainer who binds us all in perfect heel position. Morris Lamb had died because he'd been foolish. If Morris had had a heart attack or if he'd perished in a plane crash, Doug would still have inherited Morris's estate, and Morris's obviously natural or accidental death would still have banished Doug's worry that Morris would slip up and inform the elderly Winers that their son was gay. Stephanie would still have everything she wanted. She had received no crank phone calls. The ultrasound device, if it existed at all, was a malfunctioning Yap Zapper that Morris had tucked away somewhere, or a neighbor's long-range kennel silencer never aimed deliberately at Ruffly's sensitive ears. Alice Savery was not trying to rid Highland Street of dogs; Ivan was not playing Robin Badfellow outside Stephanie's windows; and Matthew was not trying to drive away the mother who had left his father to follow him to college. Standing outside the ring, I had discerned an elaborate heeling pattern where none existed. What I'd been observing were not, after all, the exercises of my own sport, but random drawings in a lottery that Morris Lamb lost.

"Matthew is probably murdering those helpless moths," Stephanie was saying. "I hope he isn't asking Leah to watch."

My mouth tasted like bitter coffee. With his uncanny ability to read my intentions, Rowdy stood up and made a brief request that consisted mainly of *rrr* and *www*. Ruffly's head turned. His eyes brightened. He bounced from his perch on Stephanie's lap, and his wiry black-and-tan body shot across the room and vanished. Rowdy's bulk followed.

"Not again!" Stephanie laughed. "The phone isn't . . . ?"

"No," Doug assured her.

I looked at Steve. He shook his head. "Not a sound."

"I'd better find out what he wants." Stephanie rose.

"Shouldn't Ruffly be barking?" Rita asked. "He isn't, is he?"

"No," I said, "he isn't. He does his whole routine if it's one of *his* sounds. Otherwise, he might just show some kind of interest. That's why Stephanie's supposed to watch him."

"Probably the fireworks," Steve said. "From the Esplanade."

Stephanie's voice reached us from the kitchen. She was conversing with a partner different from herself but highly intelligent, a gifted child, perhaps, or a wise and kindly extraterrestrial. "What is it? Tell me what it is," we heard her say.

"We'd better let her know about the fireworks," Rita said. "Steve's probably right, and she can't hear them."

As Rita stood up, Doug's face took on a look of boyish mischief. He boomed like the cannons that get shot at the conclusion of *The 1812 Overture* and, when Rita gave a startled glance over her shoulder, switched to the "Marseillaise." With an upswing of his arms, he led all of us in a march toward Ruffly. Doug's rich, trained voice was infinitely better than Morris's enthusiastic bellowing, and Doug lacked Morris's expansiveness. Even so, the performance was unmistakably Morris's.

Once we were assembled in the kitchen, Doug became himself again. "Stephanie, I am *so* sorry. I never thought. This is unforgivable. Ruffly is *working,* and we've gone and interrupted him."

But we hadn't. Ruffly's concentration was so intense that if the Boston Pops had deserted the Esplanade for Highland Street, the dog would probably have kept to his task, which consisted of posing stiff-legged before one of the glass doors to the deck while becoming all ears. The dog's little body was so rigid that the air around him seemed to vibrate. No one spoke. To prevent Rowdy from breaking the respectful silence, I caught his eye, raised a finger to my lips, and rested a hand on his head. Ruffly suddenly quivered all over, veered around, pawed at Stephanie's dress, gave one sharp bark, and again pointed his nose at the glass door.

"Ruffly, what *is* it?" Stephanie spoke exactly as if she expected a verbal reply.

Like an adept translator, Rowdy whined a question.

"Shh!" I told him.

Ruffly's answer came suddenly and almost violently. He barked so loudly that Rita and Stephanie's hands shot to their aids. His black-and-tan head twisted around toward Stephanie; his paws frantically scraped the door panels.

"Desperate to do his doo-doo?" Doug asked frivolously.

Stephanie's perfunctory smile was half-frown. Her hand fingered the squash blossom necklace as if she were counting rosary beads. "This isn't how he asks. Whatever it is, he thinks it's important. I'd better check it out. Ruffly, I'll find out. I understand. We'll go see what it is. My turn now. Good boy."

She reached for the door. I grabbed Rowdy's collar and tried to remember where I'd left his leash. Reading my mind, Steve spotted the leash on the counter, fastened it to Rowdy's buckle collar, and handed it to me.

"Training collar?" I asked. I usually remove the slip collar and leash together. Then I remembered that to prevent Rowdy from choking himself, I'd taken off the chain when I'd tethered him to the deck post earlier in the evening. I'd probably left it outside.

Doug, Rita, and Steve had followed Stephanie and Ruffly to the deck, where Doug was bending over the gas grill.

"Doug, that's not what Ruffly means." Stephanie followed the determined little dog down the steps to the yard.

Rita was fiddling with the controls on her aids. "Holly, do you hear anything?"

I listened. "No. Not really. Steve, can you hear the fireworks?"

"No. Rita? Turn the volume way up on those things."

Rita had once explained to me that the pioneers of psychology studied mental processes by examining their own inner lives. It seemed to me that if the introspective method ever came back in vogue, I could switch careers and dredge a book out of the depths of my own stupidity. Never before had it crossed my mind that Rita might hear better with her aids than I did with my so-called normal ears.

Doug straightened up. "Does anyone smell smoke?"

I sniffed. "It's the charcoal. Could that be what Ruffly is — ?"

"Probably not, unless it's generating sound," Steve said. "Rita, are you picking up anything?"

"Static. Loud background noise. Cars. Rowdy's tags." She paused. "Where's Ruffly?"

"Down here somewhere," Doug called from the yard.

I abandoned my search for the training collar, and Rowdy and I descended the stairs. As we did, I could smell the glowing charcoal and a lingering hint of steak and salmon. So could Rowdy, who lunged toward the Weber grills. "*This* way," I told him. "And there's nothing there. All you'll do is burn yourself."

The immediate vicinity of the house was bright with floodlights, but Stephanie's voice came from the darkness. "Damn! Where is he? Ruffly? Ruffly, I know you mean it, and I'm trying. Where *are* you?"

Ruffly's answering bark carried a note of exasperation. As I headed toward the back of the lot, the white of Stephanie's dress appeared ahead of me, and as my eyes adapted to the dark, I saw that she was next to the shrub border that separated Morris's yard from Alice Savery's. Leaves rustled.

"Maybe he's after an animal," I said to Steve. "There's an old carriage house back there, and there are supposed to be raccoons living in it."

"There *are,*" Doug said. "Morris used to insist on feeding them."

"Christ," Steve muttered.

"That's what I told him," Doug said. "After all, they are wild animals."

"Oh, God, it's not a skunk, is it?" Rita cannot be talked out of the belief that skunks not only can direct their spray, but will aim it straight at her.

"Oh, all right, Ruffly. If we really have to. But wait for me." Stephanie pushed her way through the shrubbery.

Doug followed her. "If *someone* finds us in her yard, we're going to get a good scolding, and if someone sees a dog violating the leash law, God forbid, are we ever going to catch it. Do you know that you-know-who once tried to file an official complaint against Nelson and Jennie for playing in their own yard? Can you believe it? That woman has rabies on the brain. Her carriage house is positively crawling with raccoons, and she's utterly phobic about fully-immunized dogs being off leash."

Rowdy and I had cleared the shrubs. I held a branch for Steve, who was in back of Rowdy and me, and we waited for Rita, whose high heels were slowing her down. "What is this stuff?" she complained.

"Laurel, I think, or maybe azaleas," I said. "Whatever it is, it doesn't have thorns. Rita, why don't you take off your shoes?"

She crashed out of the bushes. "This is horrible! If God had intended plants to grow wild, He'd never have invented pots." She sniffed. "I smell smoke."

"Rita, calm down," I told her. "It's probably just someone else's charcoal. I mean, it is the Fourth —" But it didn't smell like briquettes. I wished that Alice Savery's house had motion-sensitive lights like the ones on the path beside Morris's. I could see Rita, who was right next to me, but the others were ahead of us somewhere in the shadows. The white of Rowdy's face stood out, and the white of his tail was waving over his back. Ahead of us, Ruffly was hard at work. His barks were increasingly urgent. I felt a surge of irrational dissatisfaction with Rowdy. His hearing probably wasn't quite as sharp as Ruffly's, and he lacked Ruffly's passionate attention to sound, but he could at least make some effort to help.

Rita was sputtering. "These things are set wrong! Everything is so damn loud that I can't hear anything. Holly —"

Doug collided with me. "It's the carriage house," he exclaimed. He dashed off.

"He must be going to call —" Rita began.

"Of course he is. Rita —" I was going to tell her to hurry up, but at that moment Rowdy ran out of patience. I found myself hauled like a racing sled toward the carriage house at the rear of Alice Savery's property. There were no lights on in the building itself, but spots mounted high in the trees of an adjoining yard revealed a distraught Stephanie. She paced in front of the tall doors of what looked like a small barn. "Ruffly, your work is all done. I'll take over. My turn now," she was saying. "Good boy. Thank you. It's okay now. I'll take over." Ruffly, however, kept frantically barking, jumping in the air, and racing back and forth between Stephanie and the building. Catching sight of me, Stephanie asked anxiously, "Can you *hear* anything? He will not calm down. Is there a smoke alarm going off in there?"

If there'd been an alarm in the building, it would certainly have been sounding. No flames were visible, but the air stank of smoke. I tried to get my face in the light so that Stephanie could see my lips, and I spoke as clearly as I could, but my Caruso reincarnate had added his arctic canine voice to Ruffly's, and he almost certainly drowned me out. "No, not that I can hear, but the dogs are making so much noise!" I shook my head, pointed at the dogs, told Rowdy to hush, and finally clamped my hands around his muzzle.

Stephanie returned her attention to her dog. "Ruffly, I'll take it from here! What on earth is wrong with him! He's supposed to let me . . ." Her voice broke.

"Move back! Stephanie, move back!" Against the smoggy city sky, the slate roof of the carriage house showed only its usual sag; no sparks, no visible signs of a blaze, not yet. A few yards ahead of us, the espaliered tree I'd noticed from the street still shinnied its way benignly upward, its leaves blurred and blackened only by nightfall. Nothing but the burning chemical stench betrayed the shabby building's transformation to a gigantic smudge pot set to metamorphose to a blast furnace when the vapors trapped within found air and flame, and the fire reached its flashpoint.

"Stephanie, we're too close. Move back!" I touched her arm. She flinched as if my hand had seared her flesh. I waved toward Alice Savery's house and Highland Street. As I did, Steve came sprinting down the drive, and Rita finally showed up. Matthew and Leah were at her heels.

"I can't rouse anyone there." Steve jabbed a thumb toward the big house. Catching sight of Stephanie, he yelled at her as uselessly as I'd done, "Get back! Hey, get away from there!" Veterinarians are trained to act in emergencies, and they're used to shoving around large creatures. Steve gripped Stephanie's forearms and began dragging her away from the danger zone around the carriage house. The fumes became nauseating, medical, and weirdly sick now, as if within the old wood and under the slate, an evil surgeon were merrily cauterizing the raw stump of a leg he'd just had fun amputating. The stench had a pesticide taint: I imagined the sadist medico basting the severed limb in bug killer and roasting it for his own consumption.

Matthew and Leah arrived bearing flashlights. The beam of Matthew's brought me the welcome light of reality. When he ran it over the carriage house, I saw through the grimy haze a pair of wide double doors that looked as if they'd open outward. I stared at them. Smoke oozed through, I thought, but the doors remained closed. No one opened them to hurl out charred remains. No half-dead, legless creature shrieked from within.

Ruffly's leaps became ferocious, his barks menacing. Stephanie battled to shake Steve's grip. "It's a sound!" she insisted. "He hears something. It's not like the phone. He's not playing." Unable to hear her own desperate voice, she clamored wildly.

"Steve, it couldn't —" I began. A hideous phrase ran through my head, a fear-twisted snatch from a song, "the crown of creation," but grossly distorted, like words of melted wax: *the crown of cremation.* "Where is Miss Savery?" I demanded. "Matthew, Leah, *run* and see if you can find her. Bang on her doors. Yell. Do anything!"

As they took off, Doug appeared. "Morris's raccoons! This is awful! They're in there, and —"

The stench? Chemicals. Petroleum. Kerosene. Gas. And fat, maybe? Melting fat, the rendering of fat-streaked flesh. The nausea started in my throat and spread down until my stomach gagged.

Steve was calm. "At this time of night, raccoons are checking out garbage cans."

356

"Doug," I shouted over Ruffly's unremitting noise, "what if Miss Savery's in there! Where the hell are the fire trucks? Doug, would she be in there? Does she keep anything — ?"

Doug answered. "Hideous junk and the world's oldest Volvo station wagon. You must've seen her in it, sitting bolt upright going directly against the traffic the wrong way up —"

Rejoining us, Leah interrupted him. "Matthew's looking for a hose. Why isn't anyone else *doing* anything?" Leah had found a garden fork. She plunged it into the grass.

"Leah," I told her, "you were supposed to be looking for Miss Savery and not —" Leah extracted the garden fork from the ground. "Put that thing down!" I ordered her. "If you want to do something useful —"

Ruffly was still dashing to Stephanie, wheeling around, almost flinging himself against the harmless-looking doors of what now felt and stank like a giant crematorium about to blow open and shoot out half-incinerated remains, the singed bodies of small, furry animals, monstrous human limbs with flame-eaten flesh. Stephanie kept trying to assure Ruffly that his work was done. "He can't be made to feel that his efforts are ignored," she told Steve, "but when I tell him I'll take over, he's supposed to . . . Why is he *doing* this?"

She may have missed Steve's reply: "I haven't got a clue."

Yes, a single incident, one crash of a high jump, can ruin a high-strung obedience dog by making him refuse all jumps ever after. Hauled away from what he considered a vital task, Ruffly might learn a permanent lesson and never work again. *So what!* This was, for once, no time to discuss dog training. Ruffly's life was more important than Stephanie's need for his help. The fire patiently smoldered. It wouldn't wait forever. Ruffly's mad forays to the carriage house doors could place him inches from the building when the fire grew tired of this grimy, smoky waiting, gulped for air, found a spark, and exploded in glorious, greedy flames.

Angrily brandishing the garden fork in the smudgy darkness, her flaming red-gold curls standing out around her head, Leah looked like a particularly beautiful devil venting its fury on the cinders of home. She stomped into the reeking smoke around the burning carriage house and, I assumed, toward Ruffly, who had quit flying around to station himself rigidly in front of the closed doors, where he'd be instantly incinerated when flames shot out or, if the building collapsed, excruciatingly crushed to death by falling timbers and slabs of slate. I remembered how decisively Leah had dealt with Willie and how effectively she'd cut off his yapping and nipping. She, at least, could act. Over her shoulder, she chastised us: "Don't you people know the first thing about hearing dogs?"

As I tried to think what the first thing was, Leah approached Ruffly. When she reached him, the smudge around us thickened. "Hurry up!" I shouted to her. "Grab him and run!" Leah bent down. Enraged, I realized that she was murmuring to Ruffly. Starting toward her, I shouted again, "Leah, grab him! *Grab* him and *run!*" But instead of scooping up the little dog, Leah raised the garden fork waist high and began to poke at the big iron latch on the carriage house doors.

"NO!" I screamed.

Steve's voice joined mine. "Jesus Christ, Leah, oxygen is —"

Rowdy had caught the contagious excitement. My efforts to control his joyful bounding slowed me down. Before I reached Leah, she succeeded in lifting the latch. As the door swung open, Ruffly shot through and disappeared into a dense billow of smoke, visible even in the darkness of night, fetid, thick, and hungry for air.

Doug took over the task of restraining Stephanie, who'd begun to scream; Steve appeared at Leah's side and started dragging her away; and in one smooth, heart-stopping motion, Rowdy backstepped, twisted his head, and slipped his collar. I dashed after Rowdy and nearly caught him. Only a few yards from the gaping door to that smoldering furnace, I lunged for his tail, even felt its coarse guard hairs brush my fingertips, but there was no stopping him. Before I caught my breath in the smutty air, a streak of white trim and dark wolf gray zoomed after Ruffly, straight into the black smoke, straight into the furnace, straight toward fiery death.

Burned alive. Rowdy. The crown of creation. The crown of . . .

For a second, I froze. Crazed with fear, I groped desperately for smothered memories of fire-safety films and dormitory drill procedures. A lungful of smoke brought me a terrible vision of Rowdy's thick, beautiful stand-off coat ablaze in an aura of crimson flames. The memories kindled and caught. *Stay low. Avoid the real hazard: smoke.* At the open door of the still-smoldering building, I dropped to my knees and crawled. *Find something to breathe through.* My black dress. I tugged the skirt up over my mouth and nose. "Rowdy! Rowdy, come! I love you!" The smoke ate at my eyes like drops of burning acid. "Rowdy, don't do this to me, you son

360

of a bitch! Rowdy, *come!*" Blinded by smoke and darkness, I edged forward. My knee whacked a hard ridge in the floor. A sharp object that felt like iron sliced into my right shoulder. Then something hit me in the face and bounced off. Little dog claws cut through the jersey. A small dog, low to the ground. Ruffly! In seconds, he was gone.

My chest ached, but the choking and coughing seemed to come from far outside my body. My left hand, searching, palm down, found cracks and grit. With no warning, huge, sharp spikes hammered so fiercely through flesh and tendons that I could have sworn my hand was being nailed to the concrete floor. When a bone-hard mass grazed my cheekbone, pain radiated to my ear and across my scalp and down my neck. Human fingers wrapped themselves around my ankles. I saw nothing and heard nothing, but I know Steve's touch. I knew his hands as surely as I knew Rowdy's big-dog nails and that massive, malamute-perfect heavy-boned chest.

"Move, for Christ's sake! Holly, *move!* Open your damn eyes!"

And then, miraculously, I was on the grass. Thick smoke swirled around me. "Rowdy! Steve . . . Oh my God, where is he?"

A flashlight played on the open door to a hell now backlit by luminous flames. From

361

its mouth emerged the cutout silhouette of an Alaskan malamute, a huge black dog, black face, black paws, black tail, pulling and struggling, head down and awkwardly twisted, taking impossibly slow, labored steps, jaws locked on the burden it dragged, the body of a boy too small for his nine years, light in life, heavy now.

Dead weight. Ivan.

33

In the year of our Lord 1636, two events notable in the history of Cambridge occurred almost simultaneously. The first has never recurred. Once founded, Harvard College was what it was and has stayed that way ever since. The second event took place immediately after the first. As you'll remember, God let a whole week slip by between *Fiat lux* and a well-earned rest, but the word *Veritas* had no sooner passed the lips of the founders of Harvard than they began to congratulate themselves. *(Had to be done! Knew it all along! I told you so, didn't I? Didn't I?)*, and before long, when they'd reached a jolly state of puritanical merriment in which no one would listen to a single word that anyone else had to say, an unusually modest and witty founder became responsible for the second notable event, the one that's been endlessly repeated ever after, the cracking of the old Cambridge joke (A.D. 1636), "You can always tell a Harvard man, but you can't tell him much."

When I listen to Leah, I sometimes reflect

that, in this regard, Harvard women have finally achieved a status equal to that of Harvard men. "*I'm* supposed to be the novice," Leah announced, "and *you* people are supposed to be the experts. So how come not one of you remembered the first thing, the *first* thing, about hearing dogs? Watch your dog! Trust your dog!" She caught her breath. "Remember? *Trust* your dog."

We were sitting outside Morris's house. Matthew had located a couple of garden hoses and two faucets on the foundation of Alice Savery's house, and he and Doug were making what I suspected were futile efforts to contain the carriage house blaze. Stephanie and Steve had taken Ruffly indoors; Steve needed the bright kitchen light to examine and treat the burns on the dog's feet. Rita was using Stephanie's phone to place another 911 call and to call Ivan's mother, Bernadette. It had been minutes, not the hours it seemed, since Doug had originally called, but as it turned out, he'd innocently given Alice Savery's name and address. Thus he might as well have told 911 that he wanted to report a false alarm. I'd left Rita with the receiver of the big white phone clamped to her left ear. The hearing aid she'd removed before making the calls was resting on the counter. Or that's where it was until I palmed it.

"Trust your dog!" Leah repeated.

"Leah, that will do," I said. "You are being —"

"Leah?" a small voice echoed.

"Ivan, the fire trucks are coming," she told him. Ivan was determined not to miss their arrival. That's what we were doing outside. "They'll be here any minute."

"Leah, God is everywhere, right?"

"Ivan!"

"This is important, Leah." Scraped and black-smudged, Ivan's face had lost none of its intense curiosity. Those round violet eyes commanded attention. "Leah, I was thinking: God is everywhere, is everywhere to *start* with. But if I go into a room, and the windows are closed, and the doors are all locked, and it's a, uh, confined space . . . Does that mean that now there's less of Him? Or does He just get squished up?"

"Ivan," Leah said gently, "you don't need to worry about locked doors any more. Just, from now on, stay out of people's yards."

"Raccoons don't," he countered. "Matthew told us —"

I stopped listening. Except for the weak, scratchy voice, Ivan sounded like himself. He remembered screaming for help. He also remembered resting his head on the floor by the side door of the carriage house, where, he'd reasoned, a little fresh air would seep in through the crack. It had. He looked horrible, though. So did I. In one of the most politically correct cities in the world, I wore blackface — and black arm and black leg, too. Rowdy still looked like the malamute from hell, but the pads of his feet were fine, and, although he'd taken more smoke than I had, he wasn't wheezing. I stood up, smacked my lips to him, then led him down the illuminated path next to Morris's house, through the shrub border, and across a little stretch of lawn to Alice Savery's back door.

Light was no problem anymore. The smoldering carriage house was now a bonfire that had attracted a crowd of neighbors. The cautious clustered in a group at the end of the drive; the bold formed a scraggly line near Matthew and Doug, who were soaking the area around the building with their hoses. The smoke was steamy now. Everyone faced the fire. No one watched Rowdy and me.

The back door had glass panes. After I'd tried ringing the bell, I tapped on one of them. Then I took off one shoe, placed the sole against the pane, rested my left elbow on the upper, and used the flat of my right hand to deliver a hard whack to my left fist. I'm not an experienced housebreaker; what I am is a landlady who does her own repairs, including glazing. In almost no time, I'd removed enough glass to let me reach in, locate the knob, and open the door. Most houses in that neighborhood had expensive security systems. I'd half expected to hear an alarm like the one Ivan had triggered by pounding on the front door. Nothing happened. My fingers found a light switch.

Careful not to let Rowdy step on the broken glass, I led him through a little mud room, where we paused. I inserted Rita's aid in my left ear. Then I removed the wide jersey belt from my waist, wrapped it around and around Rowdy's head, and tied it on top. He looked ridiculous, of course, a large charcoal-colored dog wearing a hair ornament, but I didn't happen to be carrying any canine ear plugs, and the belt effectively pinned down his ears and added a few layers of muffling.

Beyond the mud room was a shabby, ugly kitchen with yellow-speckled green linoleum, greenish-yellow walls, and restaurant-size cabinet space. Everywhere, and I mean everywhere, were brown paper grocery bags packed with junk mail, newspapers, and bright-colored, neatly folded boxes that had once contained such diverse items as graham crackers, cornflakes, radon detectors, and at-home kits to test water purity. The sour air certainly smelled as if it could use testing, and the layer of grease that clung to every surface was so thick that if you'd scraped it into cans, you could've supplied the shortening needs of a bad diner for six months. Perched on the edge of a counter, ready to fall off and break someone's foot, was a great big red fire extinguisher.

"Miss Savery!" I called.

My left ear felt as if someone had jammed a full-size radio into it. When my fingers explored the aid, they felt huge and clumsy, and when they finally located the minuscule volume control, one touch in the wrong direction cut off all sound to the ear. In an effort to turn the damned thing back on, I made what I intended as a fine adjustment. The air came to buzzing, crackling life. Rowdy's tags clanged like cymbals. Almost in the ear itself, a fully inflated five-wad bubble of Bazooka in the mouth of an infant Dizzie Gillespie burst with a weirdly metallic *POP!* The origin of the deafening explosion proved to be my own mouth; I'd lightly clicked my tongue. But I left the volume set high. If an ultrasonic blast cut off the aid, I'd definitely notice.

With every step Rowdy and I took, the floor creaked like a rickety bridge about to drop out from under us. We made our cacophonous way through a butler's pantry. When I pushed a swinging door, it shrieked on its hinges, and

Rowdy shoved ahead of me. I flipped a switch on the wall, but the brass chandelier over the mile-long table had fake-candle-flame bulbs that gave only dim light. Propped on the mantlepiece over the fireplace at one end of the dining room were two tarnished candlesticks with no candles, a china shepherdess, a beautifully framed watercolor of a flower garden in bloom, and two plastic boxes that turned out to house little gadgets with warning lights. One gadget would indicate gas leaks; the other would warn of the presence of carbon monoxide.

"Miss Savery!" This loud, hollow bray was a stranger's. In what felt like an effort to demonstrate my control of the alien sound, I repeated, "Miss Savery!" We reached the large entrance hall at the front of the house, where my foot caught in a braided rug. To regain my balance, I rested a hand on Rowdy's back. I raised my chin, opened my throat, and let the strange voice boom up the wide staircase ahead. "Miss Savery!"

A momentary burst of silence hit my left ear. Rowdy jerked his head and pulled away from the stairs. "Buddy, I am so sorry," I told him. Far above us, something moved. We headed up the stairs. On the second-floor landing, I hit every light switch and saw no one. Straight ahead, a door opened to a filthy green-tiled bathroom that looked like the stage set for a film on home safety hazards. Teetering on a little marble shelf above the ancient sink, as if deliberately positioned to tumble into the basin, was a battered electric radio plugged into the same four-way adapter that also sprouted the cords of a grungy Water-Pik and a new-looking rotating-bristle toothbrush, both of which sat on top of a toilet you don't want to hear about. On a filthy bath mat rested a rusty electric heater heavily patched with duct tape. A three-legged stool next to the empty tub supported a little student lamp positioned like a duck ready to dive into the water. Alice Savery evidently enjoyed reading while she soaked. Her taste in books, it seemed to me, should have run toward sizzlers, but cosied up next to the lamp as if prepared to nudge it into the tub was a beautifully bound volume of *À la recherche du temps perdu*. Proust's *In Memory of Things Past*. Courting lost time. The old venetian blinds that covered the window had ivory-colored slats like the thinly milled tusks of poacher-killed animals. Maybe Rowdy smelled them. I had to drag him out.

On the landing, I again shouted to Miss Savery. Then I headed up the worn wooden servant stairs to the third floor. On both sides of the treads, books were stacked so high that

Rowdy and I were forced to ascend single file. I went first. On top of one stack of especially scholarly-looking tomes were two dismantled smoke detectors, their battery compartments gutted. Chunks of plaster from the hospital green walls crunched underfoot.

When we'd finally picked our way up, I was sweating from the trapped heat, and my lungs sounded like an artificial respirator in need of a tune-up. The landing offered a choice of four closed doors. A foot or so above the knob of one door was a large blotch of smudges that looked like a nonrepresentational finger painting grudgingly produced by a depressed child. Working on scent rather than sight, Rowdy headed for that door. He had raised a paw to add a bas-relief to its decoration before I tugged him back, gave him an informal version of the down signal, and murmured that I'd be back soon. I turned the doorknob, wormed past Rowdy, entered the room, and quickly pulled the door shut behind me, leaving Rowdy's leash securely caught in it.

The room I entered had a low ceiling, but it was long and wide, and its walls were so heavily lined with books that it looked like some out-of-the-way section of the stacks of a university library. Despite three open, unscreened windows that admitted smoke-tinged air, it smelled predominantly of old paper.

Directly ahead of me was an ugly, beat-up teacher's desk. The only light came from an old-fashioned gooseneck lamp on the desk top, which also held three or four Harvard Coop notebooks, a mug of pens and pencils, a large red fire extinguisher like the one in the kitchen, an antique Underwood manual typewriter, a black telephone wired to what looked like two answering machines, and three or four other electronic devices that I couldn't identify. I'd found Alice Savery. I no longer needed Rita's aid. I popped it out of my ear and dropped it into a pocket of the black dress.

She was sitting at the desk. She faced away from me. As approaching sirens finally began to wail, she rose from her seat. Before she had finished turning around, I said, "Your carriage house is on fire, but the little boy got out. Now you need to come with me."

Her gray hair with its Roman cut made her head look like a steel helmet with the visor raised, and the khaki clothes that had seemed practical and above style when I'd first seen her in her garden now looked unmistakably military. Her eyes were fiercely narrowed, as if she suffered from some form of chronic conjunctivitis that made vision painful. Although I'd removed the aid, Alice Savery's voice was loud and somehow impersonal. Her tone was at once authoritative and pitiful: "Alfred would never have let them get away with it," she said firmly. The small gray-and-brown figure peered to the left, then to the right. "They *stole* my garden. I had roses, beautiful roses. And in my white garden, there were two weeping pears that they cut down. They brought in a machine to tear up their roots."

I found myself speaking very simply. "Miss Savery, your carriage house is burning. The fire could spread. It could be dangerous here. We need to leave. Come with me."

Her slate gray gaze moved systematically back and forth without pausing even briefly on me. "Can you smell it in the air?" But she was voicing an observation, not asking a question.

"Of course. The smoke —"

She blew out a scornful breath. "At first, one finds it all so very easy to dismiss. It can be so dreadfully, dreadfully subtle. One learns to adopt a multifaceted approach. There are some who disagree, but I count myself among those who subscribe to the theory that aluminum does indeed play a contributory role." The strained expression on her tight face suggested a painful struggle with some complex problem of logic. Once again entirely sure of herself, she gave a stiff smile accompanied by a mechanical jerk of the chin. "Secondary smoke is an entirely different matter." She paused a moment. When she spoke, her voice was still loud, but her tone now suggested the expectation and fear that she might be overheard. "They have very powerful lobby groups." Projecting her voice as if aiming it at the most distant seat in a large lecture hall, she added a single word in a confiding stage whisper: *"Viruses."*

As I understood the tobacco industry and its lobby groups, the term was apt enough. Alice Savery, however, turned out to be speaking literally. Her objection to cigarette smoke was based not so much on the threat it posed to human lungs as on its capacity to infect plants with something called the tobacco mosaic virus. I wondered whether it existed at all. The rabies virus certainly existed. So did HIV. As Alice Savery saw it, those were the two principal viral weapons directed at her, and their chosen agents of contagion were, respectively, dogs and homosexual men. "This *Lamb,*" she almost shouted, "made no effort whatsoever to disguise it. One knew immediately." She shook a boney fist. "When one works in one's garden, insect bites are an inevitability, not to mention two potentially rabid —" She broke off. Her eyes blazed at me. "He committed suicide. He was an extremely foolish person."

"Come with me," I said gently. But, again, Alice Savery paid no more attention to my words than she did to the wails of the sirens or to the shouts of the firefighters that now reached me through the open windows. Desperate to communicate with her, I went striding to the big window that faced the backyard, and I pointed dramatically at the carriage house. Flames seemed to leap out to kiss the thick streams of water from the hoses.

Alice Savery followed me. At last taking in what I'd been trying to convey, she stared briefly at the scene, but then moved away from the window and back toward her desk. "They *stole* my garden." She was enraged and grieved. "And now they're burning down my carriage house. The children have done that, you know. They steal my flowers. Only yesterday, they came and ripped them out. They hide in my carriage house, and they think I don't know. They sneak in there, and they smoke cigarettes. My poor —"

I approached her slowly and cautiously, as if she were a strange dog that might suddenly turn on me without warning as I tried to rescue it from danger. I offered her my arm. She took it. I led her to the door. As I turned the knob, I told her, "My dog is waiting in the hall, but he's very friendly, and I promise you that he's had all his shots. He won't hurt you." Rowdy's leash was jammed in the closed door. In opening the door, I freed him.

Only when Alice Savery caught sight of Rowdy did I finally realize that my assurances — indeed, every word I'd spoken — had been utterly wasted.

"Miss Savery, you can't hear anything I'm saying, can you?" I asked softly.

Even if Alice Savery had heard me, her terror would probably have blotted out my voice, and even if she'd been a dog lover, Rowdy would have been a bizarre sight, a big smoke-black dog, his pink tongue hanging out as he panted from the heat, a black jersey bow on top of his massive head. Alice Savery's steely fingers dug painfully into my arm. Then she let go and sped across the room toward her desk, presumably in search of whatever ultrasound device she'd used on Ruffly. I tried to beat her to it. We reached the desk almost simultaneously. Her hand grabbed for one of the gadgets. I snatched the gadget. "He won't hurt you!" I bellowed. I tried to let her see my lips, but she wasn't watching. *"He's perfectly friendly!"*

As if to prove my claim, Rowdy moved toward Alice Savery. She sidestepped, threw panicked looks left and right, and suddenly darted toward the dim end of the room that lay at the front of the house. As I bent to pick up the leash that trailed from Rowdy's collar, I heard what sounded like the rattle of chain. When I looked up, Alice Savery was at the window that overlooked Highland Street, her back toward me. I shouted her name. Anyone who can hear finds it almost impossible to believe that someone else cannot.

Hooked over the windowsill was a wide, sturdy-looking metal bracket, and out through the open window, Alice Savery was dropping the metal chains and rungs of the emergency escape ladder the bracket was meant to support. Years of manual labor seemed to have given her the strength and agility of an athlete. When I was halfway to her, she had one leg over the sill. Her hands clutched the bracket. I dropped Rowdy's leash and sprinted, but she'd already swung her lean body over the sill, and one of her feet must have found a rung.

"Don't!" I hollered. *"Stop!"*

She transferred her full weight to the ladder, and the bracket dug into the rotten wood of the sill. Then, as her frozen face vanished beneath the window, the bracket moved, and its hooks shifted. In seconds, the old wood gave way under Alice Savery's weight.

34

A month later, Rita's freshly streaked hair was long enough to cover her ears completely and reliably. Even when she shook her head, the aids didn't show at all. *Aid,* I should say. To leave her left ear free for the telephone and to give herself a chance to adapt to amplification without total bombardment, she'd taken to wearing only the aid that went in her right ear. Three days earlier, however, she'd stepped into the shower, soaked her head, poured on shampoo, and discovered only when she was halfway through lathering her hair that one of the unbearably uncomfortable foreign objects to which she would never adjust was still firmly lodged in her right ear canal. It was now at the audiologist's for repair or replacement. Consequently, I was walking on Rita's left. Rowdy was ahead of us at the end of his six-foot leather lead, sniffing bushes and, early on the warm summer evening, making sleddog-sure that we didn't hit a patch of thin ice. Willie trotted merrily along in what Rita considers perfect heel po-

sition, that is, anywhere that might even remotely be considered vaguely in the vicinity
of her left side. His eyes crackled, his beautifully trimmed black coat gleamed, and every
one of the tiny black Scotties running around
his new red collar and down his leash looked
exactly like him.

"I keep telling you." Rita shook her head.
"It's much more complicated than that. The
hearing loss alone was *not* what made her paranoid."

"Well, it didn't help," I said.

"If she'd done anything about it, it wouldn't
have hurt, either," Rita snapped.

I'd found Rita and Stephanie amazingly un-
sympathetic about Alice Savery's hearing loss.
The news had come as no surprise at all to
Stephanie. "If the only thing the person's
doing about it is denying it, I can always tell,"
Stephanie had said. "There's a certain expression one sees on people's faces when they're
missing a lot of what's being said and trying
to pretend that they're getting it. Of course,
I have an advantage. I watch people's faces."
She had paused, cleared her throat, and added,
"Also, one tends to assume that other people's
hearing is more or less like one's own. My
starting assumption with Miss Savery was
probably rather different from yours."

Willie greedily eyed the ankles of a passerby, but they belonged to a runner who was too quick for him. Looking almost regretful that Willie had missed an early evening snack, Rita said, "Holly, the point about this woman, Alice Savery, is that everything was part of a pattern of cutting herself off so that she became quite literally alone with her own thoughts. Yes, she had trouble hearing, but, from what I can tell, her attitude was, to a large extent, well, so what? What do other people have to say that's really worth listening to? So, in part, when she dominated interaction, she was covering up her hearing loss. But, at the same time, she was expressing a certain arrogance that has more to do with character structure than it does with hearing or not hearing. Admittedly, there is a theory that there's a link between uncorrected hearing loss and paranoid ideation. But what's often overlooked is that it goes uncorrected because the person doesn't *care* about what other people have to say, or, quite unconsciously, discovers that *not* hearing is a handy way to avoid potentially corrective input. The hearing loss and the paranoia sustain each other."

Moving at Rita's sore-footed pace, we'd reached Huron, walked up a block, and crossed to the intersection with Sparks Street, which leads to Brattle. Like Highland, Sparks is affluent, verdant, and beautiful. Like Highland, it had also been the site of a murder. A feminist law professor, a very pretty woman, had been walking down Sparks Street early one evening when she'd been stabbed and killed by an assailant who was never caught. Since then, even with my big dogs along, I'd superstitiously avoided Sparks Street. But Rita minces along so slowly that it made sense to take the shortest route to our destination.

"Except . . . Except, Rita, Alice Savery wasn't totally cut off, you know. She listened to the radio. She could hear well enough for that. She had a TV. She got *The New York Times*. Her house was filled with books. And a lot of what she said was *true*. Rabies *is* incurable. The tobacco industry *does* have powerful lobby groups. And . . . Did I tell you this? There really is a tobacco mosaic virus, and it actually *is* spread by —"

"But a carefully selected reality," Rita said crisply. "And with several gross distortions. Like the insects?"

"Yes, but . . . Rita, when the AIDS epidemic first started, there really was some concern about that. Some little town in Florida? I forget the details, but it was in all the papers. And it's true that mosquitos spread heartworm and malaria and some other diseases. AIDS just isn't one of them. And about rabies, everyone in England — the entire country — is as paranoid as Alice Savery was. There's a six-month quarantine on all dogs entering Great Britain, even if they've had their rabies shots, and if you sneak one in and get caught, they destroy the dog. It's ridiculous, because there is absolutely no way that an immunized dog could introduce rabies, but if you point that out, all you hear is this huffy, pompous, 'Well, there is no rabies in Great Britain.' It's their big fear about the tunnel to France, that it's going to let in rabies. They're completely paranoid about it."

"Phobic," Rita corrected. "Paranoid is what Alice Savery was. Not only did this woman project her fears and impulses and whatever onto the external world, and not only did she latch onto realities that happened to mesh with her inner life, but, once having done so, she proceeded to *elaborate* the elements, to manufacture connections, to hook them up with one another in ways that they just aren't hooked. The other crucial thing about this system of hers — and this is always true in paranoid people, Holly — is that this was a system in which she herself was the central object. Yes, radon is dangerous, and, yes, so are viruses and cigarette smoke and all the rest, but, in reality, they pose separate and *impersonal* threats. Alice Savery was not, in fact, at the center of anything."

"What I still can't get over is . . . Obviously, I realized that there was something radically wrong with her."

"So did she. That business about aluminum? There used to be some theory that aluminum caused Alzheimer's, and what that was about was her sense of her own deterioration."

"But, Rita, I honestly thought that Morris's property *had* been stolen from her. She had me convinced that someone, a shady lawyer, I don't know, but someone had gotten hold of it. Or I thought that maybe her brother owned it and got into a poker game with a card shark and —"

Rita nearly tripped. "*Savery?* Holly, Savery was —"

"I don't trust people with no first names. Hitler. Mussolini."

"Adolph. And . . . Benito, wasn't it?"

"You see?"

"Well, Savery's was Alfred, and according to the biography I just finished, he was a perfectly decent person. The poor man died of pancreatic cancer when he was only in his midforties. In fact, I've wondered. This is pure speculation, but I've wondered if the events surrounding his death weren't what triggered her paranoia. To all appearances, she was completely devoted to him, but at the same time there must've been a certain amount of envy there, too. Savery really was important; he was at the center of things. Alice was peripheral. She went to Radcliffe; she probably started out with as much potential as he did, for all we know. She must've felt short-changed. Then he gets sick. She nurses him. He dies anyway. *Major* loss. And guilt? Normal anger that he'd deserted her. Anger when she discovered her financial position? Anger that he was Savery and she was just Alice? I don't know."

"Maybe Alice blamed that on a virus, too," I said. "Maybe she thought that's what caused the cancer."

"Maybe she blamed it on herself. Unconsciously, of course. There's no way we can know what her feelings were. What we do know is that she had them — everyone does — and that she couldn't acknowledge them."

I said, "What Alice Savery really couldn't acknowledge was her own responsibility. I still can't believe that she was the one who sold that lot. I mean, she had to sell it. It was either that or sell the whole place, the house, the garden, everything, and move somewhere else. If she wanted to keep living on Highland Street, it was a perfectly sensible thing to do. And one of the amazing things is that she actually went around telling people this story about how it had been stolen, and everyone just thought that what she meant was that it had appreciated. And if you look at what it's worth today and what she probably got for it, and if you ignore everything else, well, it *was* a steal. You know, Rita, in a sort of simple way, what really killed her was that she honestly didn't have enough money to keep up that house."

"Bullshit," Rita said bluntly. "Well, not total bullshit. But, look, nothing could be more characteristic of paranoid people than this bizarre portioning out of the resources that are available. Alice was existing on cornflakes, and at the same time she was buying all those electronic gadgets, and they couldn't have been cheap."

I'd been correct in supposing that the ultrasound device used to torment Ruffly had come from a mail order house. I'd just been wrong about what kind. As it turns out, just as dog fancy has its catalogs, so does paranoia. Phobia? Whichever. The police found the catalogs in Alice Savery's house, and Kevin Dennehy told me about them. The catalogs had sad, misleading names that sounded like brands of over-the-counter sleeping pills and lines of feminine hygiene products: *Rest Assured. Security Plus.* They had been the source of the test kits and monitoring devices I'd seen, and of the emergency escape ladder as well. They'd also supplied Alice Savery with three ultrasound devices, one for each floor of the house. Weirdly enough, some of the protective gadgetry was useless to someone with a major hearing loss and no assistance dog. The front door alarm Ivan had triggered was meant for travelers to hang on the inside knobs of hotel room doors. Alice Savery probably couldn't have heard it unless she was standing next to it. Besides, she never went anywhere. Instead, she stayed home and watched. Here and there throughout the house were little observation posts, chairs positioned to face windows.

The post in the kitchen was where the police found the most powerful of Alice Savery's ultrasound devices. The Bark Quell emitted 140-decibel bursts pitched above the range of human hearing. Although the Bark Quell had an automatic, yap-activated mode, Alice Savery had evidently preferred to operate it manually. My hunch about why she pushed the button herself is that she wasn't trying to quell barking at all. Why silence a dog she couldn't hear? I suspect that she was trying to drive Ruffly and especially his viruses away from the open windows of Morris's house that faced the open windows of her own. It's possible that Alice imagined that ultrasound could repel not only dogs but their supposed germs, too. Maybe ultrasound really does scare away viruses. Matthew Benson might know. I don't. The squirming and wiggling of microorganisms doesn't interest me at all. Why settle for mere pseudopodia — false feet — when you can have real paws?

"She bought those gadgets," Rita said. "But that's comparatively trivial. Years ago she could've sold that carriage house or fixed it up and rented it. She had plenty of options."

"That's not how she felt. Like the carriage house? You know, Rita, if she'd lived to collect the insurance money for that, she wouldn't have realized at all that what she'd done was tantamount to burning it down herself. I don't know whether she *was* responsible, but she didn't *feel* responsible."

"You certainly are determined to let her off the hook," Rita observed.

"Not really. No, I'm not. Alice Savery murdered Morris. She did it in a sneaky way so that she could tell herself that she wasn't responsible, but she did murder him. And when she made Avon Hill warn the kids not to go into her carriage house to sneak cigarettes, she deliberately lured Ivan there. She set him up. She was the one who poured gas around in there, and when Ivan did what he was *bound* to do, she locked the door and trapped him inside. She opened the valve on Stephanie's gas grill. No one made her do it, and she knew that Stephanie smoked out on the deck. But if you look at what Alice Savery did, then evading responsibility was the whole point, wasn't it? If Stephanie didn't smoke, if Ivan hadn't —"

"And Morris Lamb?"

"If Morris hadn't been the way he was, if he hadn't been Morris, maybe, but . . . We've been over it and over it, but I'd still like to know exactly how she did it. You know, my best guess is that Morris didn't just go around sort of randomly picking things. Morris was, uh, exuberant, but he wasn't stupid. For what it's worth, I think that he stayed strictly with the stuff in the raised bed, and I think that Alice Savery planted things there knowing that they'd at least make him sick. There's no shortage of ordinary plants that'll do it. In fact, I'm working on a new column about that, and it's worse than I remembered. It's practically enough to make you scared to take your dog outside. Lantana, foxgloves, lupine, aconite, laurel, rhododendrons, flowering tobacco, larkspur, and, of course, delphiniums, and Doug had already planted some fairly weird stuff that is safe — some special kind of marigolds and violas and a whole variety of greens for *mesclun* — so it isn't as if she'd stuck one big hemlock plant in the middle of a bed of lettuce. The other thing is, even though the plants were in a plastic tunnel, it was still pretty early in the spring, so the plants must've been immature and not necessarily all that poisonous, except . . . except, of course, that she believed Morris had AIDS. I mean, when I heard he died, I stupidly thought he had AIDS, too, and so did everyone else. Of course, that was after the fact. But it's still no excuse, really. Anyway, I think that Alice watched Morris pick the stuff from the raised bed, and I think that she saw the light stay on in his bathroom — it's on her side of the house — and I think that she went out and did some selective weeding in his garden. And after that, I think it was like selling the lot next to her house; as soon as she'd done it, she talked herself into believing that she just was not responsible. Her land was stolen; Morris poisoned himself; she'd never even told Doug that raised beds existed, never planted the idea to begin with. And I am positive that if she'd survived that fall, she'd have put the blame for it all on Rowdy. And on me, too."

"For the hundredth time, it really was *not* your fault."

"I shouldn't have taken Rowdy with me. It's just . . . I didn't want to go in that house alone, and I had no idea that anyone could be *that* afraid of dogs."

"Loose dogs," Rita said. "*Unleashed*. Unbridled impulse."

"Whatever. I still shouldn't have —"

"Holly, look. One of the tragedies of paranoia is that, so often, it's a self-fulfilling prophecy. Sometimes these people behave in ways that really do force other people to conspire against them, in the sense of making secret plans to manage them. But it's perfectly characteristic of someone like Alice Savery to take all those elaborate precautions to ward off imaginary dangers while failing to take ordinary measures to protect against real hazards. It's virtually diagnostic."

"Rita, Rowdy did move toward her."

"He and Ruffly also saved Ivan's life. Speaking of whom —"

We'd almost reached the entrance to the little Sunday school playground that lay in back of St. Margaret's Episcopal Church. Approaching from the opposite direction were Ivan and Bernadette, with one of the smallest Alaskan malamutes in existence and definitely the smallest malamute who'd been available for adoption anywhere in the United States. She'd arrived at Logan Airport a week earlier on a flight from Houston. Bernadette, Ivan, Leah, and I had gone together to pick her up. Ivan knew that she came from Alaskan Malamute Rescue of South Texas, and I'd expected him to give her some kind of cowgirl name. But the one he'd chosen without the slightest hesitation was Shakespearian and thus perfectly Cantabrigian. Helena, Ivan had patiently informed me, was a character in *All's Well That Ends Well*. Ivan's Helena, who had a sweet, gentle temperament, weighed only fifty-eight pounds, small for any mal, tiny for a Texas mal. But she was the right size for Ivan, and, of course, fifty-eight pounds less for the Houston landfill that year.

"Now, Rita, keep Willie hugged in right next to you," I ordered. "Rowdy, watch me! If Willie tears into another —"

But Rita didn't hear the rest of the warning. Neither did I. At the sight of another Scottie, Willie had gone into a frenzy of yapping that ended only when Leah handed Kimi's leash to Matthew Benson, loomed over Willie, and commanded him to cut it out. Matthew kept a grip on Kimi, but he locked his eyes on Leah's breasts. I reminded myself to pray for the safe return of Jeff and of Lance, the Border collie.

"This was a big mistake," Rita told me. "Why did I let you talk me into this?"

The playground was, I'll admit, becoming a little crowded and rather zoolike.

"Relax," I said. "Just think. If I hadn't talked you into going to the audiologist, you might've ended up paranoid, just like Alice Savery."

"Holly, for Christ's —"

"Rita!"

"Sorry. But . . . You know, we really don't belong here. We aren't even Episcopalian, and the dogs —"

"Well, who knows," I said. "There really is no such thing as an Episcopalian dog, is there? And there's a little kid over there with a chameleon, and there's definitely no such thing as an Episcopalian chameleon."

"No, but the *owners* of the other animals —"

"It's a Blessing of the Animals," I pointed out, "not a Blessing of the Owners." I lowered my voice and spoke directly into Rita's aided ear. "And, believe me, one thing about Stephanie is that if she didn't want us to be here, we wouldn't be here."

"You still don't get it, do you?" Rita demanded. "You still cling to that same unexamined attitude."

"I admire Stephanie," I whispered. "It's just that I don't really —"

"Of course you don't," Rita interrupted. "Bright, controlling woman, unusual career, very competitive, with an absolutely marvelous dog. So how could you possibly — ?"

"All right!"

"There's no need to be defensive," Rita informed me. "There's no way to assimilate reality without distorting it. Most of the interesting things in life don't happen way out there somewhere, you know; they happen right in here." She raised her hand to her temple.

If Rita is correct, the Blessing of the Animals occurred not amid the greenery of the play yard behind St. Margaret's Episcopal Church on a warm summer evening, but within the minds and souls of the Reverend Stephanie Benson, who conducted the service, and the people who joined her. Stephanie wore clerical garb, a long white gown with loose sleeves. Around her neck was draped a wide multicolored shawl that probably has an ecclesiastical name that I don't know. Doug Winer wore white, to match Morris's Bedlingtons, I assumed. Doug didn't belong to St. Margaret's, either, but Morris had, so maybe Doug disagreed with me about the existence of Episcopalian dogs. Besides, if canine breeds got assigned to human religious denominations, the Church of England and its U.S. affiliate would certainly have first claim on the Bedlington. Nelson and Jennie were as perfectly groomed as Morris always kept them.

I hoped he was admiring them. In fact, I hoped that Morris never took his eyes off his dogs. Doug held Jennie's lead, but I wasn't sure that Morris would be pleased to see that the human end of Nelson's lead rested in the hand of the waiter, Fyodor, whose striking eyes focused lovingly on Doug. Doug's parents were not there. They were alien to the part of Doug's life that had included Morris and now apparently embraced Fyodor.

Ivan Flynn-Isaacson didn't go to St. Margaret's, and neither did Steve Delaney, who is a devout member of the veterinary profession and regularly attends the services of the American Kennel Club, as does his shepherd, India, who was at Steve's left at the far side of Lady, Steve's timid pointer. Leah had been reared to believe primarily in Harvard and only secondarily in God, but her parents perceived no difference between the two, so at any Cambridge assembly, she fit right in.

Most of the other people there seemed to know one another. They were, of course, Stephanie's parishioners, and they'd brought with them an astounding variety of creatures great and small, the great on leash, the small in carriers, cages, and containers of water: two gerbils, a lop-eared rabbit, several noisy guinea pigs with long black coats, a Siamese fighting fish, a bowl of goldfish, a parakeet, a small snake, a newt, a Burmese cat, two kittens that were part Abyssinian, a handsome tabby, a Great Pyrenees, a show-quality German shorthaired pointer, two beagles, the Scottie who'd provoked Willie, a golden retriever, and four or five dogs for which the politically correct term used to be mixed-breed but is now random-bred, meaning God only knows what, and She does, too, and loves them eternally.

Stephanie called us together. She had us gather in the kind of circle of people and animals that was perfectly familiar to me from the rites of the Cambridge Dog Training Club, except, of course, that Roz seldom has us bow our heads.

I expected a vague ecumenical blessing. Stephanie's was not. She spoke formally. "O merciful Creator, Your hand is open wide to satisfy the needs of every living creature: Make us always thankful for Your loving providence; and grant that we, remembering the account that we must one day give, may be faithful stewards of Your good gifts; through Jesus Christ our Lord, who with You and the Holy Spirit lives and reigns, one God, for ever and ever. *Amen.*"

For the children, I think, Stephanie translated the prayer into simple English. Then, with Ruffly prancing at her side, his miraculous ears still scanning heaven and earth, Stephanie made her way slowly from animal to animal, blessing all with equal dignity, newts and snakes and all. When Stephanie and Ruffly reached us, I was astounded to see that she had not merely been resting her hand on the bowls and on the cages and on the animals themselves as she murmured her prayers. Gently placing her fingers on the crown of Rowdy's head, she drew in his dark, furry cap what was unmistakably the sign of the cross.

I felt shocked and guilty, but if gerbils, newts, and snakes could be blessed, so could we: Stephanie Benson, Alice Savery, Doug Winer, Morris Lamb, Fyodor, Ivan, Bernadette, Steve, Rita, Leah, and even the godless Matthew. As for Holly, Rowdy, Kimi, and the sign of the cross? Instead of dispatching hideous little gray aliens to abduct me and stick needles in my innards, the firmament had sent beautiful wolf-gray companions to steal nothing but my heart. There might well be Christian breeds, I thought, but the Alaskan malamute was not one of them. Malamutes believe in food, sex, and social hierarchies. So do I. I also believe in the Alaskan malamute and in all dogs, which is to say, in all-forgiving love. I felt heathen. I felt absolved.

X